BRIDES OF THE WEST

Glory

LORI COPELAND

Tyndale House Publishers
Carol Stream, Illinois

Visit Tyndale online at tyndale.com.

Visit Lori Copeland's website at loricopeland.com.

TYNDALE and Tyndale's quill logo are registered trademarks of Tyndale House Ministries.

Glory

Designed by Libby Dykstra and Jacqueline L. Nuñez

Edited by Diane Eble

Published in association with the literary agency of Alive Literary Agency, 7680 Goddard St., Suite 200, Colorado Springs, CO 80920.

Scripture quotations are taken from the *Holy Bible*, King James Version.

Glory is a work of fiction. Where real people, events, establishments, organizations, or locales appear, they are used fictitiously. All other elements of the novel are drawn from the author's imagination.

For information about special discounts for bulk purchases, please contact Tyndale House Publishers at csresponse@tyndale.com, or call 1-800-323-9400.

Previously published in 1999 under ISBN 0-8423-3749-0.

First repackage first published in 2007 under ISBN 978-1-4143-1537-9.

Second repackage published in 2020 under ISBN 978-1-4964-4196-6.

Printed in the United States of America

26	25	24	23	22	21	20
7	6	5	4	3	2	1

To four very special men in my life:
my grandsons, James, Joseph,
Joshua, and Gage

1

"Well, well, the least you could do is stay for supper!" Glory choked on dust as Ralph Samuels's buckboard spun out of the yard on one wheel. Sighing, she glanced toward the shanty, hoping that was squirrel she smelled frying and that Poppy had cooked enough for two.

Bending over, the petite young woman with a boyish frame picked up the knapsack holding her extra pair of denims and shirt. *Poppy isn't going to be happy about this,* Glory thought. It was the third time in as many months that an almost-husband had brought her back. The eager suitor would call on her proper-like; then Poppy would propose marriage. The besotted swain always agreed, only to go back on his word before vows were spoken. Glory didn't understand it. This time she'd nearly made it through the whole day before this fickle lout got cold feet.

Men were just too picky. Yes, she'd corrected Ralph a few times this morning—only *corrected* the man. So what? She hadn't said that she knew everything. He was thin-skinned and took her harmless observations for a sign of bossiness. Bossy? Her? She wasn't bossy—just happened to have more knowledge about turnips than Ralph could ever hope to have, and it was his pained expression, not hers, that put a blight on the outing.

She glanced at the shanty again, wondering if Poppy would be upset with her for coming back—or being returned—a third time. He shouldn't be. Seemed to her that she was lucky to have discovered Ralph's headstrong tendencies now rather than later. Wouldn't it have been dandy to be hitched to a man who couldn't discuss *turnips* without blowing up?

"Poppy!" Glory sniffed the late afternoon air, her eyes traveling to the piece of metal pipe stuck through the tin roof. Only a faint waft of smoke curled from the chimney. *Odd,* she thought. That was meat she smelled frying.

Climbing the steps to the porch, she kept a firm grip on the knapsack. Wasn't any need to unpack. When Poppy had gotten it in his mind a few months back that he wasn't going to live much longer, he'd set out like a man possessed to get her married off. No amount of arguing could have convinced him otherwise. She didn't need a husband; she was able to take care of herself. Been doing it since she was knee-high to a grasshopper. But the old hermit had argued—something Poppy didn't do that often. He'd fretted day and night about how she couldn't live in these parts alone—not these days. He'd contended that if Indians didn't stir up trouble, men with no-good intentions would.

How could Poppy worry? Glory could fire her old Hawkins rifle better than any man; Poppy couldn't dispute that. She could haul water and chop wood and skin a bear in less time than it took to talk about it. She wasn't much on cooking and cleaning, but Poppy did all of that. She knew all she needed to get by. She didn't want any man telling her what to do.

Why, if she hadn't fallen off that wagon when she was a baby and if Poppy hadn't found her lying on the trail, she probably could have raised herself.

Her resolve stiffened. She had to talk Poppy out of this foolish notion of marriage; it wasn't going to work.

"Poppy?" Glory pushed the front door open a crack and peered inside. Late-afternoon sunlight fell across the dirt floor. A remnant of morning fire had turned to white ashes. The iron skillet was on the stove, and the scent of frying meat—and burnt bread—teased her nose.

Squinting, her eyes shifted to Poppy's cot across the room. Poppy, hands across his chest, lay sleeping peacefully between the rumpled blankets.

Shoving the door open, she came inside. Sleeping at this time of the day! Poppy would be up all night. Pausing beside the cot, she smiled down affection-ately on the only father she'd ever known. She didn't know her real pa's name, but when she'd fallen off that wagon and nobody had noticed, Poppy had become her family from that day on. If her real ma or pa had come back looking for their infant daughter, they hadn't found her. Poppy said he'd stayed around the area for over a week, waiting for someone to come back to claim their baby girl. Then bad weather had set in and he'd been forced to bring the infant to his shanty, and that's where she'd lived ever since, with Poppy; Molasses, the old mule; a cow; and a few settin' hens.

For years afterward, every time a wagon rattled by the shanty, the old hermit would flag it down and ask if anyone was looking for a lost child. The weary travelers would shake their heads, saying how sorry they were to hear about the tragedy, but they hadn't known anyone who was missing a young'un. So Glory had stayed, and the years had passed, and now the old man was worried about dying and leaving her all alone.

"Poppy?" She gently shook Poppy's shoulders. "Wake up, sleepyhead. It's gonna be dark soon, and you'll not sleep a wink tonight."

The old man lay deathly still, his blue-veined hands resting lightly across his frail chest, a faint smile on his weathered features. "Poppy?" she repeated, her breath catching as she bent to press her ear to his upper body. Her heart sank when she realized that he wasn't breathing. The beat that was once hearty and strong was silent now.

"Oh, Poppy." Tears smarted in her eyes, and she gathered the kind old man into her arms. "Why did you have to go and leave me?"

Sunbeams stretched across the shanty floor and gradually faded to shadows. Glory sat on the cot and cradled the old man like an infant, rocking him gently back and forth, singing a lullaby that he'd sung to her so many times before: "'Sleep my little child, sleep and run no more. Someone who loves you holds you tight and will forever more.'"

Poppy was gone. Memories flooded her heart: memories of how the old hermit had taught her to hunt and fish, to track wounded animals to either put them out of their pain or attempt to heal their wounds. He'd taught her to laugh at herself and to care about others, though it was a rare treat when they ever saw another living soul.

They lived deep in the Missouri hills with only animals and each other for company. Poppy's brother, Crazy Amos, came around occasionally looking for a handout. Glory was scared of the ferocious-looking giant. He stood heads taller than Poppy, and his massive hands were as big as the hams Poppy had hanging in the smokehouse. Poppy didn't cotton to his younger brother either. Said he was a freeloader, and Poppy didn't hold with freeloaders. Had "gold" in his eyes, Poppy contended; all Amos ever wanted was money. Poppy said iffen a man was able-bodied but didn't work, then it weren't fittin' he should eat. Amos lived a spell away and came around only once or twice a year, but that was enough to sour Poppy's disposition for days.

Tenderly smoothing her hand over the old man's forehead, Glory buried her face in his hair and cried. "What am I going to do without you?" She was alone now—completely alone. She'd never had anyone but Poppy, and the cow, the old mule, a few chickens. And now she didn't have Poppy.

* * *

It took her two days to dig the grave. Glory washed the old hermit and dressed him in a clean shirt and pants. Afterward, she set his battered hat on his head, tilting it at a rakish angle the way Poppy liked it. Stepping back to survey her work, she smiled. "You look mighty perky, Poppy." Then she dissolved into tears and couldn't do a thing for the next few hours.

She didn't know how to let Amos know about Poppy's passing; the thought brought only relief. The farther away Amos stayed, the better she liked it. He wasn't right in the head, and worse, he was mean. Once she'd seen him hit his mule so hard with one of his big hands, the animal wore the mark a week later. He'd boasted about the men he'd killed and the women he'd mistreated. Glory didn't think he should be proud of his actions, but they seemed to amuse him.

Amos would pin her with a black-eyed stare until she'd squirm in her chair, heat igniting her cheeks. Finally he'd laugh and look away but not until he was satisfied that she was weak from fright. He was an evil man, and she hoped she'd never have to set eyes on him again.

It took all of her might to get Poppy from the shanty to the graveside. She didn't weigh much, but she was sturdy. Poppy had been proud of her strength, and today she worked hard to live up to his praise. Grasping him under the arms, she dragged Poppy's lifeless form down the ravine, careful to keep his pants and shirt as clean as possible. The journey to the grave site thirty yards away took most of the afternoon.

She shoveled the last spadeful of dirt onto the grave and mounded it up. Straightening, she listened to the silence. The stillness overwhelmed her. No Poppy's voice calling her to supper, no sounds of him putting the animals down for the night.

Not one other living soul to share the empty days.

"I cain't help but feel like I'm leavin' something undone," she said to no one, pondering what that something might be.

She remembered the time Poppy brought home a picture he'd found, saying it'd probably fallen out of a passing wagon. It showed some people standing around an open grave. The women were weeping into their handkerchiefs, and the men held their hats over their hearts, real respectful-like.

"Surely they must have spoken a word or two over whoever was in that hole." Glory thought long and hard. "Well, I reckon I ain't rightly sure one way or the other. . . . I would sure hate to find out later I was supposed to say something and didn't."

She tried to gather her thoughts as she kicked at

a rock. Seeing as how she didn't own a handkerchief, she took off her hat and held it over her heart.

For a moment she searched for words. "Don't rightly know what to say. . . . Poppy, you was a good man, and you sure was good to me. I thank you for pickin' me up off that trail when I fell out of that wagon. Weren't something that just any ole body would've done. . . . Well, guess most anyone would've picked me up, but not everybody would've kept me and loved me the way you did. I'm much obliged, Poppy. I loved you too—a powerful lot—and I'm gonna miss you something fierce." She had to stop now because tears were choking her.

The cow waited nearby, wanting to be milked. Molasses, the old mule, munched on late-summer grass near the lean-to. A couple of hens shook their feathers before flying to the nest to roost. Everything seemed normal, yet nothing would ever be the same.

Sighing, she laid a clump of sunflowers on the fresh dirt, wishing for a proper marker. Rocks would have to do for now, but she fashioned them in the form of a fish. Poppy loved to fish. She'd spent many a day on the riverbank catching catfish with him. She carried the shovel back to the lean-to and stored it before she milked Bess, who by now was looking a mite uncomfortable.

After the burial, days blurred. She got out of bed at the same time, did the same chores, listening for the sound of Poppy's voice. Every night she visited the grave site and wept from loneliness. It was the first time she'd experienced separation, and the empty feeling deep inside her hurt something awful. She had no one to talk to, no one to explain the hollowness.

"I don't know what to do, Bess," she whispered, leaning against the cow's warm flank while she milked. The fragrant smell of Bess's coat and the warm milk hitting the cool bucket gave her a measure of comfort. This animal was a friend, someone she knew when the rest of her world was void of anything familiar.

Warm weather gave way to blistering heat. Fireflies kept her company at night. By day, she hunted her food and cared for the animals in silence. At night, when the isolation felt as heavy as an iron blanket, she talked to the mule for companionship, sharing stories of her day.

"Though it don't seem it, winter will be here in a few months, and I'm afraid," she whispered to the old mule. "Saw a woolly worm this afternoon. His coat was black and thick; it's going to be a bad winter."

Poppy had taken to town a few times, so she knew there was one not more than a couple days' ride. Should she leave the shanty before the snows came? The thought terrified her. Life in the woods was the only thing she knew. Squirrels and chipmunks were her friends; she wouldn't know how to live around other people. But she wasn't sure she could survive a brutal winter alone in the woods, either.

● ● ●

One night Glory sat straight up in bed, reaching for the rifle when she heard someone pounding on the front door and shouting, "Let me in, girl! I know you're in there!"

Amos! He continued banging on the door with his enormous fists, muttering drunken threats between poundings.

Sliding out of bed, she crouched beside it, her fingers tightening around the gun's stock. When Amos was drinking, he was mean as a wolverine. Poppy had warned her to never let him in when he was in such a state.

The heavy bar across the door rattled. "Come on, Glory girl! Open up the door and let Uncle Amos in! It's hot out here!"

He wasn't her uncle—he was no kin to her, and now that Poppy was dead, she didn't have to pretend that he was. What did he want? Why was he here in the middle of the night pounding on her door? Her heart thumped in her throat. Had he found out that Poppy was dead? How could he know?

Amos's voice dropped to a menacing growl. "Open the door, Glory. I've come for my money." He shoved his weight against the oak, and Glory slid under the bed. Her fingers closed around the trigger, fear choking her.

He knew. Somehow he knew Poppy was dead, and he was here to take the gold Poppy kept hidden in a pouch beneath the floor.

Amos slammed his bulk against the door, trying

to break it down. Glory closed her eyes, silently praising Poppy for building the shanty out of strong oak. Trembling, she listened to Amos's repeated attempts to enter. Over and over, he threw his weight against the door. She could hear him swearing violently under his breath, threatening her with unimaginable, vile acts.

Trembling, she gripped the Hawkins until her hands hurt. Other than hunting food, she'd never shot another living, breathing thing, but she intended to shoot Amos if he broke that door down. She could hear her own breath coming in ragged gasps as his threats became more threatening and vile now.

She kept her eyes shut and waited. If he gained entrance, he would kill her and take the gold. Images raced through her mind—images of the rage burning in his dark eyes, corn liquor coursing through his veins, his big hands doubled and ready to hit, greed spurring him to madness.

"I want that gold, Glory! It's mine and I mean to have it!"

She kept quiet, refusing to answer. *Give up and go away, Amos. You're not coming in!*

Then there was silence, and the night seemed endless. It sounded as if Amos had left, and then she knew he was back. She could hear him chopping at the door with something, but the oak still held. A bottle shattered on the porch, and he bellowed in rage. The stench of corn liquor drifted under the crack beneath the door.

Fueled by whiskey, Amos slammed against the door—over and over until Glory was certain he would come flying into the room at any moment.

Getting out from under the bed and standing up, she positioned herself a few feet away from the doorway, waiting for him. She hefted the loaded rifle to her shoulder, squinted, and took aim. The room was dark. She couldn't see a thing, but she knew where to point, and there weren't many better with a gun than she. If Amos came through that door, she'd drop him like a hot rock.

Suddenly silence fell over the cabin again. The pounding stopped. Straining to hear, Glory eased closer to the door. Had he given up and left? Long seconds passed while she waited, conscious only of her frayed breathing.

The windowpane behind her shattered. Whirling, she fired, aware of the sound of more breaking glass. Her heart threatened to leap out of her chest as she dropped to her knees and crawled toward the front door. He was at the back of the house now; she had to escape. If he trapped her in the cabin, she wouldn't have a chance.

Bounding to her feet, she lifted the bar, threw open the door, and bolted outside. The night was pitch-black, a heavy cloud cover obscuring the moon. Racing toward the lean-to, she bent low, her bare feet covering the ground silently. He wouldn't be able to see her, not in this blackness.

The smell of hay and cow dung rushed over her when she slipped inside the crudely built shelter and threaded her way to the back of the stall. When she was a child, she'd hidden here from Poppy many a time when they were playing hide-and-seek. She could hear Amos shouting her name, cursing as he staggered about in the dark searching for her. The hunt went on for hours. Toward dawn, he finally staggered onto the front porch and collapsed from drunken exhaustion.

Seizing her chance, Glory shot from the lean-to and raced to the back of the cabin. She climbed through the broken window and hurriedly gathered her knapsack with her extra pair of pants and shirt, a jacket, some bacon and a few cold biscuits, and the pouch of gold that she took from beneath the shanty floor. She quickly pulled on her scuffed leather boots.

Amos's besotted snores filled the cabin as she carefully eased the front door open and gingerly stepped over his sprawled form.

His right hand snaked out and latched on to her ankle. "You're not going anywhere, girlie."

Bringing the butt of the gun down on his hand, Glory broke his hold. Howling, he struggled to sit up, but Glory swung the rifle a second time and knocked him cold. With a moan, he slumped to his side and lay lifeless, blood seeping from a wound on his head.

Scrambling off the porch, Glory raced to the lean-to and swung open the door. "Shoo!" she yelled at Bess.

The chickens started on their nests, squawking

as she raced through the coop and opened the back door. She drove the cow out, making a clear passage for the hens' freedom.

A moment later, she fastened a bedroll and her knapsack on back of the mule and swung aboard. The last she saw of Amos, he was sprawled on the front porch, lying amid the remains of a shattered whiskey bottle.

She didn't know if she had killed him or not. But by now, she didn't rightly care.

2

"Oh, Molasses!"

Hands on her hips, Glory stood beside the lifeless mule a day and a half later, feeling helpless. She'd depended on that mule to get her to—well, somewhere. They weren't very far from the cabin, and she was sure that Amos would try to follow her, once he regained consciousness. *If* he regained consciousness. Had she killed him? The thought gave her a bellyache. She hadn't intended to kill him, just escape him. When it came to gold, Amos was determined.

She studied the dead mule. Molasses, on the other hand, had never been determined about anything, except going to the barn.

"Well, ole friend, you gave us the best you had, and I thank you for it." Glory knelt and patted the mule's rough hide. Poppy had brought Molasses home one day when Glory was very small. He'd bought him from a down-on-his-luck trader. Now Molasses was dead, and she was afoot.

Hefting the bedroll, her pack, and the Hawkins

over one shoulder, she struck off. She was not sure where she was going, but she knew she couldn't sit in the middle of the road and twiddle her thumbs. Poppy had headed this direction every spring when he'd gone to town for supplies. To her way of thinking, there had to be people in this direction, and where there were people, there was opportunity to start a new life. A new life was what she needed the most right now.

That and a mule.

She plodded along the faint trail for some time, shifting the pack from one shoulder to the other until hunger made her stop and dig into her meager cache of supplies. She was glad she had fried up the last of the bacon and made that batch of biscuits the day before Amos arrived. She'd have enough food for another day or two if she was careful.

Sitting down on the pack with her rifle across her knees, Glory munched on the bacon and biscuit slowly, trying to make it last. The sun was straight overhead when she heard the creak of wagon wheels. Both excited and apprehensive, she waffled between the choice of flagging down strangers or hiding until they passed.

"Better a ride than blisters on your feet," she decided, quickly jamming the last bite of biscuit into her mouth. Wiping her face with the back of her hand, she peered down the road, waiting for the wagon to come into sight. She hoped it wasn't Amos—if it was, she'd bolt like a jackrabbit.

The tall ribs of a prairie schooner with a double

hitch of oxen came over a rise. Glory's mouth went dry. A man—a big man—much younger than Poppy, sat on the driver's seat; his hat was pulled low over his face.

The mid-July sun was hot, so hot she could hardly breathe. Swallowing, she eased out in the road, thankful that it wasn't Amos and hoping it wasn't something worse.

● ● ●

Coughing, Mary Everly leaned forward on the wagon seat. "Is that someone standing in the road?" she asked, squinting.

Jackson Lincoln was wondering that himself.

"The owner of the dead mule we passed a ways back, I'd venture."

Jackson smiled at the earnest youngster who hovered near his shoulder. He'd had his doubts when he left Westport a few days ago to escort five women to Denver City to be mail-order brides. It was the most unusual assignment he'd ever undertaken. When he'd first seen his charges, he'd almost backed out of the job; they seemed awfully young to be traveling such a long way. They were orphans, too old to be adopted and, therefore, an unwanted liability. The head of the orphanage had allowed the girls to sign marriage contracts with Tom Wyatt, a broker who had promised to secure a good husband for each one of them.

But a couple of days into the trip his worries

had been proven false. The girls were pleasant and helpful, passing the time amicably. Mary was fifteen, he guessed. Patience, Ruth, Harper, and Lily—all around the same age. Not one of them was certain about anything except that she had no home unless he could safely deliver her to Wyatt in Colorado.

Jackson suspected why some of the girls had never been adopted. Mary was sickly and pale with a persistent cough. Patience, at sixteen, he figured, was gentle in nature but addled at times. She'd stop talking in midsentence to think about something, and he'd found her more than once conversing with a bird on the limb of a tree.

Harper was a hard one to figure out. Her mother had soured her on all men, leaving Harper tough as leather. Thought to be fourteen, she was the youngest and a clear-cut troublemaker with a razor-sharp tongue. Harper looked out for herself and tended to irritate people. Just the opposite of Patience, who would mother the others, making sure everyone was comfortable before she took to her own bedroll.

Then there was Ruth—the serious, most educated one, who looked on the positive side of the worst circumstance. Ruth was certain a wonderful new life lay over the next rise. Jackson wasn't so sure of that. Experience had taught him otherwise. Caution made him one of the best wagon masters around, even if there was only one wagon on this assignment.

Ruth's opposite was Lily, who laughed easily, her eyes dancing with mischief. Jackson strongly suspected that this fifteen-year-old was bound for trouble before the trip was over. She was too full of life for him to think otherwise.

"Who is it, do you suppose?" Lily leaned out of the wagon over Jackson's left shoulder, straining for a better look.

"I don't know, but we're about to find out."

Hauling back on the heavy reins, Jackson drew the team alongside the thin youth. Clearly the teenage boy had outgrown his dirty cotton trousers. The hems crowded the tops of his scuffed leather boots. Jackson's eyes touched on the faded flannel shirt that was too big across the shoulders. The brim of the battered leather hat hung down over his forehead, obscuring half the youth's face. One thing for certain: he handled the Hawkins like someone accustomed to having it close at hand. The wagon rolled to a halt, and the boy shuffled his feet.

"Got a problem?" Jackson asked.

The wiry youth squinted up at him, and Jackson noticed his smooth cheeks. He wasn't even old enough to shave, and he looked almost feminine under all that grime.

"Mule up and died on me."

"Where're you going?"

"To town."

The boy was young; Jackson noticed his voice hadn't dropped yet.

"Climb aboard, but the rifle goes in the back."

The stranger hesitated briefly before handing it up. Jackson passed the weapon back to Lily.

The youth fixed him with a stare. "I want it back."

Jackson met his troubled gaze, then scanned the dirt on the youth's face. "You'll get it back once you reach where you're going."

The girls didn't like handling guns, which suited Jackson just fine. Then he didn't have to worry about their getting hurt. But the boy was another matter. He could be an outlaw, or he could be down on his luck as he claimed. Jackson wasn't taking any chances.

The boy slung his bedroll and pack up into the storage box and shinnied up beside Jackson, who caught a whiff of the young man and regretted the invitation. The kid stank—smelled as bad as rancid meat. The girls, who had crowded to the open flap at the front of the wagon to eye the stranger curiously, immediately moved farther back. Mary joined them. Jackson hoped he could keep the boy downwind as much as possible.

Slapping the reins over the rumps of the oxen, he kept an eye on the newcomer from the corner of his eye. "Lost your mule, huh?" The loaded wagon slowly traversed the rutted trail.

"Yes, sir. Died on me clean as a whistle."

"Where's your family?"

"Don't have any. Mostly just had the mule and Poppy. Poppy died a few weeks back."

"That right."

The boy watched the road. Jackson noticed he was gripping the seat like it was going one way and he was about to go the other. When the lad noticed Jackson staring, he turned to eye him and asked, "Where're you heading?"

"Colorado."

"Colorado. Is that far?"

"A dreadfully long way," Mary declared from the back of the wagon. "We're going to Denver City to be mail-order brides."

The youth turned to look over his shoulder. "Brides? You're gonna marry someone you've never met?"

Mary nodded, a friendly expression in her hazel eyes. "A gentleman by the name of Tom Wyatt is paying our way. Mr. Wyatt arranges marriages for young women. We've signed a contract with him, and he in turn will provide us with suitable husbands."

The boy turned back to look at Jackson, who was working the reins to avoid a deep pothole.

"How far have you come?" Patience asked the boy. The girls all gradually shifted back to the front to join the conversation while keeping upwind of their guest.

"Don't know . . . left the cabin 'bout two days ago." The boy kept his eyes trained on the road. "Buried Poppy there . . . dug the grave myself."

"Poppy?" Harper poked her round, coffee-colored face over Lily's shoulder. "Who on earth's Poppy?"

The boy blinked as if he'd never seen a dark-skinned person before. "Don't rightly know—just a man, I guess. He found me on the trail when I fell outta my pa's wagon and took on the job of raising me."

"Found you?" the girls chorused.

Lily's eyes widened. "Where are your real folks?"

The boy stiffened. "Don't know that either. It's always been just me and Poppy." The boy shifted as if he'd rather not continue the discussion.

"Then you're an orphan like us," Ruth said.

"Don't know about that, but I'm mighty glad you came along."

Jackson smiled as he listened to the friendly chatter. The boy was so candid.

"What happened to your Poppy?" Ruth asked.

"Went to sleep and never woke up. Guess that was good. He didn't suffer, I suppose."

"You buried him?" Jackson asked. "And started off on your own?"

"Yes, sir. Off to find me a new life."

"So are we." Mary scooted closer. "A new life, with husbands and hopes for families and children one day. They told us at the orphanage that more and more people are moving west and building towns with stores and houses."

"It's an exciting adventure," Lily bubbled, "and we can hardly wait to get there. But Mr. Lincoln says Denver City is a long way off."

Jackson grinned. "A very long way, ladies. With any luck, we'll be there in plenty of time before the snows."

Right now, that was Jackson's main concern—to

complete the six-hundred-eighty-five-mile trip to Denver City before late September, and he wanted nothing to slow them down. What concerned him most was getting through the high divide between the Arkansas and Platte Rivers before snow, even though it was now July and snow seemed a long way off. It was a crucial pass, and wagons were advised to get past the spot as early as possible.

"I'll just be riding to the next town," the boy said.

Jackson nodded. "Should be there sometime tomorrow."

• • •

Late that afternoon Jackson pulled the oxen off the road and went another mile before stopping in a grassy field beside a running stream. "Black Jack Creek is a good place to camp for the night. Good grazing for the animals with fresh water nearby."

"Why, it *is* almost evening," Ruth said, surprise registering on her flushed features.

The afternoon had passed pleasantly enough. The boy had warmed up to the girls when they'd stopped for a half hour to rest the team and let the group pick the blackberries growing thick along the roadside.

Jackson got out of the wagon and unhitched the team. The boy leapt down nimbly, dragging his bedroll and pack with him.

The girls quickly set about making camp. As

they did their chores, the newcomer pitched in to help. Jackson was happy to see the youth was no shirker. The young man gathered wood, and by the time Jackson had watered the oxen, he had a fire going in a circle of rocks and a coffeepot bubbling to one side.

Jackson staked the oxen where they could graze during the night, then joined the others at the fire. The boy jumped up to pour him a cup of scalding black coffee.

Jackson smiled and thanked him. "I didn't catch your name."

The boy glanced away, and Jackson wondered if he was shy.

"Glory."

The wagon master's smile slowly faded. "Glory?"

"That's right. Name's Glory." The kid looked straight ahead.

"Glory." Jackson took a sip of coffee. He hadn't expected this. "What's your last name?"

"Don't have one. Name's just Glory."

Lily burst into laughter. "You're a girl?"

"Of course I'm a girl," Glory spit out. "What'd you think I am?"

Mary blushed. "Well, your trousers—"

"And the way you look . . . all dirty—"

"Harper!" Ruth scowled.

"You thought I was a *boy*?" Glory sprang to her feet, ready to fight, until Jackson calmly reached out to restrain her. The waif's eyes moved to the simple gingham dresses the others wore, and she frowned. "I ain't no boy."

"We can see that now." Patience smiled. "We just didn't expect to find a girl alone on the trail."

Glory glanced at Jackson, then back at the girls. "Well, I didn't expect to see a covered wagon with five girls and a man in it either, but I recognized a wagon when I saw one."

Lily giggled, and Mary smothered a cough. The tense moment passed, and Jackson poured himself a second cup of coffee.

"How come you don't have a last name?" Lily asked.

"I've been *trying* to get one. Poppy tried to find me a husband, but that didn't work out."

Jackson choked on a swallow of coffee that went down the wrong way. Glory leaned over and whacked him on the back until the spasm passed.

"Married?" he choked.

Glory nodded. "Been trying to get married, but men are fickle. They keep bringing me back."

Patience's eyes widened with surprise, and the other girls snickered.

Jackson pinned them with a stern look. "Ladies."

Glory shrugged. "Poppy found three likely candidates before he died, but each one brought me back home before the day was out. Almost made it to supper with one, but Ralph didn't like it when I told him he didn't know beans about turnips. So I've got just *Glory* for a name."

She pulled off the battered hat and thrust her hands into the released mass of curly, cinnamon-colored hair. Jackson frowned. If she'd taken off her hat earlier, he'd have realized that she was a female. She was a comely young woman, perhaps a bit older than Ruth, with slightly tilted gray-green eyes in an oval face. Despite the dirt, Jackson noted a few freckles sprinkled across a finely carved nose above a neatly defined mouth. If only she didn't smell so bad. Poppy clearly hadn't emphasized regular baths and clean clothing.

"Well, far as I know, there's no law about not having a last name." Jackson finished the coffee and pitched the grounds into the fire. "Best we get supper over with early. We leave at first light."

Weary from the day's journey, the group ate supper and washed dishes. Each girl took a bedroll from the back of the wagon but seemed hesitant on where to spread her blanket. One waited for the other to make a decision. Jackson spread his bedroll at the front of the wagon, giving the girls privacy.

Standing upwind, Ruth glanced at Glory. "You get first choice on where to sleep."

Glory's eyes surveyed the possibilities, and she shrugged. "Don't rightly matter."

Lily licked one finger and held it up in a clear effort to determine the direction of the slight breeze. Then the girls spread their blankets upwind from Glory.

• • •

Glory wondered if she'd done something wrong. She'd been real polite, answered all their questions best she could, and she thought they were getting along right well for strangers. But clearly nobody wanted to sleep near her.

Jackson issued a gentle reminder from the front of the wagon. "Ladies, it's getting late."

Tucked in her bedroll, Ruth opened a leather-bound book and smiled at Glory. "We were reading in Psalms last night. Psalm 23."

Glory listened to Ruth's melodic voice as she read words that Glory had never heard before, beautiful words. She didn't understand what they meant, but they kept her attention. She'd seen a book like that once. Poppy had brought it home and said a lot of people put store in the words, but since neither she nor Poppy could read, they didn't know what it said. She glanced at Jackson, who lay listening to Ruth read. Did he know what the strange words meant? Did he count them useful? He must, she decided, because he didn't make Ruth stop.

When Ruth finished reading and closed the book, the girls bowed their heads and Patience began to speak. "Lord, we thank you for a safe journey today and for food tonight. We thank you again for Jackson, who is taking us to a new life in Colorado. And we pray for a restful night of sleep and a good day tomorrow. Amen."

The other girls echoed, "Amen."

Ruth started to put the book back into its water-proof pouch.

"What is that?" Glory asked.

Ruth turned. "This?"

Glory nodded. "It has pretty words."

"Why . . . it's a Bible. Haven't you seen a Bible before?" Mary asked and then dissolved into a fit of wheezing and coughing. Glory noticed that Mary coughed more as the sun went down. She seemed to have a powerful affliction.

"Don't reckon I have. . . . Poppy had something like it that he'd found on the trail." She looked away. "Couldn't neither one of us read."

Patience looked shocked. "I thought everyone knew about the Bible and read it."

"Well, I didn't. And I ain't read it," Glory admitted softly.

Harper's head popped out of her bedroll. "You can't read? Even *I* can read. Some."

Ruth leaned closer to Glory. "Don't pay any attention to Harper. I'd rather hear someone read the beautiful words that God has given us than read them myself."

"Dawn comes early," Jackson called. "Time to turn in." He doused the lantern, and the girls settled down for the night.

Poppy had said that same thing every night before blowing out the lamp. *"Time to turn in."* The familiar phrase reminded her of her loss as she rolled into her blankets. She lay on her back and stared up at the stars and wished that she could have Poppy back. Knowing that she couldn't, she wished she were already in "town" starting her new life.

"Good night," Patience whispered.

Rolling to her side, Glory smiled. "Good night."

For the first time in weeks, she wasn't alone, and it felt good. So very good. And she'd learned a few things this day. Not all people were as bad as Amos; and if she tried, she could walk a long, long way.

Oh, Poppy, I wish I was back home in my own bed and you were sleeping across the room. Her eyes stung, and she rubbed them. The wind must have kicked up some dust. She coughed, mumbling under her breath.

Jackson's gentle voice drifted to her. "Go to sleep, Glory."

"Yes, sir. Thank you for giving me a ride. I'm much obliged."

"You're welcome."

If nothing else, Poppy had taught her manners, but she suspected there was a lot Poppy hadn't, or couldn't have, taught her.

Closing her eyes, she listened to the fire crackle and burn lower. It was good that she'd run away. If Amos had followed her, maybe he'd given up by now and gone back to wherever he'd come from.

And it was good that this wagonload of girls and Jackson had come along when they had. Real good. She didn't feel so alone now.

She fell asleep thinking how nice it felt to be with people—people who talked and laughed and knew about places called "town."

3

The sun was below the tops of the trees when the prairie schooner rolled into Squatter's Bend the following evening.

Glory was dumbfounded by the bustling activity; she couldn't do anything but stare openmouthed at the wide, dusty street and all of the funny-looking buildings. She'd only gone with Poppy when she was a young child, before she could be left alone at the shanty. She didn't remember the buildings being so tall and odd looking, as if they were more of an afterthought than an honest-to-goodness intention.

Mary leaned over to tap Glory's mouth shut. "You'll catch a fly. Haven't you ever seen people before?"

"I've seen a few, but never this many in one place."

Glory couldn't get enough of the strange sights. She was reminded of the picture Poppy had of all those men standing at a graveside, all those women crying. She had thought it was really something and had stared at those bawling folks for hours on end. But gawking at a picture full of people had been nothing like the spectacle playing out before her

today. In her eyes, Squatter's Bend bested a burying
scene any day of the week.

If she and Poppy spotted a passing wagon twice
a year, they were lucky, leastways she'd thought
so. Then there'd only been a ma and pa and a few
young'uns in it, never this many people and never
all bunched in one place. Fact was, she hadn't known
there were so many people in the world! On second
thought, she decided that there weren't any more
people; they all had to be here in Squatter's Bend.

Buggies and wagons pulled in and away from
the fronts of buildings, their wheels rattling on the
dirt road, kicking up dust. Men whistled to their
teams and threw friendly shouts at each other as
they rode off. Mamas, their arms full of fat bundles,
herded small children across the street like protective
hens. Glory strained to get a better look at the pack-
ages. What could they have bought? Probably most
anything they liked. And the smells! She sucked in
drafts of mouthwatering aromas, most notably that
of baking bread, wishing with all her might that she
could smell butter, too. Her mouth pooled at the
thought of hot bread and butter, and she swallowed
repeatedly, craning her neck to try to see everything
at once.

Mr. Jackson Lincoln sawed on the reins, and the
wagon rolled to a stop in front of the tallest building, which sported a wide, white porch. After setting
the brake, he carefully wrapped the reins around the
handle before he turned to the girls. "Stay close. I
don't want to have to hunt you up when I'm finished."

"Yes, sir, anything you say, sir." Harper's dark eyes flashed back at him as if he'd said something he shouldn't have. Glory wondered if the girl plain flat out carried a chip on her shoulder. This morning at breakfast, Jackson Lincoln had asked Harper to pass the butter, and she'd told him to get it himself—she weren't his servant. Jackson had gone on eating like the butter wouldn't add to the biscuit, but Glory had known it would. She had jumped up and gotten the butter for him herself. Even dug around in the box and found some apple butter to go with it. No, it just seemed to her that Harper didn't like taking orders from a man—least of all Jackson Lincoln.

"It won't take me long to get staples ordered. We'll pick up the supplies before we leave town in the morning." He glanced at Glory. "You gonna be all right here by yourself?"

"Yes, sir." Glory swallowed the sudden, growing lump in her throat. "I'll be just fine. Thank you, sir."

Leastwise, she sure hoped so. She'd never been away from the shanty, and she didn't know what to expect. Fact was, nothing she'd ever known had prepared her for this, but she guessed now that she was on her own, she'd learn to handle it.

The wagon master smiled, a right nice smile, and she noticed a dimple in his left cheek. She couldn't say his age—hard to tell. But he was older than she and probably forty years younger than Poppy. As she watched, he jumped lithely from the wagon to the ground and disappeared into the general store. A bell over the door tinkled when he opened it, a sound

Glory had never heard before but liked. It made a nice, welcoming noise that she thought sounded peaceful.

Harper climbed onto the seat Jackson had vacated and sniffed the fragrant aroma of baking bread. Closing her eyes, she grinned, her even white teeth flashing in the early morning sun. "Now don't that smell like paradise?"

Glory thought it smelled better than anything she'd ever smelled before, especially since she hadn't eaten much lately. With Poppy gone and supplies running low, she'd gone to bed hungry more often than not the past few weeks. And there hadn't been an abundance of vittles since she'd left the cabin. Shooting game hadn't seemed worthwhile, and then she'd accepted a ride with Jackson Lincoln and the girls, and she hadn't wanted to be any more trouble than she already was. That thought reminded her of why she was here with Jackson Lincoln: Amos.

A shudder leaked out when she thought of her narrow escape. Was Amos trailing her? Of course he was. Last night she'd told herself he'd give up, but she didn't really believe it. The more likely question was how long would it take him to find her? And when he did, he'd take her pouch of gold and leave her with nothing to her name. She wouldn't have the slightest means to start a new life. She didn't know how to do anything but hunt and fish, and from the looks of things in Squatter's Bend, there wasn't much call for the like.

Mary coughed, and Patience leaned over to

gently arrange the shawl more snugly around her thin shoulders. "Put your handkerchief over your mouth, Mary," she said softly. "The dust will make your cough worse."

Mary nodded and complied. Glory could see the two girls were fond of each other.

Harper squirmed on the seat. "Shouldn't we get out of the wagon? Mr. Lincoln might be a while, and I'd surely like to stretch my legs."

"Me, too," Ruth agreed.

The girls climbed out and Glory followed, her gaze drinking in the frantic bustle that didn't stop. Up the street, fire billowed from the blacksmith's pit, and the even rhythm of his hammer as he pounded the hot iron into shape echoed up and down the rutted street. Poppy had done what shoeing was necessary at the shanty; she'd tried her hand once but hadn't been good at it.

Glory edged closer to Mary, her bewilderment overwhelming at the moment.

"Don't be afraid," Mary whispered, clutching the hankie over her mouth. "Towns are always noisy places."

Glory didn't want the others to know how frightening the town was to her. She wasn't a baby—she could hold her own. "Ain't afraid. Just like to be near you." To prove it, she joined hands with Mary. Only seemed proper, seeing how nice they'd been to her.

Holding hands, two by two, the six young women ventured down the sidewalk, Glory gripping Mary's hand tensely. The girls paused in front of a dress shop to admire the array of pretty store-bought dresses and other goods in the window.

"Ain't those pretty," Harper breathed, and Glory thought maybe she'd forgotten her usual fierceness in the excitement.

"I had a red dress once," Ruth said softly. "It wasn't near as pretty as this one, but I liked it, and it fit better than most." She sighed. "I loved that dress."

Glory didn't want to mention that she'd never owned a dress in her life. Dresses like her new friends wore seemed to be the thing most young women wore instead of trousers. Another thing she learned from being in town.

"What happened to your red dress?" Lily asked Ruth.

"Wore out," Ruth replied wistfully. "Wore it until one day when I washed it, it fell clean apart."

A murmur of sympathy passed among the girls.

"How come you couldn't get another one?" Glory asked.

"When you live in an orphanage, you get what other people don't want," Patience explained. "Sometimes folks pass on things that are better than others. Occasionally a dress or coat that still has a few wearings left in it will be donated, but not often. An orphanage depends on the goodness of others, except folks couldn't afford much goodness at the one we came from."

"We learned to take what we got, make the most of it, and be grateful," Ruth added.

Glory studied the shiny material displayed on

a form in the window and wondered how women could stand to wear such things. Why, getting through the brush with all that material dragging behind would be nigh to impossible. And the wind would whip up that skirt right smart-like.

"Never had a dress," Glory murmured, almost before she knew she was saying it.

"Never had a dress?" Lily moved to stand beside Ruth, upwind of Glory.

"No."

"Not ever?" Harper frowned. "How come? I thought every girl had a dress."

"Not me. Never had much use for one."

The women on the wagons who had come by the cabin wore faded dresses that more often than not hung loose on them, the hems sometimes ragged. None wore anything like what she saw in the window or even like those the women in this town wore. This dress was a pure wonderment. All that frilly lace and rows of ruffles would choke a horse.

Glory spied the boots sitting beside the dress in the window and grinned, pressing her nose against the cool glass. Now there was something she could use. Her boots had holes in the soles. She'd patched them with a bit of leather, but nothing lasted long, and the stitches let in water.

If she was careful where she stepped, she could wear her old boots out in the woods, but thick briars punched through the patches and the leather was soon eaten away again. When the snows had come, she'd padded the soles with rags to make do, but that was powerful lumpy to walk on and caused hurtful blisters.

Eyeing the durable leather boots, she thought about the gold in Poppy's pouch hidden under her belt. She didn't know how much it amounted to, but it was enough to get Amos riled. She could spend some of the money on a new pair of boots, but she didn't dare show it. If Amos was so bent on getting the gold, then others would be too. Besides, if she were to begin a new life without any skills, it would take every bit of the gold she had to stay alive until she figured a way to make a living.

"It is quite remarkable handiwork," Ruth observed, her eyes fastened on the window display. "Look at the fancy stitching along the bodice, and the way the skirt hangs so beautifully from that point in front."

Harper made a disgusted noise. "Where would anyone wear something like that?" But Glory noticed Harper didn't look away; she just kept staring at the pretty red dress like it was a pork chop bone and she was a hungry pup.

Jackson Lincoln came out of the mercantile and whistled shrilly. Glory jumped at the sound, but the girls, apparently accustomed to this signal, turned immediately from their daydreaming and started back toward the wagon. Glory trailed behind.

Jackson grinned as the girls approached, and Glory admired his right fine-looking eyes. They were blue, the color of eggs she'd found in robins' nests each spring. And when he smiled, his white teeth flashed and his cheeks creased like he smiled a lot. "All set, ladies?"

Ruth nodded, smiling back at him pretty as you please. "Got the supplies ordered?"

He chuckled as if he really liked her, and Glory felt funny inside, kind of empty.

"They'll be ready first thing in the morning." He glanced at Glory, and his smile reappeared, making her feel warm inside. "Had decided to buy our staples when we reached this point of the journey. We'll be camping right outside town tonight. You're welcome to stay with us."

"No," Glory said, dying inside to accept his kind offer. She wasn't looking forward to seeing that prairie schooner leave without her. "I'm starting my new life, so I might as well get to it."

Swallowing against a dry throat, she glanced up the street, her gaze taking in the orange glow of the setting sun. Things were settling down a bit, not as busy as they'd been earlier. Loud music now spilled from a doorway; men were coming and going from the building.

Gunshots rang out suddenly. Glory jumped, automatically crowding closer to Jackson. The crowd scattered like buckshot, ducking behind posts and water troughs. Then two men wearing tin stars on their shirts appeared from another building and quickly took in hand the two men who'd been staggering down the street and shooting off their guns. Glory didn't understand what was going on, but she'd just as soon it hadn't happened.

When the excitement cleared, Jackson took her arm and steered her down the street. "You're sure you won't stay the night with us? This town looks kind of rough."

"You don't have to start your new life this very minute," Mary encouraged. "You can spend the night in camp with us, then return in the morning when we come for our supplies."

The other girls chimed in to agree, and Glory felt real proud to have such good friends. She'd never had even one friend before, unless she counted Poppy, and now she had a bunch. But she couldn't accept their generosity. She'd already declared her independence, and Poppy would expect her to take care of herself.

There wasn't a better place to start than here, right now, in this town . . . among all these strange people. "Thank you much, but I'll be staying here tonight."

"All right then, load up, ladies. It will be dark soon."

Before they got into the wagon, each girl gave Glory a parting hug. She would have liked for those acts of kindness to go on longer, but the girls kept the friendly embraces brief.

Handsome Jackson Lincoln swung himself onto the wagon seat, as the women scrambled aboard. Ruth claimed the bench seat beside Jackson, Glory noticed, and she didn't blame her. That's the spot she'd have chosen.

Then it was time to leave. Glory stood on the

edge of the road, waving until the wagon disappeared from sight, trailing a faint cloud of dust. She drew a deep breath to settle her quivering stomach and tried to ignore the wave of loneliness that washed over her, the likes of which she'd never felt before.

Squaring her shoulders, she sighed. Wasn't nothing left to do but get to making her new life.

She set off down the walk, having no idea where she was going or where she'd spend the night. Smells coming from a building with a wide window drew her. She peeked in to see people, happy people who smiled at each other, eating at long tables. Her stomach knotted with hunger. Her noon meal had been a biscuit and bacon left over from breakfast, and it had satisfied her at the time, but that had been a long time ago. Wondering just how one got to eat in there, she forgot where she was until a gruff-looking woman with gravy stains on her white apron came out to shoo her away.

"Get on, girl. Quit annoying the customers."

Hurt, Glory turned and strode down the planked sidewalk, head held high as if she had somewhere to go. Before long, she slowed. The rough planks hurt her feet through the thin soles of her worn boots. She hadn't noticed before, but a wind had sprung up, a wind with rain in it if she knew the signs. And it was getting dark. She pulled her thin jacket closer, wishing it fit better. It wouldn't do much to block out dampness. She scanned the black sky. If it rained, it would take days for her clothes to dry, and wearing wet clothes was miserable, even in July.

She'd gotten caught in storms a few times while out hunting, and she didn't look forward to it again.

She kept moving, following sounds and dodging threatening-looking men who eyed her either with pity or with another look she didn't understand at all. One threw her a coin. At first she was insulted and refused to pick it up, but then she decided that maybe the man would be upset if she didn't accept it. She didn't want charity, but then she'd never known anyone who had enough money to throw away. So she picked up the coin and stuck it in her pocket, hunched her shoulders against the dampness, and continued on down the street.

When she felt water well up in her eyes, Glory blinked hard and reminded herself of Poppy and how ashamed of her he'd be if she couldn't make her own way. She couldn't keep feeling sorry for herself. Stiffening her spine, she crossed the street and hurried toward a white clapboard building where men and women were gathering. Expensive buggies and fine-looking teams filled the yard, where a mellow light shone from lovely narrow windows. As she approached, the first stinging droplets of rain spattered on the dry road. The scent of rainwater hitting dry dust filled her senses.

A laughing couple carrying a baby entered the building, allowing warm light to spill out the door momentarily. A woman's lilting laughter and children's happy voices drifted to her, and she wished with all of her might that she could be a part of the festivities inside. Overhead, a bell tolled from the tower, its sweet sound filling the stormy night. She paused to look up, blinking rain out of her eyes. That sound called out to her, its friendliness beckoning to her. *Welcome, welcome, welcome,* it tolled. But then one of the finely dressed men spotted her and smiled, shooing her out of the way when he and his family passed. He was eyeing the Hawkins rifle she still clutched in one hand.

"Run along now," he said. "Services are about to start."

His little girl stared back at Glory with wide blue eyes before her mother pulled her forward and they disappeared inside the building.

Glory backed away, and the man pulled the big doors closed. A moment later, singing began, singing like she'd never heard before, and she was caught by the sound. How wonderful it was! The melodic sweetness washed over her like rich, thick honey as she stood in the rain and listened. Shutting her eyes, she pretended that she was in the warmth and light, singing the beautiful songs with all those nicely dressed folks.

Rain peppered down harder, reminding her that she was not part of what was happening inside, but still she hesitated to leave. The music was so beautiful. Finally the thunder and lightning drove her to seek shelter, and she hurried across the street toward a row of tall buildings. Water soaked through the shoulders of her jacket and began seeping through the soles of her boots.

Driven into an alley for protection against the

blowing rain, Glory found a large, wooden crate that offered temporary cover. Scrunching into the box, she ate a cold biscuit from her pack and watched the rain turn the street into rutted strips of mud.

Oh, Poppy, I miss you so much. Her heart ached nearly as much as the chill in her bones.

She wondered what Mary was doing tonight. She imagined her sitting by a warm fire, eating some of Ruth's fine cooking. Salt pork and brown beans. And of course, the girls would be talking and laughing. Then, due to the rain, they'd go into the wagon to sleep. It might be close quarters, but they'd be dry and cozy, having each other for company.

Leaning against the back of the crate, she pulled her feet in tight and closed her eyes. Gripping her rifle tightly to her body to keep it dry, she thought of handsome Jackson Lincoln with eyes the color of robins' eggs. He'd been good enough to give her a ride into town, and he hadn't charged her a cent. How lucky Mary, Patience, Ruth, Harper, and Lily were to be traveling with a fine man like Jackson Lincoln, who would protect them and make sure they get to their destination, their new lives.

She drew a shaky breath and wished she were going somewhere, too. Wished with all her might that she had somewhere to go. Maybe she should have accepted one more night of their hospitality. It wouldn't have affected her independence. At least she would have been dry. It was still up to her to find her own way, to make a new life, but she regretted starting out on her own on this night, this cool, rainy night. A few more hours with her new friends would have been nice. A few less hours of being so alone.

A fierce wind rattled the brittle crate, and she pushed farther into the corner. Curling into a fetal position, she listened to the rolling thunder, her fingers still gripping the rifle, her teeth chattering more from fright than from cold. Men ran in and out of a building with the loud music, passing by the end of the alley. Women laughed louder. One woman had come out to roll a cigarette, the lantern light catching the red in her hair. She looked strange. Glory heard strains of the other music from across the street—the sweet, pure music coming from the building with the warm light. It seemed the two sounds warred with each other. One, loud and disturbing; the other, sweet and comforting. The sweeter singing told about a place called heaven and how they were all going to go there someday and walk on streets of gold.

Streets of gold. She closed her eyes.

Just imagine.

Gritting her teeth to keep them from chattering, she tried to find a comfortable spot. She'd heard Poppy mention that town called Heaven once. He'd said it was a place some folks hoped to go when they died, but he wasn't sure how they planned to get there. For days after, she'd lie in the grass in front of the shanty and stare up at the sky, trying to figure a way up there. It would take a mighty tall ladder, taller than any she'd ever seen, taller than any ever made.

Keeping her eyes shut, she listened to the glorious voices coming from the warm building, hoping that Poppy had gone to live in that town called Heaven and that someday she could go visit him. Wasn't likely, though. She didn't know where this Heaven was or how to get there. Right now, she wasn't overly fond of Squatter's Bend and not so sure it was where she wanted to start her new life.

And truthfully, she couldn't imagine how Poppy could have gotten to Heaven, because he certainly wasn't going anywhere the day she'd buried him six weeks ago.

She dozed, huddled against the blowing rain. Sometime during the night the music from both ends of the street stopped. Toward dawn, the rain slowed to a foggy drizzle.

It was full daylight when Glory awoke with a start, nearly dropping her rifle. Soaked to the skin, teeth chattering, her hair falling into her face, she crawled out of the crate. Stamping her feet, she tried to get the feeling back. She looked like a drowned rat and felt worse. If her new life was going to be anything like the past few hours, she hoped she would die young.

The town was strangely quiet, nothing like the day before. Creeping to the mouth of the alley, she watched from the shadows to see what was happening. Vapors of fog rose from the muddy streets, and the stillness was almost as frightening as the rowdiness of the day before.

Not many people were about. The few who

stirred were shopkeepers removing shutters from store windows. The blacksmith's fire was flaming up again, fanned by bellows pumped by the same big man who had worked there yesterday. The thin man at the livery stable yawned sleepily as he scooped grain into a bin for the horses.

Glory turned at the sound of a lone wagon rolling into town. The prairie schooner appeared through the gray mist, and she almost cried out with relief when she spotted the tall form of Jackson Lincoln on the driver's seat and Mary's pale face peering over his shoulder.

A more welcome sight Glory had never seen. She longed to rush out to greet them, but she didn't. Instead, she shrank farther into the shadows, wishing she could hide somewhere until the traveling party collected provisions and left town. She couldn't bear for Jackson to see her like this: her boots sucking water, her clothes soaking wet and muddy, her hair stringing in her face and dripping inside her collar.

Frightened, Glory held on to the corner of the building and ignored the hunger gripping her belly.

"Glory?"

She recognized Ruth's voice and quickly shrank farther into the shadow of the alleyway.

"Glory!"

But she wasn't quick enough. Seconds later a strong grip lifted her to her feet. She peered up into Jackson Lincoln's handsome face, and she felt faint with embarrassment.

He eyed her condition; his cleanly shaven jaw

was set with anger. "What did you do? Sleep under a downspout?"

Before Glory could respond to his query, the girls arrived, all talking at once.

"Glory!" Ruth exclaimed. "Why, you're wetter than an old hen!"

"Come, get out of those damp clothes before you catch your death," Patience exclaimed.

"Girl? What's *wrong* with you?" Harper's hands sprang to her hips. "Don't you know enough to get in out of the rain?"

Jackson interrupted the girls' excited babble. "Girls, you can ask Glory all the questions you want later. Right now, she needs dry clothes and, by the looks of things, hot coffee, and some eggs and bacon are in order." He turned back to eye Glory. "That won't slow you down but an hour or so, getting on with your new life, will it?"

Glory nodded meekly. No use lying to him now. He could clearly see that the first night of her new life hadn't exactly been a bragging success. "No, sir, hot coffee and eggs and bacon sounds real nice— thank you, sir."

He leaned close enough that she could smell the scent of his shaving soap as he chided gently, "The name is *Jackson*."

Glory glanced at the other girls. Mary nodded. "It's all right—we all call him Jackson."

Glory smiled between chattering teeth. "Yes, sir. Jack . . . Jack . . . Jackson."

She allowed the girls to lead her to the wagon, which Jackson had hitched to the rail in front of the mercantile. The girls helped her into the back, and Patience wrapped a light blanket around her shoulders.

Ruth rummaged in the food box and handed Glory a biscuit and bacon. "Here, have these for now. You must be starving," she said.

Glory's stomach clenched with hunger, but she forced herself to accept the food without snatching it out of Ruth's hand. "I'm all right," Glory said.

"No, you're not. You should have stayed with us."

Glory folded the whole biscuit into her mouth and chewed. It wasn't mannerly, but she wasn't in a mannerly mood this morning. She was mad—plain mad that she couldn't take better care of herself. What did Jackson think of her now? He probably thought she was a helpless, sissy female too foolish to get in out of the rain.

"My, it's a wonder you didn't catch your death last night," Lily scolded as she fished inside a trunk, sorting through clothing. "We slept warm as toast in here."

Patience toweled Glory's wet hair while Mary stripped her out of her wet clothing.

"Why didn't you come looking for us?" Lily asked. "We were camped just outside of town. You could have found us easily."

"Didn't need to find you." Glory wedged a fat strip of bacon into her mouth.

Lily and Patience exchanged a look that Glory couldn't make out.

Clearing her throat, Patience smiled. "Why don't we go over to the hotel and get you into a hot tub of water? Cleanliness is next to godliness, you know."

Ruth shook her head. Her penetrating gaze seemed to silence Patience. Glory wondered if Ruth knew she felt they were ganging up on her.

"Nowhere in the Bible does it say such a thing, Patience."

"Oh." Patience blushed. "I'd always heard—"

"Well, if it don't, it should," Harper grumbled.

Ruth gave her a stern look.

Lily reached for the dry clothing, and Glory shook her head and wadded another piece of bacon into her mouth. "Already had my bath."

Lily's face fell. "You did?"

"'Course." Glory felt both resentful and puzzled.

"You did *not*." Harper towered above her, hands on hips. "You slept in that alley in the rain. That's how come you smell like a wet dog."

Glory refused to look at her. She'd already decided they weren't going to be friends, though Glory felt beholden to her for her help. "Did too— had one the day I buried Poppy, and before that I had my spring bath, same as usual."

"Well . . . you can put these on." Lily handed Glory a dry shirt and a pair of trousers. "I used to wear these when I helped in the orphanage garden. They should be about the right size."

Glory hoped her eyes conveyed her appreciation.

The last thing she needed was to fuss with one of those dresses on top of all her other troubles.

*   *   *

Jackson Lincoln emerged from the mercantile as Glory climbed from the back of the wagon wearing Lily's trousers and shirt. They'd fit someone who ate more biscuits than she did, but Glory wasn't complaining. The warm clothing was a heaping sight better than her wet ones. Harper intercepted the wagon master on the sidewalk, her dark eyes flashing.

"You know Glory slept in that alley last night? Sat there in the rain all night."

"I suspected as much." He fixed Glory with a tolerant look, setting his Stetson more firmly on his head. "You got a hankering to be a duck?"

Glory hastily braided her hair and stuck the braid under her hat. "No, sir. Just don't want to be a burr under your saddle."

He patted the top of her head, then picked up a box of supplies and loaded it into the back of the wagon. "You let me worry about that, short stuff. The only burr under my saddle is getting these ladies to Colorado ahead of winter snows." He stored the box and turned back to face the girls. "Mary, take Glory to the café and get a hot meal in her. Ruth, Patience, Lily, Harper? You help load supplies. It'll take most of the day, so let's get about it."

Mary and Glory set off for the café, and the others started toward the mercantile.

"We tried to bathe her," Lily whispered when she passed Jackson on the way into the store.

He frowned. "No luck?"

"Said she had her bath the day she buried Poppy and one last spring."

A laugh started in Jackson's throat and bubbled up into an amused rumble in his chest. The girls paused on the mercantile porch and turned to determine the source of his amusement.

"Ain't funny," Lily whispered, struggling to keep up with the wagon master's long strides. "She just plain *stinks*." She pinched her nose daintily.

"The dousing she took last night didn't help?"

Lily made another face. "Made it worse—she smells like an old dog when he's been out in the rain too long."

"Well, we can't hurt her feelings. If she doesn't want to take a bath, we can't make her. If she won't join up with us, guess it won't be a problem come morning."

"Yes, sir, suppose it won't. She's right sweet—a shame she won't agree to come with us. I'll bet that nice Mr. Wyatt could find a husband for her, too. Can you talk to her, Jackson? She hasn't got anywhere to go, and I think she's afraid but too stubborn to admit it."

"She's a grown woman, Lily. She's welcome to come with us, but I can't force her."

"Yes, sir. I suppose you're right."

Jackson opened the door to the mercantile and gave the young woman a lopsided grin. "But on the off chance that she changes her mind and decides to come with us, keep after her about that bath. Okay, Lily?"

Lily shuddered. "Intended to do that anyway, Jackson."

4

"Shove that barrel to this end!"

"There's room for another pound of bacon over here!"

The Lincoln party worked until the sun hung like a red-hot globe over the town. Sweat poured off temples, and tempers cooled as quickly as they flared. At the end of the day, Lily collapsed on the general store's porch step and declared that her back was near broke. Worn to the nubbin, the others agreed. Every last one of them.

Perched on the stoop, the travelers shared dippers of tepid water from the rain barrel and looked back on their long day. Bacon had been stored in boxes surrounded by bran to prevent fat from melting away. They'd packed fat slabs of pork in the bottom of the wagon to keep them cool. Flour had been stitched inside stout, well-sewn, double-canvas sacks, twenty pounds in each bundle.

Ruth had stood over an iron pot behind the store, preserving butter by boiling it thoroughly and skimming off the scum as it rose to the top until it was clear like oil. She'd placed it in tin canisters, and Jackson had soldered them shut. Mary had sacked sugar and put it in a dry place.

Dried and canned vegetables were stored in tins for travel. Lily said she would make pemmican later: buffalo meat cut into thin strips and hung up to dry under the sun or over a slow fire.

It had taken the better part of the day to prepare for their long trek from Westport, Missouri, to Denver City, and eventually to the foothills of Pikes Peak, where Tom Wyatt lived.

As far as Glory was concerned, it had been the most exciting day of her life. Helping out made her feel like she was part of a family. At times during the day she found herself daydreaming. She longed to go with her new family, to witness sights she hadn't known existed until today. The women chattered as they worked, excited about the prospect of new lives, exhilarated at the thought of sturdy young men awaiting each of them at the end of the long, hard journey. Glory was tempted to forget about independence—especially when Mary and Lily kept after her all day to join them. She hadn't mentioned a word about Amos, and she didn't intend to. Wasn't any use to upset anyone, and besides, Jackson Lincoln and the girls would be gone in the morning, and they wouldn't have to know that she'd struck Amos, taken the gold, and run away. That was stealing to some folks, but the way she figured it, she hadn't had much choice. It was Poppy's money, and though she wasn't his blood kin, Poppy had meant for her to have it if anything ever happened to him. Of course, Amos thought the gold belonged to him because he *was* blood kin—guess that's where they had a fuss. She didn't care a whit about the gold, but right now she was in no position to be giving anything away to Amos or anybody else. She was on her own, and she had to take care of herself first.

"There's nothing keeping you here," Mary had argued when they'd stored the sugar.

"Nothing but pride," Harper had said.

Glory hadn't let the remark rile her; pride had nothing to do with her feelings. If she left, she'd never see Poppy again—leastways, his grave. He might be gone, but right now she knew where she could talk to him if she needed to. She might buy a horse and ride the distance back to the cabin occasionally. Likely she wouldn't do that for a good long spell because of Amos, but she'd go back sometime. If she traipsed off to Colorado, she'd never see the likes of these parts again, and it didn't seem right to leave Poppy lying there, day after day, without her visiting. Especially considering the way he'd looked after her all these years.

"Pride don't have a thing to do with it," she'd argued. "I got to start my new life. If I went with you, before long I'd be depending on you, and Poppy raised me to fend for myself."

"It's going to get real lonely around here," Ruth had murmured. She carried a pan of bacon to the back of the wagon. "Once we're gone, you'll have no one to help you—no one who cares deeply about you."

Glory had already considered that; there wouldn't be a soul she could call on if she were to get sick, so sick she couldn't look after herself. Wasn't likely that she would; she'd always been healthy as that old mule.

When she'd caught a chill, Poppy had rubbed bear grease on her chest and put a steaming cloth hot from the fire over her heart. Phew! The medicine had stunk like all get-out, but it had done the job. By morning, she'd usually felt fit as a fiddle. But the old mule had given out, and she supposed she'd go the same way someday.

She'd thought plenty about all the advice the girls had given throughout the packing: why she should go with them, and how she shouldn't be alone. But she had to give independence a try. Wouldn't seem right otherwise.

● ● ●

Glory did concede to have supper with the traveling party that night. Jackson shot and dressed some squirrels by the stream just before dark. Glory perched on a nearby rock, watching him work.

Jackson Lincoln was a mighty handsome man— not that she'd seen that many men in her life. She'd spied a couple when they hunted near the shanty during the winter. One had been older than Poppy, and the other one had passed by so quickly she'd hardly gotten a glimpse of him. Poppy had told her not to be thinking about men, and she hadn't because she didn't know what she was supposed to think.

But Jackson Lincoln was different from those other men—handsome, strong, real gentle-spirited, it seemed. She had the feeling she was coming down with something every time she was around him—something feverish and bad. Like right now, her mouth was dry as day-old bread, and her stomach felt like she'd eaten something sour though she'd barely eaten at all.

Glory studied his large hands gutting and cleaning out the squirrels' entrails, pitching them aside for a wild animal to find later. Her mind worked furiously to think of something interesting to say—she wasn't much on conversation and didn't know a lot about many a thing. Sometimes she and Poppy sat for days on end and never said a word; reckon they'd about said everything there was to say before he'd died. But there were a lot of things she didn't know about Jackson Lincoln. A lot of things she'd like to know.

"Did you know that Lily wanted me to take a bath today?" She eyed Jackson at a slant to see if he thought the idea was as outrageous as she did.

"That right?" He pitched a skin onto the bank.

"Told her I'd had my bath—bathed *twice* this spring already. Once at the usual time and once the day I buried Poppy." She'd thought that was proper in view of the sadness of the circumstance.

Jackson smiled and kept working. "The girls take

a bath once a week and take a sponge bath nightly. They even wash their clothes twice a week in that big tub hanging on the side of the wagon, if the weather cooperates."

Glory turned to look at the object. "Once a week?"

"Once a week."

"Don't that plumb wear their hide clean off?"

"Nope." Jackson rinsed the blade of the knife and then washed his hands in the stream. "Their skins are pretty as a picture. The young ladies like to keep themselves smelling good."

Glory stared at the gurgling water. Did she smell good? She'd had those two baths—surely she did. "If I was to change my mind about coming with you, would I have to wash once a week?"

Jackson grinned and handed her a pan of fresh squirrel. "Yes, you would."

Well, then, that was one more reason for her to stay put.

She trailed him up the steep bank, and an hour later the party was sitting around the fire, lazy and replete from fried squirrel and gravy that Ruth had prepared. Lily picked up a guitar and strummed it, joining with the chorus of night creatures enfolding the camp in peaceful solitude.

Glory saw Ruth open the Bible and read to herself for a few minutes. That Ruth was real regular with her reading. She was smart, book smart. Glory admired that, though she didn't have any book learning herself.

Glory nodded in Ruth's direction. "Why does she do that every night?"

Mary stirred, her cough more pronounced tonight. "Ruth loves the Lord; she wouldn't miss reading his Word." Getting more comfortable, Mary laid her head on her forearm and stared at Glory across the fire. "You don't know much about the Lord, do you?"

Glory shook her head. She'd heard Poppy mention the name when he talked about that town called Heaven.

"He's our heavenly Father," Mary murmured. She closed her eyes, and Glory watched the fire pop. Everyone seemed to know about that town except her. Her eyes roamed the sleepy group. Tonight was a far cry from the terror she'd felt last night; she wondered about each of her friends, where they'd come from, what they hoped to find once they reached Colorado.

"Mary? Tell me about the others."

"Ummm," Mary said softly. "Well, Ruth came to the orphanage about a year after me. We'll be sixteen on our birthday. Ruth's folks and two brothers died during an outbreak of cholera. She was the only one left. A Sioux warrior brought her to the orphanage and left her on the doorstep.

"Lily came when she was five. Her ma couldn't keep her after her pa was killed in an accident." The girl's eyes shifted to Harper, sitting away from the others, huddled in a blanket.

"Why is she so cross?"

"Just her way. She really isn't so bad once you get to know her. She keeps her distance—scared, I suspect. Her ma didn't know who her pa was."

"What happened to Harper's mother?"

"Potter, the man who tended garden at the orphanage, didn't want Harper's ma coming around much. Seems she took men home with her—men she didn't marry. After a while she stopped trying to see Harper. Don't anyone know what happened to her. She left one day, and nobody's seen her since."

Turning, Glory smiled at Mary. "And you? What happened to your folks?"

Mary sighed. "The cough. My folks were on their way to California, and I was so sick they couldn't take care of me. Ma was afraid I'd die, so she wrote me a note and told me how much she loved me, but that she loved me enough to want me to live. They went on, and I stayed behind." Glory thought she saw moisture in Mary's eyes now. "Don't blame them—I cough all night and keep everyone awake."

"Must have been a real hard decision for your ma and pa."

Nodding, Mary huddled deeper into her blanket. "Patience's folks were killed by a band of renegade Indians when their farm was raided. A young squaw brought her to the orphanage one day. She knew she was in danger of being killed herself, but she brought the baby anyway. Patience was scared and had dirtied her britches. Took a long time for her to warm to folks. She likes to talk to birds—you noticed that?"

Glory nodded. She'd seen Patience talking to a sparrow behind the mercantile earlier that day. Her eyes moved to the one in the group who interested her most. "What about Mr. Lincoln?"

Mary smiled, opening her eyes. "Nice-looking man, isn't he?"

Glory shrugged. "Guess so."

"Nice-looking and kind. The kind of man a papa would want for a daughter."

"Is he married?"

"No, he's soured on women. We consider ourselves lucky to have him leading us. Supposed to be the best wagon master around. Don't think he would have taken the job at all if he hadn't been a close friend with Mr. Potter. Jackson leads large trains—hundreds of people—to California and Oregon, but Mr. Potter wrote and told him about our situation and how he needed to get us to Colorado safely because Mr. Wyatt had good husbands waiting for us. The orphanage is too crowded for us older ones. I suspect Jackson didn't want the job or the responsibility of five young women, but Mr. Potter had done him a favor once, and Jackson nearly had to agree. Think he's afraid that we've gotten off to a late start, and he's worried about early fall snows."

Glory frowned. "Is it time for the snows to come?" It seemed so hot; it was hard to think about cold weather.

"No, they're months away, but Colorado is a long way off, and it snows early in the Rockies."

Jackson got up and turned down the lantern. Glory knew it was time for her to leave. Getting to her feet, she said good-bye for the last time, knowing she would never see the group again. The thought hurt almost as bad as losing Poppy.

Jackson saddled his horse and took her the short distance to town. Concern filled his eyes when she slid from the animal to the ground, clutching her pack. Gazing up at him, she wished with all of her might that she didn't need her freedom so bad. His eyes fixed on hers and caused that funny feeling to erupt in her stomach.

His features sobered. "I respect your decision, but I think you should come with us, Glory. Squatter's Bend is no place for a young woman alone."

"I'm much obliged, Mr. Lincoln—"

"Jackson. Remember?"

"I remember. Jackson." She took a deep breath, liking the sound of his name on her lips. "I need to do this on my own."

Nodding, he tipped his hat. "You're a mighty brave young lady." Flanking his horse, he gave a friendly wave and rode off.

Not brave at all, she corrected, turning around to view the town of Squatter's Bend. It looked as scary as it had the night before, only scarier now, since she knew that not a mile down the road were a warm campfire, new friends, and Jackson Lincoln. The building that had been filled with warm light last night was now dark and quiet. Loud music spilled from the brightly lit building, where men and women were laughing and dancing. She drew another long, fortifying breath and trudged toward the music.

•   •   •

Glory took a few halting steps down the uneven plank sidewalk. The rising moon shed a narrow strip of light beneath the building eaves. Careful to remain in the shadows, she slid her right hand along the rough walls, while keeping the Hawkins tucked firmly under her left arm.

If she were to begin her new life in this town, she might as well learn her way around. She wondered if she could make friends here—friends like Ruth, Patience, Mary, and Lily. Even Harper's companionship, despite her sharp tongue, would be welcome now. Glory thought of Jackson, his strength and calmness. A lump crowded her throat. She'd spent her life trying to be self-sufficient, but at this moment, the quiet protectiveness of Jackson and the warm consideration of the girls would be a comforting haven.

Unaccustomed to the kindness of strangers, Glory wondered if the people in this town would be as generous and caring as Jackson and the girls had been. If that were the case, she might be able to start her new life here.

A short distance ahead, a couple emerged from

a shop. The handsome boy and girl appeared to be no more than a few years older than Glory. Shyness swept over Glory, making her drop her gaze.

Seconds later, a thread of hope caused her to glance up. Maybe these two well-dressed folks would introduce themselves and offer her kindness like the girls and Jackson had done. The couple strolled casually toward her, eyeing her curiously and whispering to each other as they drew closer.

Perhaps six feet away, the girl suddenly pressed a lace handkerchief to her nose and turned away. The boy cast Glory a disapproving frown. Grasping the girl's elbow, he steered her sharply around Glory, then quickened their pace.

"Whew," he muttered, "you'd think a girl would take more pride before mingling with decent folks!"

Glory dropped her chin and rushed to the first alley she saw; she scampered around the corner, craving solitude. She kept moving until she found a dark corner. Wedging herself between two abandoned crates, she slid down the wall and folded her arms around her knees.

What did that boy mean by "take more pride"? Glory couldn't count the number of times Poppy had accused her of having too much pride for her own good—"stubborn pride," he'd called it.

Glory wasn't sure what the boy had meant, but she was certain of one thing: rejection. The young couple had forsaken her at first sight. She didn't have to understand the meaning of his words to interpret the looks of disgust and revulsion on their faces.

Why, the girl had acted like she was too superior to breathe the same air as Glory.

Stung and humiliated, Glory buried her forehead against her knees. Pain pricked the backs of her eyes like needles, and an unfamiliar wetness slipped down her cheeks.

So much for starting a new life in this town. When people her own age wanted nothing to do with her, there wasn't much chance of being accepted by older folks. How could they be so quick to find fault? She hadn't spoken a word. She hadn't done a thing to them. Who did they think they were?

Glory tossed her head back and sniffed, wiping her cheeks with the backs of her hands. Well, if they didn't want her, she didn't need them! There had to be other places she could go where people were nice like Jackson and the girls.

Although she'd spent only a short time with the party, they were never far from her thoughts. How could she have fooled herself into believing that others would be as considerate as they had been?

More likely most folks were like Amos. Her heart pounded at the memory of her narrow escape from him. What if he found her here? She shivered at the thought.

Shadows lengthened in the muddy alley, and a dampness rose from the ground, sending a chill through her thin clothing. She gazed at the strip of stars overhead. It was clear, no rain likely, but definitely a cool night ahead.

She heard manly voices at the end of the alley

near the street. Cautiously she peered over a crate.
She saw silhouettes of men passing by, a few in pairs,
others alone, all headed in the same direction. Each
looming shadow looked like Amos. Throaty laughter and harsh shouts reminded her of the vile man
and his taunting threats, his promise that she could
never escape him.

Glory wanted to spring to her feet and run for
her life, but she was frozen with fear. If she left her
hiding place, she could likely run smack into him.
One of those men could be him. If he tried to grab
her, would anyone stop him? She remembered the
young couple. Not likely anyone in this town would
come to her defense.

Behind her, through the wall, she could hear a
tinny piano and the clink of glasses, followed by
loud voices and the scrape of furniture pulled across
wooden planks.

She crawled into an overturned crate, similar to
the one where she'd sought shelter the night before.
It was tight and cramped, but she'd be safe here.
Maybe her luck would hold out again. Her fingers
tightly gripped the rifle stock. She'd never shot a
person, but if Amos appeared, it might have to be
her last resort.

She remembered his rage. Surely Amos was in
pursuit. Greed had sent him to Poppy's cabin. He'd
been prepared to do whatever it took to get his
hands on Poppy's gold.

Now something more would drive his search:
revenge. She had escaped, and in the process she

had hurt him. She knew that he would never tolerate that. Even when Amos had visited Poppy on earlier occasions, even when he'd acted friendly upon arrival, his good humor had always exploded into rage when Poppy had refused his demands. Poppy had warned her that his brother was evil. At the first sight of Amos, Poppy had sent her to the shed or anywhere so that she wouldn't be around him.

A week before his death, Poppy had demanded that Glory promise him never to share the gold with Amos. The whole conversation had made Glory uncomfortable. She hadn't wanted to discuss a life without Poppy, but he hadn't been satisfied to drop the subject until she'd given him her word.

At this point, Glory was tempted to give up the gold in exchange for her safety, but she could never break her promise to Poppy. He'd asked so little of her over the years. Only one promise. He'd insisted that he'd saved the gold for her, to give her the start she deserved.

She'd gladly trade all the money to have Poppy back, to go back to her life with him in the cabin. She sighed; she couldn't go back to that life. Poppy was gone forever. And Amos? Would he ever give up trying to find her and the gold?

She shook her head sadly. Not likely Amos would ever give up. She'd been foolish to think she could start a new life in this town. It was too close to Poppy's cabin, only a few days' ride. Sooner or later, Amos would show up here . . . if he wasn't here already.

The thought filled her with dread, and a realization dawned on her. She had refused to continue with Jackson Lincoln and the girls, not because this town appealed to her. It had been because she knew that when Amos found her, and she had a scary premonition that he would, he would not hesitate to hurt her or anyone with her.

Her heart ached for the girls and Jackson, but she felt protective and loyal where they were concerned. They were the only people besides Poppy who'd ever been good to her.

The noise in the building behind her grew louder, the voices more raucous. Drunken shouts like those she'd heard from Amos startled her.

Poppy had mentioned that Amos spent most of his nights in saloons. Just her luck. In her embarrassment, she'd darted into the first alley she'd seen. Of all things, it was next to what had to be a saloon, and probably the most likely place for Amos to visit if he'd chosen to stop in Squatter's Bend.

The night seemed endless, and sleep impossible. It was too dark to travel, only a sliver of moon. Glory vowed that she would leave this town at dawn's early light.

As the noise diminished and the crowd thinned out, Glory allowed her eyes to close for just a moment. They felt so dry, they ached.

Through the thin wall behind her, she heard a sudden crash. Her body jerked convulsively, and her head thudded the top of the crate. "Ouch," she muttered, rubbing the growing bump.

"Hear somebody?" a man asked, his words slurring.

Glory's eyes flew open in alarm. Shuffling feet sounded nearby. She must have dozed, and someone had moved into the alley without her knowing.

"Yeah," someone said gruffly, kicking over an empty barrel. "Suppose we got company?"

"Could be."

Glory clutched the rifle in her stiff fingers. Her body hadn't moved for hours, and she felt rigid. Cold fear made her shrink back into the crate as far as she could.

Closing her eyes tightly, she strained to hear footsteps drawing closer. Her eyes flew open again when she heard the crash of another barrel, this one very near.

"Come out, come out, whoever you are," a man's voice sang out in a mocking tone, followed by rumbling laughter. A howl echoed down the alley as someone kicked an empty crate. It tumbled until it crashed into the crate where she was hiding.

Desperately Glory scooted out of the crate, her stiff knees slowing her down. She scuttled backward until she hit something hard. She pushed herself to her feet. Drawing the rifle to her hip, she called out hoarsely, "Stop. Don't come any closer; I'll shoot."

The two men paused and swayed in the early light of dawn. They looked too thin to be Amos, but instinct told her that they could be equally dangerous.

"Sounds like a kid," the tall man muttered, squinting in the shadowy light.

"More like a girl, if you ask me," the short man chortled. "Well, well, now," he said smugly. "This could be our lucky day."

The two shared a meaningful chuckle as they spread their arms and shuffled toward Glory to block her escape.

Glory glanced over her shoulder. At the end of the alley was a fence, flanked on either side by doors to buildings, most likely locked from the inside. No time to test them, she knew. The men were effectively closing off her only avenue of escape.

"I'm warning you," she said, panic lending her a menacing tone, "I'll shoot you, both of you."

"Oh, my," mocked the short one, "I'm sooo scared."

"Me, too," the other agreed with a raspy laugh.

As they drew near, the short man lunged toward her, landing heavily on both feet. "Boo!" he hollered.

Instinctively, Glory swung out and caught the side of his head with the butt of her rifle. The man staggered, then keeled over backward.

The tall man sank to his knees beside his companion. "Charlie? You all right?" He touched the side of the man's head, then jerked his hand back and stared in stunned silence at the blood on his fingers.

Glory seized her chance and raced past the two, keeping as far away from them as possible.

The tall man on his knees looked up as she

raced by. "You killed Charlie," he declared. "You killed Charlie Gulch!"

Glory raced down the middle of the street without looking back, but the man's last cry came clearly to her as he shouted, "You'll hang for this, you hear me? You'll hang!"

5

"We're burning daylight, ladies!"

Jackson saddled the mare while the women finished breakfast. Overhead, the first pink rays of dawn filtered through oak branches.

Ruth took a pan out of Harper's hand and extended it to the wagon master. "Care for the last biscuit and bacon?"

Jackson smiled, patting his flat abdomen. "The way you've been feeding me, I'll have to start walking beside the wagon instead of riding in it."

Ruth flushed beneath his praise. "Figure a man needs a square meal under his belt if he's going to see a group of women safely cross-country."

"Well, you're going to make some lucky man a fine wife." He grinned at her as he tugged the saddle cinch tighter.

Color flooded Ruth's cheeks, and she turned away to dump the coffee grounds on the fire. "Seems the least we can do for you, Jackson."

The girls pitched in, gathering up the plates and

cups. Patience tucked the remaining strips of bacon inside the last biscuit and folded a napkin around it. "For later," she murmured as she handed it to Jackson.

"Thanks." He tucked the napkin into his shirt pocket, then shook out his coffee cup, his eyes scanning the hills behind him. A movement in the brush some hundred yards away caught his attention, and he froze. Was someone trailing them?

Casually he turned back to the group and handed his cup to Harper, who stood at the bucket rinsing the dishes. "Thank you kindly," he said quietly. "Yeah," she replied without a glance. "I'm just a real sweetheart, ain't I? Gonna make some man a real fine wife." She threw back her head and laughed.

Jackson turned toward the hills and bent to pick up his gear, keeping an eye on a thin line of brush running the length of the ridge. This time he saw a speck of fabric and the quick bob of a head. He groaned as he looked down and shook his head. Glory. Now why on earth was she following them?

"Something wrong?" Ruth asked.

Jackson considered telling her that Glory was following them, but he dismissed the idea. No use getting the girls stirred up. If Glory was following instead of joining them, she must have her reasons, though he couldn't imagine what they would be.

"Just falling behind schedule," he said. "Let's get a move on."

● ● ●

Sighing longingly, Glory parted the thicket for another look. The aroma of frying bacon still scented the air, and her stomach knotted with hunger. What she'd give for a serving of that breakfast. When the wagon started moving, she was going to search the camp for scraps. Her shoulders slumped. She knew that Jackson and the girls were careful not to waste food or leave anything behind.

She couldn't run down the hill and join them, much as she wanted to. She'd told Jackson that it was time she started a new life on her own. Of course, then she'd thought she would stay in Squatter's Bend. That was before she figured out that people didn't like her there. Truth was, she didn't like the people. And now she'd killed one of them. She sighed heavily. She could still see the two men who'd cornered her in the alley, the spurt of bright red blood after she'd struck one of them . . . could hear the snarled threat: *"You'll hang for this!"*

Not only would she have to hide from Amos, who was surely pursuing her for Poppy's gold and his own personal revenge, but now she would also have to dodge the law.

Hiding here in the dark woods, she had considered returning to Squatter's Bend to explain to the sheriff what had happened in that alley. It had been a desperate act of self-defense. She'd never meant to hurt anyone, only to get away from those awful men who'd given her no means of escape. But would anyone believe her? She doubted it. Surely the folks in Squatter's Bend would believe otherwise.

She was a stranger, and the tall man obviously lived there with Charlie. "You killed Charlie. You killed Charlie Gulch!" that man had shouted. She swallowed the lump in her throat as she corrected herself: the man who *had been* Charlie Gulch.

No one would believe her, and if she went back now, it wouldn't bring the dead man back to life. If she returned, Amos would likely be there ready to tell his story, a pack of lies about her stealing gold that belonged to him.

No good could come of her going back. She gazed wistfully at the wagon below as the girls scrambled into the back. How she wished she could race down that hill and join them—let Jackson Lincoln protect her. The small party had provided the only warmth and security she'd felt since Poppy had died.

She shook her head and sank back on her heels. She couldn't drag them into her troubles. Amos was on her trail, maybe lawmen, too. Jackson had enough problems. Besides, when he'd offered to let her join them, she'd flatly refused, told him she could take care of herself—been almost high-handed about it.

"Well, I've done a fine job of taking care of myself so far," she muttered ruefully to herself as she watched Jackson climb onto the wagon seat and gather the reins, ready to leave camp.

As if he'd remembered something, he handed the reins to Ruth and hopped to the ground, then strode back to the campfire, now just a pile of damp ashes. With his back to the wagon, he took something out of his shirt pocket and set it on a large flat rock.

He returned to the wagon and swung onto the seat. Without a word, he took the reins from Ruth and gave them a shake, setting the team on its way.

Moments later, Glory crept toward the abandoned campsite, keeping an eye on the disappearing wagon. She knew before she touched it what was inside the tightly wrapped item Jackson had left on the rock. The aroma was unmistakable. Bending down and snatching up the small package, she pulled back the corners of the napkin and inhaled the pungent tang of bacon seconds before sinking her teeth into the delectable meat. She sat on her haunches, chewing. Her eyes scanned the area nervously.

She darted into a shadow behind the trunk of an oak. In a moment, she had devoured the biscuit and was beginning to feel better. She sensed that she was completely alone, other than the scurrying squirrels and the noisy birds.

Eventually she padded down to the creek and sipped several handfuls of cool water. For a moment, she examined the napkin that had contained the biscuit.

Why had Jackson left food behind? Did he know she'd been out there, watchful and hungry? Usually she could outwit her prey, moving quietly and undetected through the woods, but Jackson was no fool. Somehow, he must have sensed her presence or the presence of someone he thought might need the food.

She warmed the napkin in her hands, grateful for the wagon master's kindness. Bending down, she dipped the napkin into the cool water and wiped it across her forehead and over her cheeks and mouth.

Feeling better now, Glory decided to follow the wagon, keeping out of sight. She could shadow the traveling party all the way to Colorado, remaining far enough behind to keep them from seeing her but close enough to not feel so alone.

●　　●　　●

"Looking for something?" Ruth asked as Jackson scanned both sides of the trail.

"Just enjoying the fine weather." He winked at her. "The trail is full of surprises—need to keep an eye out."

When they'd stopped for a noon meal, he thought maybe he'd spotted Glory in a grove of sycamores. When he'd looked again, no one was there. He'd resisted the urge to leave food behind. If he made it easy, she wouldn't make herself known. He didn't need another girl along, another responsibility, but it would be easier for him to have her with the others than to worry about her out there trailing the wagon.

He berated himself for having left the biscuit that morning. Feeding strays was sure to make them hang around. At the same time, something about the homeless waif brought out his protective side. Could it be pity? he wondered.

In many ways, she had been very sheltered. She could move through the woods, hunt like a man, and put meat on the table, but she was unprepared for the world and its threats. She'd made him want to shield her . . . until he'd encountered her stubborn pride. That was a nuisance he could live without.

That night they made camp at Rock Creek. Jackson checked the perimeter of the rolling terrain where he'd tethered the stock to give them access to the lush grass. However, he saw no signs of Glory or anyone else for that matter. Bidding the girls good night, he turned in early. If Glory decided to join them, it was going to have to be on her own terms.

•   •   •

Several days later, Jackson saddled the mare instead of tying her behind the wagon. They'd crossed Dragoon Creek late yesterday; about a mile up was Second Dragoon. After the girls had broken camp and climbed into the wagon, he handed the reins to Ruth. "Think you can handle the team by yourself?" he asked.

She smiled. "Yes."

He returned the smile, grateful for her quiet competence. "Good girl."

"Ladies," he announced a moment later.

The girls poked their heads out of the wagon behind Ruth, who was sitting on the driver's seat.

"Up ahead, we'll encounter another stream. Usually has a rapid flow over a sandy, level bottom. But with recent rains, it could be out of its banks. It might be a tough crossing. I'll ride beside the team to steer them to solid footing. Ruth will drive.

Harper, be ready if she needs a hand. Everybody stay in the wagon and do as I say."

"We're ready," Ruth called cheerily. "I've yet to see the righteous forsaken, and I'm fully confident that the Lord will see us safely to the other side."

"Yes, ma'am! He's never failed me yet." Jackson scanned the group, and every head nodded.

"Yes, sir," Harper added with a trace of mockery in her tone. "Like Ruth said."

"Let's move out!"

Jackson glanced around, hoping he'd made his announcement loudly enough for Glory to hear. He'd seen no sign of her this morning, but he'd felt compelled to leave their scraps behind in a small bundle beside the campfire before dousing it. He couldn't let the girl starve.

When they reached the stream, Jackson studied the swollen waters and swift current. It was worse than he'd imagined. The girls watched in silence as he reined his horse up and down, studying the bank. At one point, he clucked to the mare and tapped her with his heels. The horse responded, leaping into the water that swiftly rose to her shoulders. He maneuvered her against the current as he carefully threaded their way across and up the opposite bank.

"We'll cross here," he shouted from the other side, a distance upstream.

Ruth sawed the reins and clucked to the team of oxen, guiding them upriver as Jackson made his way back across to them. In a few minutes, he helped her line up the wagon.

"Got everything secured in there?" he called.

"Got everything tied down," Lily shouted.

"And knotted twice," Patience added, poking her head out between the canvas.

"Could get bumpy, ladies, so find something solid to hold on to."

Ruth glanced back over her shoulder and then bobbed her head. "Ready," she announced.

"Let's move out," Jackson called as he took a position close to the team. The animals slid down the bank into the river, the wagon wobbling behind.

Jackson kept an eye on the wagon as the oxen stretched their necks to keep their heads above water and dug their hooves into the sandy bottom. Slowly they worked their way across, Jackson reining his mare and pulling on the oxen's harness, and Ruth sawing the reins to support their direction.

As they approached the other side, Ruth slapped the reins and Jackson hauled on the oxen as they scrambled up the muddy bank. Safely across on dry ground, the wagon master turned to face Ruth. "Everybody okay?"

"Everybody's okay here." Ruth glanced overhead and added, "And we thank our Lord."

Jackson bowed his head respectfully and sat back in his saddle for a moment. When he looked up, his heart leapt in his chest. "Oh no," he muttered, kicking his horse into action.

In a flash, the mare bolted back into the water and under Jackson's urging swam toward the center of the swollen stream, her eyes wide with fright. The girls leaned out the back of the wagon to see what had gotten into him.

"Glory!" the girls shouted in a chorus when they spotted her a few feet from the far bank, her head barely above water as she struggled to hold her rifle above her in one hand while treading water with her other hand.

Glory moved farther into the river where the current strengthened, making it impossible to maintain her balance. Her eyes rounded in panic. When she opened her mouth to call out, she gagged on a gulp of muddy water.

Jackson guided his mare downstream, anticipating the inevitable, hoping he'd reach Glory in time. Her head disappeared beneath the surface of the water and then bobbed to the surface.

He urged his horse into what he prayed would be the path of the girl as the river clutched her in its undertow. He would have only one chance to grab her. If she got by him, the current would take her faster than he could follow.

The mare grunted as something solid collided with her broadside. Jackson plunged his hand into the water and grabbed the first thing he felt. Up came Glory, held tightly by the hair of her head. She sputtered and howled in pain as Jackson drew her up behind him astride the mare.

For a moment the horse thrashed for a solid foothold under the added weight, then scrambled forward. When he was able, Jackson turned the animal in a slow circle and headed toward the bank.

The girls had climbed out of the wagon and were anxiously pacing the bank. As the mare drew near, Patience and Lily grabbed the bridle on either side and helped haul the horse up the slippery bank.

Weakly, Glory slipped off the horse and collapsed on dry ground, struggling for breath. When she lifted her head to look gratefully into the eyes of the man who had saved her life, Jackson seared her with the heat of his scornful gaze.

"You could have been killed," he muttered between clenched teeth. He had nearly missed snagging her in the churning water. For a few seconds he had felt helpless to save her, and he hated feeling helpless; it was something he could ill afford when he was responsible for the lives of others.

"I'm sorry," Glory choked out, gagging on dirty water.

"I'm tired of your games." The rebuke came out harsher than he'd intended, but the little twit had scared him senseless. "Get yourself into *that* wagon and *stay* there before you get your fool self killed!"

Glory met his gaze squarely, her quivering chin the only sign of how much the effort cost her. "I can't," she replied in a small voice.

"Can't or won't?" he snapped. He tossed a look to the sky. "Keeping an eye out for you has slowed us down for days. Thanks to the delay you've brought us, we won't make Council Grove this week."

"Will that be a problem?" Ruth asked.

Jackson shook his head. "It could be." He shot a glare at Glory. "We'll make better time if you're with us than letting you traipse along behind, slowing us down."

"I'll only bring you trouble."

"Trouble?" Jackson muttered, glancing away. "What do you call what just happened?"

"Trouble—but I was trying to stay back!"

Ruth knelt beside her and brushed matted hair off her face. "Glory, you have to listen to reason. We understand your need for independence, but you must cooperate now. Let's get you into some dry clothes. After a bite to eat, everything will look brighter."

Glory grasped Ruth's arms. "I can't join you. Bad things follow me. I'd only bring you harm."

Patience touched Glory's shoulder. "You're talking nonsense. Now let's get you into dry clothes before you catch your death."

Glory shook her head, staring at Jackson, who was gazing stonily ahead. He knew she realized he thought of her as a burden. She wanted to prove she could fend for herself, but after what just happened, how could she blame him for doubting her ability to survive on her own?

She struggled to her feet. "I have to go."

Ruth reached out to cajole her. Jackson saw the stubborn pride in the tilt of her chin and knew she had a will that would be nigh onto impossible to break. He had two options: He could tie her up and haul her aboard against her will, or he could let her go her own way. The last thing he needed was for someone to accuse him of abducting a young woman and holding her against her will. Drawing a deep breath, he knew his choices. None. He'd have to let her go until she made up her mind to join them.

He glanced at the others. "Well, ladies, you heard her. Let her go. We've wasted enough time."

•   •   •

The girls stared at him in disbelief, but the set of his granite jaw effectively stated his case. Eyes downcast, the girls rose and shuffled toward the wagon.

Ruth hung behind, whispering to Glory. "I'll leave you dry clothes and food. Please, think it over and change your mind. You must walk by faith, Glory."

"How do I do that?" she questioned, puzzled.

"By being sure of what you hope for and certain of what you do not see."

"I'm not so trusting as I can do that." Glory was deep in thought. "Leastways, not right now."

"Sure you can! You have to practice at it. Like putting one foot in front of the other, knowing that when you do so, eventually you'll get to where you're going. The more you practice walking by faith, the more natural it will become. Pretty soon, it will get downright easy." Ruth's eyes reflected deep compassion. "Besides, it's impossible to please God without faith."

"Oh." Glory's mind was bombarded with weighty thoughts. Poppy's gold. Crazy Amos. And the voice in the darkened alley echoing, *"You killed Charlie!*

You'll hang for this, you hear me? You'll hang!" Glory didn't even think to ask who this God was that Ruth spoke of.

"Please think it over and change your mind. You can't look after yourself. Come to Colorado with us. Please, Glory!"

"I can't, Ruth, but thank you just the same." Glory shot an unfriendly look in Jackson's direction, which he shot back.

Ruth hurried to the wagon, and as promised, she set a few items on the ground before climbing onto the seat to take the reins.

As the wagon rumbled over the hill, Glory pushed herself to her feet, frowning at her boots that squished with muddy water. It was then that she realized her rifle was missing. She turned to stare into the dark, surging waters and remembered. When she'd slipped underwater and felt the undertow, she'd released the Hawkins to fight her way to the surface with both hands. It was long gone now, downstream by a mile at least. She was alone and unarmed.

Defeat washed over her. How long could she last without Jackson's protection?

6

A few nights later, Jackson sat opposite the fire, deep in thought. The damp air held a renewed promise of rain. Ruth picked up the plate of fried apple pies and walked around the fire. "Have another one, Jackson. You only ate two at supper."

"Thanks, Ruth. I've had enough." He got up and handed her his cup with a warm smile. "I have some business to take care of. I'll be back in a few minutes." He picked up a lantern to take with him.

Lily frowned. "Where're you going?"

"Be back in a few minutes, girls. Nothing to worry about."

Ruth followed him to the clearing where he proceeded to saddle the horse. Worry dotted her youthful face. "Where are you going at this hour?"

"Don't worry, Ruth. I'll be back in a few minutes." He dropped the leather strap through the cinch ring and drew it up tight, then mounted his mare, whirled her in a circle, and rode out of the clearing.

A shadow of the moon darted in and out of the clouds. The horse picked her way slowly through the overgrown path. Holding the lantern aloft, Jackson searched the bushes for the object of his nocturnal search. Glory still trailed the wagon, hanging back in hopes she wouldn't be discovered. Was she playing some strange, childish game? Was she trying to get on his bad side? If she was, she was doing a fine job.

A deer darted out and leapt across a gully up ahead, momentarily spooking the mare, causing her to shy. Jackson tightened the reins in his left hand. "Easy, girl."

Where was Glory hiding? She'd been on his tail for days, so where was she now? Was she crouched in a bush, hungry and scared? The mare settled down, and he gently nudged her flanks. He'd seriously considered letting her remain out there tonight. He'd asked her twice—no, three times—to join them, but she refused. If the fool girl was headstrong enough to refuse his help, he didn't have time or patience to worry about her.

That's what he'd considered, but his conscience wouldn't let him do it. Rain was brewing, and she didn't have a lick of shelter. The nights were unusually cool for early August, and she had no protection from the elements. She seemed proud of her self-preservation skills, but he doubted that she'd ever had to use them for an extended period of time. The old hermit had kept her sheltered, teaching her only the basics of self-survival, certainly not enough to remain on her own in the wilderness. She'd proved that when she'd taken a river dunking.

Weather could turn on you fast this time of year,

and she barely had adequate clothing. Chances were, she had a minimal food supply, if any. The way he figured it, the Lord had just appointed him Glory's keeper, whether he liked it or not. And he didn't like it—not one bit.

Lord, I'm not questioning your judgment; I'm asking for patience. Patience to take care of these women and get them safely to Denver City. If you want me to look after Glory, grant me fortitude, because right now my supply is running low. Amen.

The moon disappeared behind a storm cloud, and the night was blacker than sin. Holding the lantern aloft, he scanned the thicket. If he yelled out, he'd startle her. She'd bolt, and he'd never find her. He didn't want a death on his hands, though he was tempted to wring her neck like a Sunday chicken. Why was she being so stubborn about joining them? He didn't need a sixth girl to look after, but neither did he want Glory's safety on his conscience.

Something darted across the road, and he hefted the light higher. The bushes rattled, then stilled. A deer? A two-legged one? He chuckled at his own humor. Glory was anything but funny to him. He was using valuable sack time to hunt her, and he didn't like it.

Nudging his horse's flanks, he eased closer, his hand resting on the butt of a Winchester. He reined in, listening. Silence. Clucking softly under his tongue, he squeezed the mare's flanks. The horse took another step.

Stillness surrounded him.

His eyes skimmed the darkness, instinct telling him that she was there. He tightened his thighs, and his horse took another step. *Playing games, sweetheart?*

Minutes crawled by. The rustle of leaves and the sound of his own breathing filled his senses.

Flanking his horse, he burst into the bushes. Glory screamed and bolted. Hoisting the lantern higher, he threaded the mare through the underbrush, following the sound of trampled thicket. Glory, spooked now, ran straight for a clearing, and he had her.

He wheeled his horse and galloped back to scoop her squirming form up with one arm. Madder than a hornet, words spilled out of her mouth no lady would be caught dead uttering.

"Put me down!" She took a swing at him and missed as he cantered back to the overgrown path. She hauled off and swung again, letting him have it. This time she connected. Tightening his hold, he grunted, wondering what he'd done to deserve this.

"Settle down! You've been a nuisance for days, lady. You're sorely testing my patience."

"You saw me!"

Yes, I saw you, he silently mimicked. Watched her trail the wagon three days, and it had gotten on his nerves. "You're going to get yourself hurt out here alone."

"I can take care of myself—" She squealed as he hoisted her up in back of him and rode toward camp.

When the mare galloped into the camp, the girls ran to meet them.

"Glory?" Mary ran alongside the mare, her eyes wide with bewilderment.

"Don't run, Mary," Glory warned. "It'll make you cough!"

Jackson reined in his mare and reached back to give Glory a hand down. She slid to the ground, shooting him a resentful look. Mary, Ruth, Lily, and Patience gathered around; Harper waited close to the fire.

Mary was breathless now. "Glory? What in the world?"

Glory glanced at Jackson, and he shook his head. The girls weren't aware that she'd been trailing them. They'd assumed she'd traveled on alone; he'd let them think what they wanted. They couldn't spend their time worrying about a pigheaded girl, and neither could he.

• • •

Glory nodded, her eyes reflecting her gratitude. He nodded back. He'd spared her one embarrassment; it was up to her to tell the girls why she was hanging back.

Lily alleviated the need for an immediate explanation. "You've changed your mind! You've decided to come with us after all."

Glory looked at Jackson. "I've decided to come with you after all!" Glory glanced at Ruth, her smile was a tad sheepish. "Figure this is as good a time as any to start walking by faith." Draping her arm around Lily, she walked the young woman back to the campfire.

Lily smiled, discreetly squirming out of the hold. "I'm so glad; we've been worried about you."

Ruth's face lit with elation. "I'll read you the book of Hebrews. It's full of Scriptures about faith."

Glory nodded in agreement. She hadn't meant to stretch the truth to Ruth. And maybe in the long run, she wouldn't be. She'd sure give this faith thing a try. Especially if it meant having Ruth read to her from that mysteriously wonderful book.

"I wasn't worried," Harper announced. "Should have come with us in the first place. Knew you'd have to join up eventually."

Glory shrugged off the remark. "Worried? About me?" She laughed, still avoiding Jackson's eyes. Squaring her shoulders, she crowed, "I can take care of myself."

Jackson handed the mare's reins to Patience. "Ruth, get Glory a plate of supper, please."

"Yes, sir. Right away." The girl hurried off to do the wagon master's bidding.

•   •   •

Jackson listened to the girls' chatter as he unsaddled his horse and stored the rifle in the back of the wagon. Glory had been fortunate; he hoped she realized it. Tomorrow he'd have a talk with her and get the rules straight: As long as she traveled with him she'd give up her independence. And she was going to travel *with* them—no more hanging back and drinking a gallon of muddy river water. She wasn't going to like the rules, but then he didn't like the extra trouble. Now he had six women to safely deliver before the first snow.

All she had to do was follow orders.

Seemed to him he'd gotten shortchanged.

"Mr. Lincoln?"

He turned to see Glory standing in the shadow of the clearing. Her face was dirty, and she had corn-bread crumbs around her mouth. He turned back to the horse. "It's late. You'd better get some sleep."

"Yes, sir . . . I'm going, but I was thinking maybe I'd better thank you first."

"No need for thanks. I'd have done it for any-one." He didn't want her thinking she was special; she wasn't. She needed a bath and was ornery and more trouble than she was worth. She was older than the others, maybe had as much as three or four years on them, but that still put her young enough to be trouble. All he needed was to get personally involved with her or any of the girls. He'd seen the interested look in Ruth's eyes and had done every-thing he could to erase it. Ruth and the others had husbands waiting for them in Colorado; he wasn't the marrying kind. Ma had seen to that. When he'd been a kid, she'd run his pa off and denied Jackson the pleasure of a normal upbringing. The betrayal had left a bitter taste in his mouth.

Glory stepped into the clearing, fishing in her right pocket. "If I'm going with you, then I'm going to pay my way."

"No need—Tom Wyatt will pay your way when I deliver you."

"Well—" she paused—"that's the thing, Mr. Lincoln."

"Thought I told you to call me Jackson."

"It doesn't feel right yet—when it does, I'll do that, sir."

He picked up a brush and began to curry his horse. "I'm sorry I yelled at you. I was upset, that's all. I shouldn't have lost my temper. Go on to bed now."

"Don't have any hard feelings, sir."

When she continued to stand there, he turned around to look at her.

"What if I don't want a husband?"

"I'd say you'd better give it more thought. You got no kin and no way to support yourself. A husband's not a bad idea at this point. A good man can give you a home and food on the table."

"If I pay you to take me to Colorado, then I can make up my own mind whether I want such a man. Wouldn't that work?"

The brush paused. "I suppose it would, but where are you going to get that kind of money? Tom Wyatt pays a good price for his mail-order brides."

She took a pouch from her pocket and approached him. Extending the poke, she asked softly, "Have I got enough in here to pay my own way?"

Jackson stared at the bulging sack. By the looks of

it, she had enough to buy half the state, with money left over. "Where did you get that kind of money?"

She drew the sack to her chest, looking cautious now. "It's mine. Poppy gave it to me—I didn't steal it."

"Let me see that." He took the sack from her, untied it, and spread out the gold ore in the palm of his hand. "How many people know you have this?"

"No one . . . except Poppy's brother . . . but he doesn't care."

Jackson shook out a small nugget, examined it, and then stuck it in his pocket. Yanking the string on the pouch closed, he met her expectant gaze. "One nugget is all I need, and I'll owe you some at that."

A relieved grin broke across her freckled face. "Then you'll take me with no strings attached? I don't have to take a man if I don't want one?"

"You've paid your way; I have no say over what you do when you get there."

She flashed another grin. "No, sir. You don't." She whirled and started off, turning back around when his voice stopped her.

"I may not have any say when you get there, but as long as you're in my care, you play by my rules, agreed?"

Glory's grin faded, but she nodded. "Agreed."

"And another thing. Don't be showing this money to anyone, you hear? Not to Mary or Patience or Ruth or Harper or Lily. No one—do you understand? You keep it hidden somewhere where no one but you can get to it."

Young, rich, and naive—he couldn't think of a

worse combination for a woman alone. He couldn't think of a worse combination for him. Now he had to worry about the girls' safety and roughly twenty thousand dollars worth of gold ore.

"Yes, sir." She cocked a brow. "Figure I can start a new life in Colorado as good as right here."

His features sobered. "I'll get you to Colorado. Once we're there, you'll be responsible for your own protection." He turned back to the horse, but she stuck her hand out and insisted that he shake on it.

"We got us a deal." Her eyes searched his in the lantern light.

"We got ourselves a deal," he murmured without much enthusiasm.

She started off for the fire but turned a second time. "Mr. Lincoln?"

"Yes?"

"This Colorado town—is it anything like Heaven?"

"Heaven?" He frowned.

"Yes, sir. One night in Squatter's Bend, I heard these people in a building singing about a place called Heaven. Sounded real nice, real pretty—sort of like Colorado, I'd imagine. Is it?"

He turned around to face her. Was she serious?

"Well?" she asked.

"Colorado isn't a town; it's a territory. It's real pretty, but I don't imagine it can hold a candle to heaven."

"Really? You been there?"

"To *heaven*?"

"No, to Colorado." She frowned. "Sounds to me like it's a tad harder to get to than Heaven." She looked up, studying the sky. The building storm shot fingers of light in the distance. "Wonder what it's like there in Heaven."

"I imagine no one complains."

"Yes, sir. Imagine they don't." She hitched up her britches with a look of satisfaction. "Well, I feel a whole lot better about everything. How about you?"

Actually, he felt a whole lot worse, but he was hired for a job he intended to complete, no matter what happened. The gold nugget weighed heavy in his pocket.

Lord, I don't know what you're doing here, and I still don't like it. Sir.

• • •

Glory walked back to camp feeling a sight better. Thunder rolled in the distance, and she shivered. Truth be told, she was glad Jackson had come after her. Loneliness was a powerful thing, a hurtful thing, and she'd just as soon be through with it. Now that Jackson didn't expect her to take a husband, it made things a whole lot easier. Once she got to Colorado, she'd get busy making a new life. Until then, she'd enjoy her new friends with no false expectations on their part. The others might want a man in their life, but one would only clutter up hers.

She looked up as she walked, studying the sky. She'd never thought about having a home of her

own or babies—never seemed to need it. Poppy had
been her life, and the animals her friends. Now they
were all gone—but where? Where'd a soul go when
the body died?

To Heaven, silly. Wasn't that what the song said?
The tune hummed in her head: *"When we all get to
Heaven, what a day of rejoicing that will be! When we
all see Jesus . . ."*

Jesus. Now who was that? Since Poppy had died,
she was finding out there were a lot of folks she
didn't know. Had Poppy known about these things
and neglected to tell her? She made a mental note
to ask Ruth about Jesus. Ruth read from the black
book each night and seemed to be real knowledge-
able about it. Ruth was much smarter than she.
Glory hardly knew anything she should know, and
she'd proven it today. Falling in the river, nearly
drowning . . . she could swim as well as a fish; why
hadn't she been able to swim this morning? The current was swift, but she was strong, able to swim the
width of the river when she and Poppy had gone
fishing. Her heart ached when she thought about
how Jackson had dismissed her as a careless fool. She
cringed when she thought of the anger she'd heard
in his voice this morning. She didn't like him to be
mad at her. She might not be as smart as Ruth, but
she wasn't a fool, and sometime during the trip to
Colorado, she was going to prove it.

When Glory returned to the fire, Mary glanced
up from her sewing. Her cough was worse tonight;
Glory could hear the dry rasps a distance away. Ruth

was reading the Bible; Harper was putting a pan of bread aside to rise for breakfast. Patience and Lily were bent over the tub, washing out a few things by hand.

"Going to rain," Glory announced.

Ruth glanced up, scanning the sky. "Still a few hours away." Her gaze switched back to Glory. "Where's Jackson?"

"Tending the horse." Glory sat down before the fire, warming her hands.

Harper covered the pan of bread with a cloth and then straightened, pressing her hand to the center of her back. "A bath would feel mighty good right now."

The others murmured in agreement—all except Glory, who stared at the fire, her mind still on the day's events.

Ruth glanced at the other women. "Doesn't a bath sound good, Glory?"

"Told you, took my bath a few months back," she said absently, then looked up, still deep in concentration. "How did Jackson get his name?"

"Get his name?" Lily laughed. "Why, I suppose his mother gave it to him. Why?"

"No reason. Just thinking aloud." Jackson Lincoln. The name fit him: a good strong name for a good strong man. She thought about the play of muscles she'd seen in his forearms as he brushed the horse and wondered if Jackson Lincoln had a woman of his own. Didn't matter, she guessed. Spoken for or not, he'd never look at her the way he looked at Ruth or most likely any other woman.

Ruth pulled her light wrap closer. "His mother named him after two of our presidents: Andrew Jackson and Abraham Lincoln. President Jackson served our country in her father's time, and Mr. Lincoln served her state in the Illinois House of Representatives from '47 to '49. I believe his mother's father knew Mr. Lincoln personally and thought highly of him. When he was elected president of the United States in '61, Jackson said he and his mother attended the inaugural festivities."

Harper turned to stare at Ruth. "How do you know all of that?"

Color dotted Ruth's cheeks. "Jackson told me. Seems he and his mother don't get along anymore. He rarely talks about her."

The admission caught Glory's interest. "He told you they don't get along?"

Ruth shrugged. "Not in so many words, but I could tell by the things he was saying."

Harper sniffed. "Lots of folks don't get along. Don't mean a thing."

"Ruth? Things such as . . . ?" Lily asked.

"Such as she's domineering and complains all the time. They had words a few years back, and he hasn't seen her since. Said she drove his father away when he was a young boy. It's such a pity—mother and son losing contact with each other. She must miss him something terrible."

The girls fell silent, contemplating the situation. Glory finally broke the hush. "What's a president?"

Lily and Patience giggled. Ruth shot them a disapproving scowl. "You don't know, Glory?"

Glory blinked. "Is it something bad?"

"Bad?" Harper scoffed. "Girl, you been livin' under a rock?"

"Harper," Mary rebuked softly, "Glory hasn't had our advantages." She turned to Glory and smiled. "A president is a man whom the people elect to run the country."

"What's a country?"

Ruth stopped the astonished looks with another stern look. "Lily, tell Glory what a country is."

"Well . . . a country is where we live. We live in the United States of America. Actually, our forefathers first set sail to this land in 1492. But it took a war with the British to gain our independence, and we became a country on July 4, 1776. We are the people of this country, and the people elect a president every four years. All told, we've had seventeen presidents."

"Did you know these presidents?"

"Oh, my, no!" Ruth laughed. "Most of us were infants when Lincoln served, and Mr. Jackson was elected in 1829 and was our president until 1837. President Lincoln was assassinated by a man named John Wilkes Booth while he attended a play at Ford's Theater on April 14, 1865. It was a terrible loss for the whole country."

Glory stared at her blankly.

"Assassinated—shot to death," Ruth informed her.

"Oh." Glory didn't know anything about assassination. It sounded downright mean-spirited to her, but now she knew what a president was. "You reckon this Mr. Lincoln went to Heaven?"

"President Lincoln was a fine Christian man. I believe heaven is his new home." Ruth smiled.

"And Jackson's mother favored Mr. Jackson and Mr. Lincoln particularly."

Lily nodded. "It seems that way. She named her son after them. His full name is Jackson Lincoln Montgomery, but we call him Jackson or Mr. Lincoln."

"Jackson Lincoln Montgomery." Jackson had three names, and she had only one. She looked up and grinned. "It's a fine name." And it confirmed what she'd known all along. Jackson Lincoln was different from other men. Why, he was almost presidential.

Regardless, he shouldn't feel bad toward his mother. Glory didn't know what had taken place to anger him, but whatever it was, it couldn't be bad enough to cause a parting.

"At least he had a mother," Harper murmured.

"One that didn't give him away," Mary said, shifting and adjusting her blanket. "If I have a child with a cough, I'll love it no matter what. I'll never give it away."

Ruth glanced at Mary. "Perhaps there was a reason your mother felt she couldn't keep you, Mary. I suspect that if she could have, she would have kept you. It can't be easy for a mother to part with a child.

I've never known anyone who did things without a reason, and I'm sure your mother had a very good reason."

"Maybe," Mary conceded. "But I would never leave my child."

"Never say never, Mary. None of us knows what lies around the corner."

Scooting closer to the fire, Glory thought about the girls and their lives. She'd never once felt bad toward her real folks. She'd thought about them once in a while, wondered where they were and if they were sad about losing her. But Poppy had treated her well and given her enough love for two parents. She guessed a woman didn't have to carry a child in her stomach and birth it in order to love it as much as her own.

"Guess we all wish for things we can't have." Patience stood up and stretched. "I feel like Ruth. I wish my pa would have lived and my ma could have kept me, but since that didn't happen, I'm thankful for people like Mr. Potter and the others at the orphanage. They were kind to us, gave us a home when we had none."

"Amen," Ruth seconded. "I wish my parents hadn't died so young, but they did. Our lives could be a lot worse."

"A lot worse," Glory conceded, her thoughts returning to Squatter's Bend. Hers would likely get a lot worse if Amos or the man from Squatter's Bend caught up with her.

7

When Jackson returned to camp, Glory was putting dishes in the dry box. He noticed the other girls were clustered upwind. He shook his head. There was no getting around it; something needed to be done about the stink. You'd think after a near drowning in the river she'd smell a sight better. If anything, she smelled worse. Without soap, wet only made things worse.

He busied himself checking the harness for damage from the river crossing, grinning when he heard the girls dropping hints Glory should be able to catch.

"You know, Glory," Mary began gently, "after all the bruises you got in the river today, a pleasant bath in the stream with some nice castile soap would feel mighty soothing. We have an extra one-pound bar that could be yours."

Glory shook her head. "I'm fine."

Ruth smiled warmly. "Why, I haven't seen such a lovely stream in a long time—nice pools, not too deep."

Glory shook her head tightly. "Seen enough water today to last me for a long time."

Locating a tear in the leather harness, Jackson bent over his box of tools, looking for the right one, trying to appear as if he wasn't listening.

The girls sighed as they knelt for evening devotions. This evening someone made mention that cleanliness was next to godliness, but Ruth didn't bother to correct her. Jackson noticed the subject seemed to be lost on Glory.

A moment later, he left to check on the animals. When he returned to the campfire to turn in for the night, he noticed that the girls had their bedrolls tucked under their arms. Once again, the girls were reluctant to lay them out. They'd given Glory her bedroll but were waiting for her to pick a spot first.

"Go ahead, dear," Ruth said. "You pick wherever you'll feel comfortable. We insist; you first."

Glory looked around uncertainly. "I don't rightly know where." She shrugged. "It doesn't make any difference to me. Wherever you girls like to be is good enough for me."

Ruth shot Jackson a pleading look, and all eyes turned to him. He was not one for shirking responsibility, but he was bone weary, and the last thing he needed was a bunch of feuding women on his hands.

An awkward silence developed as the girls looked expectantly at Jackson to lay down the law to Glory. He looked back at them, figuring a delicate subject like personal cleanliness should fall to the women to discuss privately. The girls had tolerated Glory's odor when she'd been a temporary guest; now that it appeared she'd be with them for the rest of their journey, they wanted relief.

He took a deep breath and slowly released it. He'd handled just about all the challenges he could stand for one day, and he was fresh out of tact. Not that he'd ever had much to begin with, he thought wryly.

Ruth sighed. "Well, someone needs to do something."

The women prepared to take an evening dip before turning in, and Jackson discreetly moved to the other side of the wagon. Glory bounded to her feet and rushed to his side.

"Care if I join you?" She slanted her head and nodded in the direction of the others. "They're going to the stream to bathe *again*."

He stepped back, giving her room. "Look, Glory. You sure you don't want to join those girls?"

"No, sir, I want to stay here, help you with chores and the like." She smiled. "Remember? I took my bath a few months back." Then she apparently remembered her manners. "But thanks for thinking of me."

He looked at her, and for the life of him, he couldn't think of a way to explain the situation. In short, there wasn't one. "Well," he said, rising to his feet, "we tried. Sorry, Glory, but you stink."

Leaning forward, he grabbed Glory around the knees and tossed her over his shoulder like a feed sack. His long striding gait covered the distance down the ravine, straight for the stream. "Cover up, ladies," he announced loudly. "You're about to have company."

He kept his head down and his eyes shut as he flipped Glory over his shoulder and into the pool. Then he spun on his heel and trotted back to the safety of the wagon.

• • •

Glory broke the surface, spitting water, her eyes as wide with shock as those of the women who'd paused in their lathering to watch the spectacle. She slapped the water in fury.

"Jackson Lincoln! I'm sick of you grabbing me and throwing me around!" she shouted, sending a spray after his retreating back. "I'd like to throw you around—see how you like it!"

The girls stared at Glory in shocked silence.

Glory glanced at them. "What? No one ever dared to talk to Mr. Lincoln like that?" She glared at them, deciding they were probably in cahoots with the wagon master, since none of them looked sorry that she'd just been manhandled.

To retaliate, she splashed water at them in a big plume. A playful water fight erupted, and the tension dissolved into giggles. Soon, Glory was having a great time, feeling fully accepted into the group for the first time.

By the time Glory climbed out of the stream, tired but clean, the girls had persuaded her to strip off her dirty clothes, scrub from top to bottom, and rub her hair with soap until it squeaked.

• • •

Ruth had fetched a fresh outfit for Glory, and when Glory walked into camp, she looked like a different girl. Eyes aglow, freshly scrubbed hair falling to her waist—she was a sight to behold. Jackson ventured a glance from the far side of the wagon but kept his distance. He planned to give her overnight to cool off. Yet he had to smile at the transformation.

Glory looked lovely wearing one of Patience's dresses, her skin radiant and glowing, her green eyes dancing as she laughed. Her mass of cinnamon-colored hair glistened as Mary carefully brushed it dry in the firelight. As he stared at her, something stirred in him—something he didn't care to identify.

• • •

That night Glory noticed that the other girls moved their bedrolls closer to hers. When the light went out, she rolled to her side and whispered. "I have to admit," she began, compelled to show her appreciation, "this is the best I've felt since Poppy died."

"Tell us about Poppy," Mary urged gently.

"Well, he was the closest thing I had to a family."

"Was he like a real daddy?" Patience spoke in hushed tones.

"Poppy was good as gold to me, raised me from

a youngster like I was his own. Fed me, taught me to hunt and fish, taught me everything he knew."

"That's nice," Mary said wistfully. "I always wanted to be adopted by a nice couple."

"Not me," Harper declared. "I knew better. Knew better than to wait around for somebody to pick me out like a cur in a litter. All I ever wanted was for folks to leave me alone."

It was the most Glory had ever heard Harper say at one time; there was a pent-up force behind her words, like a sudden thunderstorm. Glory shook her head in the darkness. "Poppy told me he found me in the road, figured I'd fallen off a wagon when the wagon train had passed through on their way west. Said he waited at that very spot for days, in case my family came back to find me. He figured they'd have come if they could."

"He just took you home to raise by himself?" Ruth asked with a trace of amazement.

"Said he had a wife once, but she died giving birth. Baby died too. After that, he lived alone because he said no one could match her. I miss Poppy a lot, but it's better now." Better now that she felt a kinship with these girls, safe under the protection of Mr. Lincoln.

"So," Harper hissed, "you fell off a wagon headed west, and now you're in another one headed west."

"Guess I'm meant to ride west in a wagon," Glory said with a sigh.

"Well, try not to fall out this time," Patience

whispered so earnestly that the rest of them broke into giggles.

"Pipe down, ladies," a gruff voice reprimanded from the far side of the wagon. "Miles to make up tomorrow. Get your rest."

The group fell silent, and Glory snuggled down under her fresh-smelling blanket. As she closed her eyes, she reached out to capture Mary's hand in hers and give it a reassuring squeeze.

"Don't worry, Mary. I know your ma loved you. And even if she didn't, I do."

●   ●   ●

The pleasant aroma of castile soap still clung to her clothing when Glory opened her eyes the next morning. Rolling to her side, she stared at Mary, who slept opposite her. Sighing, Glory realized that she'd gotten a mite upset last night—wasn't used to being waylaid like a common criminal. A bath *this* time of year! Seemed a waste of good soap and water. Still, she had to admit it felt good to have the dirt off.

An unexpected thought popped into her mind. Had Jackson noticed? Guess he would have since he was partly responsible for the ambush. He'd said she stank. The words still made her cheeks burn. Well, someone could have told her something earlier if she smelled all that bad! She didn't powder herself or wash with soap until her skin looked plumb raw like the other girls. She sniffed the air and decided they'd expect her to smell like this all of the time. Well, if it was so all-fired important, then she'd bathe every night like the rest of them and hope her skin didn't wear out.

Mary opened her eyes and returned Glory's sleepy smile. "Good morning."

The sun was not yet up. Birds chattered noisily overhead in tree branches as daybreak rose over the camp. Glory shut her eyes and savored the smell of strong coffee perking. A smile touched the corners of her mouth. Jackson was up a full half hour ahead of the others every day. It was nice to wake to the sound of another person.

But Jackson and coffee weren't the only things on her mind this morning. These were her friends, and she was putting them in the way of danger. She hadn't mentioned Amos because until now there'd been no need to tell them about Amos or the man she'd killed in Squatter's Bend. Now she was part of their group—a real part—and being part of someone or something meant you had to be honest. You had to share.

She wasn't prone to lying. Poppy wouldn't have it, but Glory could stretch the truth as well as anybody. Didn't do it all that often, but she could when she needed to. However, this wasn't the time for fibs. It was the time for truthfulness, painful as it might be. Jackson and the girls needed to know what she'd done.

She shivered deeper into the blanket, trembling

when the voice that haunted her day and night echoed inside her mind. *"You killed Charlie! You killed Charlie Gulch!"* She'd never meant to kill anyone—wouldn't kill anyone unless she saw no other way out, and she hadn't seen another way out that night.

"Penny for your thoughts." Glory opened her eyes to see Mary still smiling at her opposite the fire.

"They're not good ones." The others were still sleeping, oblivious to the girls' softly spoken conversation. Glory could hear Jackson moving around the wagon, checking the harness for the long day's travel. Her heart ached for what she was about to do.

Would Lily and Mary hate her once she told them the truth? Seemed like they would. Killing was wrong, no matter how a person tried to excuse it.

Lily, awake now, too, reached for Glory's hand. "What's wrong? You look sad this morning. Are you still mad about the bath? Because you really need—"

"I killed a man."

The dazed silence was as loud as a gunshot.

Glory stared at the crackling fire, waiting. Apparently Lily and Mary were trying to think of a response.

"Did you hear me?"

"You said you . . . killed a man," Mary repeated.

"I did . . . and I stole money from Poppy's brother—leastways he thinks I did." Her words tumbled one over the other now. "I didn't steal that gold, because Poppy told me that if anything was to ever happen to him, I was to take the money—it was supposed to be mine." Glory rolled to her side, grasping Mary's hand. "I'm scared, Mary. I'm scared that Amos is following me and will take the gold. And the man I killed? That wasn't my fault, honest. He and his friend was tormenting me, saying awful things, wanting to do awful things, and I spooked. Before I knew it, I'd hit him."

"You killed Charlie! You killed Charlie Gulch! You'll hang for this!"

Lily, wide-awake now, with eyes as wide as saucers, pressed a hand to her mouth. "When? When did this happen?"

"The second night I stayed in Squatter's Bend."

"Oh, dear." Daylight filtered through the camp. The girls lay in the stillness, Mary holding Glory's hand.

"Do you hate me?"

"Hate you? Goodness, no." Mary squeezed her hand reassuringly. "I know you'd never kill anyone unless you felt you had to. The Good Book tells us not to kill—"

"I wouldn't, honest, Mary." Glory's voice came out in a shaky whisper. "Honest. What should I do?"

The girls thought about it for a long while. Finally Lily said, "I guess you'd better tell Jackson."

Oh, she *hated* to have to tell Jackson. "Isn't it enough that the two of you know? You can help me keep watch for Amos and the dead man's friend. If we're lucky, they'll not catch up with us."

"They'll catch up with us," Lily predicted. "If Amos lives in these parts, he'll ask around and discover you hooked up with us. If the other man is behind us, he'll catch up too. You don't have a choice really. You have to tell Jackson. He'll know what to do."

Glory felt like bawling like a baby. New friends. She'd not have a one after today. When the others found out that she'd stolen *and* killed, they would leave her beside the road and not look back. And who could blame them? Loneliness washed over her already, and she held back bitter tears.

"I don't want to tell him. He'll make me leave."

"No, he won't. He can be gruff at times, but he's fair, Glory. You tell him what happened and ask him to help you."

She'd sooner walk over hot coals barefoot, but she knew Lily was right. She had to tell Jackson; it was the only fair thing to do. "All right. I'll tell him first thing this morning."

The promise was a hard one to keep. During breakfast she watched the others laughing, having a good time, even putting up with Harper's bad mood in a charitable way. The sun rose, hot as a new-formed blister. The girls broke camp while Jackson hitched the team.

Lily sent her supportive glances, but Glory hung back, reluctant to destroy the only remaining shred of her newfound security. Still, there came a time when she couldn't put it off any longer.

"Mr. Lincoln."

Jackson glanced up from tightening a harness strap. Freshly shaven, wearing a blue broadcloth shirt that matched the color of his eyes, he looked so confident, as if he had the world by its tail. She'd be grateful for a little of his confidence this morning.

"Shouldn't you be helping the others break camp?" he asked.

"We're done." She shuffled closer, eyeing the oxen. "Fine team."

"Yes, they're good animals." He went about his business, glancing up a moment later. "Did you want something, Glory?"

"I killed a man."

It came out mighty harsh-sounding, even to her ears. She'd rehearsed more tactful versions, but somehow they all came out the same. She'd killed a man. No way to sugarcoat it.

"And a man thinks I stole money."

Jackson's face drained of color. She'd known that it would. Could have bet on it, but Poppy didn't hold with wagering either. She'd been nothing but a thorn in Jackson Lincoln's side since they'd met up, and she'd just made it worse—lots worse.

Silence built. He stood there, leather harness in hand, staring at her, probably trying to figure a way to shoot her and get away with it.

"Well . . . aren't you going to say anything?"

"You killed a man and stole his money."

"It wasn't exactly like that." She explained what she'd done as simply as she could, if murder could ever be considered simple.

"Are you sure the man was dead?"

"You killed Charlie! You killed Charlie Gulch!"

"Yes, sir, he was dead." When she saw resentment and then anger cross his rugged features, she sighed. "I'll get my things and be out of your way." She turned to step to the back of the wagon when his gruff voice stopped her.

"The way I see it, you didn't steal the money. Your guardian gave it to you, so put Amos out of your mind. We can deal with him. However, killing is a serious thing. If the man threatened you, you had a right to defend yourself. If you shot him point-blank without a reason, that's a different story."

Glory took a step toward him. "I didn't shoot him! I hit him. Him and that other man was up to no good; that's the only reason I hit him!"

"That may be, but you should have gone to the sheriff and reported the incident."

"I was scared. All I could think about was getting out of that horrible town." If she never saw Squatter's Bend again, it would be too soon for her. And truthfully, all she'd thought about that fearful night was getting back to Jackson and the girls.

It wasn't right, but that's what she'd done, and now she'd have to pay for her behavior. She should have gone to the sheriff and tried to explain. Maybe he would have taken her side, and maybe not. Either way, she wouldn't have the killing hanging over her right now, choking her like a heavy rope.

Jackson was right; the money was hers, no matter what Amos claimed. But had she been honest from the beginning, she might have been spared the frustration evident in Jackson's eyes right now.

She faced him, lifting her chin. "Do you want me to leave?"

He viewed her somberly. "Do you want to leave?"

No, she didn't want to leave. She'd do most anything to stay, to be a part of their group on the long journey west. But she wouldn't cause him any more trouble, even if that meant she'd be on her own again.

"I'd . . . be beholden if you'd let me stay." The admission hurt, but that's the way she felt.

Stepping back to the animals, he laced a leather strap through a brass ring. "Seems only fair that I'd talk it over with the girls. We'll all be affected by your decision."

Nodding, Glory stepped aside. "Seems only fair. I'll wait right here."

She watched the group huddle for a short meeting. The disdain in Harper's tone clearly carried over the other voices, and Glory's heart sank. They didn't want her to stay. They didn't want to be peering over their shoulders, running from a crazy so-called uncle, from a man seeking revenge for a friend, maybe even from a lawman or a posse.

Quietly she eased toward the wagon and reached inside to fumble for her pack and bedroll. Might as well go ahead and leave, make it easier on everybody. Tears welled in her eyes, temporarily blinding her. Didn't seem fair. Charlie Gulch had intended to hurt her; she'd had no choice but to defend herself. And Poppy told her she was to take the money if anything happened to him. Well, something happened to him and to her, too. Something neither one could stop.

Lily caught sight of Glory as she turned from the group, and she shouted, "Glory! Wait!" Breaking from the huddle, she ran to meet her. "You can stay! Everyone agreed that we want to help you."

A smile broke across Glory's face. "They did!"

"Of course. You're ours now." Lily draped an arm around her.

The other girls gathered around, adding their support. Even Harper gruffly conceded that she could stay as long as she kept out of her way. Glory didn't care; she'd keep out of everybody's way for the entire trip, just so long as she didn't have to be alone. Mary and Patience hugged her, and Lily patted her back. When she saw Jackson watching the exchange, she broke away and cautiously approached him. "I won't be any more trouble," she promised.

He nodded, his demeanor more sober than she'd ever seen it. "You keep your eyes out for trouble."

"I will, sir." She'd watch harder than she'd ever watched. She wouldn't cause him a lick more of trouble.

"Jackson. How many times do I have to tell you? It's *Jackson*." He glanced up, giving her a grin that melted her heart.

"Yes, sir. *Jackson*." The name suddenly felt right on her tongue.

He winked at her, then stepped around the front of the oxen. "Girls! We're wasting daylight!"

And as easy as that, Glory put her pack back into the wagon and prepared to walk the ten miles of travel that day with Jackson.

8

The wagon traveled across level prairie until it passed Big Turkey Creek three and a half miles up the trail. The rest of the day the Arkansas River Valley was in sight. The frequent rains left pools of water along the road. Late afternoon, Jackson spotted a wagon in a clearing up ahead and slowed the team. It was too early to stop for the night, but the girls would enjoy sharing supper with company.

Observing no activity around the camp as he drew near made Jackson uneasy. Reining in the team, he assessed the area: no one in sight, no animals, campfire in ashes, belongings scattered. Dread replaced the uneasy feeling.

"Hello," he shouted. "Anyone here?"

Ruth sat beside him on the wagon seat; the other girls peered from behind the curtain, trying to get a look.

"Let's go say hello," Ruth suggested. "They can't be far."

"Stay here." Jackson turned on the seat, his glance

taking in every curious face behind him. "All of you," he added firmly. "I'll have a look."

He sprang lithely to the ground and slowly approached the campfire. Squatting beside the ashes, he passed his hands inches above the remains. Cold. When he straightened, he noticed the dishes and four bedrolls spread out around the camp. "Hello," he called again and waited—no response, the silence eerie.

Unable to see anything around the others, Glory raised the side canvas a few inches. "Hey," she whispered, "I can help—"

Jackson lifted his hand to silence her without turning around. His deliberate manner stopped her midsentence, but she and the other girls continued to squirm for a vantage point from inside their wagon. No doubt the prospect of meeting other travelers, maybe young people their age, filled the girls with anticipation.

Jackson moved to the back of the deserted wagon and took a deep breath before lifting the flap. Sunlight spilled over his shoulder into the dark corners as his gaze moved over the faces inside—a man, a woman, between them a young boy and a small girl. All dead. Their bodies close, embracing each other.

He stepped back, dropping the flap as he turned and strode to the edge of the clearing. He released a breath and filled his lungs with fresh, cleansing air.

"Is something wrong?" Glory called.

He dropped his head briefly before he lifted his

gaze. The women's eyes were wide and inquisitive. Covering the uneven ground in efficient strides, he returned to stand beside his wagon. Glory drew back slightly at the look of despair on his face.

"What?" Ruth whispered, speaking for all of them.

"Cholera." His tone was flat.

"You sure?" Ruth's eyes flew back to the infected wagon.

Jackson nodded, his expression resigned. "Seen it more times than I care to remember."

"Are they . . . ?" Patience began and then seemed unable to finish.

He nodded. "All four of them."

"We can't take a chance of catching this sickness," he said grimly. "Do exactly as I tell you—nothing else." He made brief eye contact with each of the women. "Understood?"

Each responded with a vigorous nod.

Ruth's eyes returned to the wagon. "What do you want us to do?"

Jackson stepped to the back of the wagon and reached inside for the box of matches. "Move our wagon to the edge of the clearing and wait for me there. I have to burn their wagon. Only way to stop the contagion."

"Can we get down?" Glory asked. "Look for their stock? If they're tied up and left behind, they might starve."

He considered for an instant and nodded. "Do *not* go near their wagon."

"We should hold a memorial service for them."

Patience looked to Ruth. "It's not fitting to . . . it's not fitting to go this way."

Worry creased Jackson's brow as he glanced back at the silent wagon. "I can't afford to risk your safety."

"We can't afford to leave them without saying words from the Good Book," Ruth said quietly. "I promise we'll be brief."

Jackson nodded. "I'll scout around to check for their stock."

●   ●   ●

"I'll help." Glory scrambled out of the wagon, relieved Ruth was going to be otherwise occupied. She could help Jackson; the thought was pleasing though the circumstances were anything but happy.

Jackson and Glory searched a wide loop around the family's wagon while the girls moved the wagon. He led the way down a slope to the Arkansas River, where tethered nearby they found a nice team of red mules still under harness, tied so they could graze on the heavy bottom grass and also reach water.

Glory murmured soothingly to reassure the two large animals as Jackson freed them. She trailed behind as he led them uphill. After tying the pair of animals to the back of his wagon, he and Glory joined the girls, who had formed a loose circle a short distance from the burned-out campfire. Glory and Jackson bowed their heads.

"Ashes to ashes, dust to dust," Ruth murmured.

Glory's gaze drifted over the neat bundles near

the campfire: bedrolls, folded clothing . . . people's lives. Her eyes focused on a scrap of black leather left out in the open not far from where she was standing. She stretched her neck for a better look. Beneath the black cover, she saw a flash of gold. It reminded her of the Good Book open in Ruth's hands. She glanced up. Sure enough, the two looked practically the same: black leather covers, pages edged in gold.

Her eyes widened. Could this book be a valuable treasure like the one Ruth handled with such care? she wondered. She glanced up to capture Jackson's attention, but his eyes were closed as he stood silent with head bowed.

"Amen," Ruth intoned, and the others followed.

"Amen." Jackson glanced up and frowned at Glory, who was staring at him. When he raised his brows questioningly, she pointed to the black book on the ground not far from her feet.

"Can I . . . ?" she began haltingly. "Would it be okay if I picked it up?"

Jackson's gaze traveled from the Bible back to her eager eyes.

"Sorry, Glory. I can't let you have it. Cholera is a powerful sickness. We have to burn everything."

Glory's face fell. She'd give anything to have a book like Ruth's. She couldn't read it, but she could hold it and feel the power of its words in her hands.

Stepping away, Jackson walked to his horse and loosened the leather strap on his saddlebags. He withdrew a book, secured the flap, and walked back to the gathering. He handed the book to Glory, his features grave. "You can have my Bible."

Glory stared at the book, then up at him. He was giving her his Bible?

"I couldn't take your Bible." She handed the book back to him.

Seconds later, the black book was back in her hands. "I want you to have it."

She opened the front cover and saw lines neatly penned in black ink. With a sigh, she passed the book back to Jackson. "What does it say?"

"You can't read?" he asked gently.

Glory shook her head, unable to meet his eyes, feeling suddenly inadequate and strangely disappointed.

Jackson's eyes softened. "It's the family Bible, Glory. The names and origins of my family's tree are recorded in the front." He leaned closer, his breath warm on her cheek. "See here? My closest relatives live in Illinois."

"Illinois," Glory murmured, staring at the feathery script. No doubt Jackson's kin had written the information for future generations.

"Perhaps you and I can write Jackson's relatives in Illinois and tell them about our trip," Ruth suggested, "so they'll know where Jackson is and what he's doing."

"Thank you, Ruth. That's a real thoughtful suggestion of yours." Jackson gave Ruth one of those smiles Glory envied.

He studied the book in her hands for a moment.

"I'm placing my Bible temporarily in your care, Glory, with one important condition."

She nodded. "Whatever you say." He was actually entrusting her with something of his. She'd never owned a book before. Neither had Poppy, though he'd always put a lot of store in such. She couldn't believe her good fortune!

"If you want to keep this book, then it will be your responsibility to care for it. I think Ruth's suggestion is good; you and Ruth will write to the names in the front of the book and tell them about yourself and how you came to be with my wagon." He met her gaze directly. "This book is important to me, Glory. I wouldn't entrust it to just anyone."

She felt color spreading to her cheeks. "I can't write." He must realize that, so why was he embarrassing her all over again?

"Then you must learn to read. And write."

Now she couldn't believe her bad luck.

"*And* write?" Read *and* write. He might as well tell her to rehang the moon . . . or find an easier route to Heaven.

She sighed. For some reason, she wanted this book more than any earthly thing she could recall because it was his, but it came with strings attached. She sensed this reading and writing deal was going to be work, the kind of work she didn't like, the kind of work where you had to sit still and think. She looked at the book, felt the weight of it in her hands. At that moment, she knew she would agree to most anything to keep it.

She nodded. "Okay."

"We have a deal then?"

"Deal." She nodded, sticking out her right hand while gripping the book tightly in her left.

Jackson took her hand and gave it a firm shake, then turned to face the girls. "Ruth, I'd like for you to teach Glory to read and write."

"Of course, Jackson. I would be happy to tutor her."

Harper lifted her brows and crossed her arms. "Teach her to read? Are you addled?"

"I don't believe so," Jackson replied, meeting Harper's surly look with one of his own. "Other than you, Harper, no one has thought to question my common sense."

Harper looked Glory up and down, her eyes dark with resentment. Glory felt her face grow hot under Harper's scrutiny; she felt she was being judged like a cow taken to market.

"I-I'm not stupid," Glory stammered.

"There's times when—"

"Harper," Ruth cautioned.

"I can do it." Glory straightened defensively. She wasn't an imbecile. There were just a whole lot of things she didn't know. And reading and writing happened to be two of them.

"Well, Harper, I know you'll want to get in on Glory's education. You can teach her to cook," Jackson said.

"Cook? Her?"

"Maybe you're not as smart as Jackson thinks," Glory stated, crossing her arms smugly. "Maybe you can't teach anybody to cook."

Harper uncrossed her arms and crossed them again. "I can teach *anyone anything* if I set my mind to it. My ma was intelligent. That's what Mr. Potter said. Very intelligent. He said that's where I get my smarts."

"Ha."

"Ha."

The girls faced off hotly.

"Then it's settled." Jackson seemed eager to move on. "Harper, you'll teach Glory to cook, and Ruth will teach her to read. Ladies, return to our wagon and move on down the trail about a hundred yards. Wait for me there."

The girls followed his order, loaded up, and started down the trail. They were over a hill and down the other side when Ruth reined in the team to wait for Jackson. They could no longer see the family's campsite, but minutes later, they saw smoke rising in the sky and knew what was happening.

When Jackson topped the rise and approached, they could see the sadness on his face. He stowed the matches, then joined Ruth on the wagon seat. Without a word, he took the reins and gave them a shake. The oxen leaned into the yoke and trudged on down the trail.

Glory turned to stare out the back of the wagon, clutching the worn, black book to her chest. Jackson

had loaned her his Bible. She thought she was going
to burst with the joy of it all.

●   ●   ●

After supper that night, Ruth sat with Glory beside
the campfire, going over the alphabet. Jackson suspected that Glory would have preferred to spend her
time skinning rabbits, cleaning a fish, even washing
dishes, but she appeared determined to prove herself
a capable student.

He smiled at the frown of concentration on her
face as she carefully repeated after Ruth. Beckoning
to Lily and Patience from the other side of the
wagon, he got their attention.

"Ladies," he whispered when they joined him, "I
would appreciate it if you'd teach Glory some house-
hold skills. You two do a fine job of it, and those are
skills she's going to need in the future."

"Of course," Lily said. "I've been thinking the
same thing."

"Couldn't be that hard," Patience agreed. "If
Ruth can teach her to read and write, and Harper
can show her how to cook, Lily and I can hone her
domestic skills."

"I'd be much obliged." Jackson nodded with a
conspiratorial smile. "And, ladies, let's just keep this
among ourselves, shall we?"

Patience and Lily glanced briefly at each other
and back to him. "Of course."

Later, Jackson found a moment to talk privately

with Mary, and she agreed to teach Glory to sew. Each of the women was more than willing to help, and all had agreed to keep their arrangements with Jackson confidential. After all, they told him, they wouldn't want to hurt the young woman's pride.

Jackson grinned as he set the wagon in motion the next morning, feeling downright proud of his accomplishments. He glanced over his shoulder, his smile widening. Glory was in the back of the wagon, leafing through his Bible. There'd be no walking until she satisfied her curiosity, and that would take a while.

A girl would be ill-prepared for marriage unless she learned basic domestic tasks. Whether she liked it or not, before the trip was over, Glory would be qualified to make some man a good wife, even though somewhere in that stubborn brain of hers, she still thought that she was going to make it on her own.

● ● ●

Cooking. Now Jackson was set on meddling in her business. Glory picked up a long-handled fork and approached the fire warily. There were a hundred things she liked better than cooking. Sore bunions, for instance, or an earache would be better than standing over a hot skillet of spitting bacon.

She had more grease burns on her arms than she had freckles on her face. Uttering a bad word, she turned a piece of bacon, jumping farther back and spouting another unsavory word. Frowning, Lily shook her head. "We don't say those words around here."

Glory eyed the popping skillet, shoving it away from the fire. "I can't help it, Lily. I'm not a cook. Don't even like it. Can't I do the wash? Or shoot something for dinner like a rabbit or a squirrel?"

"You ate when Poppy was alive, didn't you?"

"He did all the cooking. I made sure he had stuff to put on the table." If Mary or Lily asked her to skin a deer, she could do that. She could shoot a jackrabbit or wring a hen's neck to throw in a boiling pot. What she couldn't do was fry a strip of bacon without burning it or make a drinkable cup of coffee! She jumped back again, sucking a burnt finger.

The group gathered at the back of the wagon to eat breakfast. Eating had turned into an ordeal Glory would just as soon avoid. For three weeks they'd been on the trail now, and for some reason table manners seemed suddenly more important.

The girls eyed Glory disapprovingly when she sopped up gravy with bread. Why? You were *supposed* to sop gravy with biscuits, not eat it with a fork like Patience. If she tried to eat gravy with a fork, it would take her all day to get a decent bite.

Jackson approached the wagon, removing his hat. The girls bowed their heads, and he blessed the food. "Lord, we thank you for this bounty and ask that you be with us today on our travels. Amen."

Ruth and Lily unfolded their napkins and laid

them in their laps. Ruth's eyes followed Jackson, and she hurriedly reached for the plate of bacon and eggs. "You must be real hungry this morning."

"Thanks, Ruth. I can always eat Harper's biscuits."

I can always eat Harper's biscuits, Glory mocked silently. Envy coursed through her. He'd never told her that he liked her cooking. Of course, she couldn't blame him. She didn't like her cooking, either.

She felt the girls' eyes on her as she dug into her eggs, anxious to be on her way. The long days were full of new adventures, and she looked forward to each new day and to the knowledge it would bring her. Breaking a biscuit apart, she dunked it in gravy. "Good thing we ain't—"

"Haven't," Ruth corrected.

". . . haven't," she amended dutifully, "come across any more families who caught the cholera."

Ruth passed Jackson the pan of biscuits and filled his coffee cup a second time. Her hand lingered a moment longer on his than what Glory thought was proper. Ruth smiled. "Jelly?"

Jelly? Glory watched the exchange, assuring herself that she didn't care. These new feelings were worse than having a shoe fit too tight. Ruth had been good to her, real nice, but Ruth clearly had her sights fixed on Jackson, and clearly he wasn't complaining.

Glory didn't like the hurtful twinges Ruth's maternal clucking caused, partly because she didn't understand them and partly because she wanted to be the one doing the fussing. Jackson didn't seem to mind who clucked over him. He took the molly-coddling in stride, like it was his due.

Scooping a bite of eggs into her mouth, Glory wiped her chin with the cuff of her sleeve. "What do you think we'll see on the trail today, Jackson?"

Yesterday they'd spotted a big ten-point buck standing along a ridge. He'd stood there proud as a peacock, sniffing the air. Glory had studied the beautiful animal as Jackson rode to the back of the wagon and eyed her sternly before he spoke. "By the size of his rack, he's been around a few years. Unless the meat is needed, nobody in this train kills for sport."

Glory wouldn't have shot the buck for any rea-son; Jackson didn't need to look at her that way, as if she were loaded with evil. Poppy had said it was wrong to kill for sport, and she'd never dream of felling that magnificent creature.

The rest of the day she'd kept busy watching geese lifting off of ponds and colorful birds taking flight, wishing Poppy could see all the new wonders.

They'd stopped at Big Timbers long enough for Jackson to check the harness, and she'd watched Patience talking to a couple of bluebirds on a fence post. When she'd asked Patience if they'd said any-thing back, Lily gave her a weary look. Well, Glory didn't talk to birds. How was she supposed to know if they talked back to some folks?

Jackson glanced up from his breakfast plate, dis-turbing her musings. "We'll be at Apishapa Creek in a month. At that point, you'll be able to see the

Huerfano Mountains and Spanish Peaks in the distance."

"Huerfano?" Glory asked awkwardly, trying out the different sound on her tongue.

Jackson nodded. "Means 'orphan' in Spanish."

"Like us," Lily murmured. The girls felt an immediate kinship with a range of orphan mountains.

"Yes," Jackson said, lying back to rest. "The Cherokee Trail comes in from Arkansas near Bent's Fort and leads to the gold diggings at Cherry Creek."

"That's in Colorado," Ruth said.

"Wow," Glory murmured in awe. She shook her head, marveling at her good fortune. She'd already been farther than she'd ever dreamed possible and seen things she never knew existed, and Jackson said they'd barely begun the long trip, and they were less than halfway there.

That day they walked only ten miles, but the trail had crossed high, broken terrain. The going was slow and difficult, and the wagon had gotten hung up several times.

For weeks, Jackson had warned them that there would be many tedious days like this one, not to let themselves be spoiled by some of the earlier days when the road had been flat and worn down by previous travelers.

Again, Jackson reminded them of what lay ahead. "The road is just as bad up ahead," he told them as they gathered around the fire that night. "Don't look for easy travel."

Glory listened to the warning, bone weary

tonight. Her sore feet agreed that the road had been hard today, though she had found previous days exhausting as well. She ladled lard into the skillet and set it on the fire to heat.

The others eyed the skillet bleakly.

Glory noted their leery looks and determined to make them eat their uncharitable thoughts. Ruth had put her in charge of cooking tonight, and they were going to see that she was improving. She cut up an onion and threw it in the hot grease. The spicy aroma added hot fuel to the late August air.

Lily sniffed the pleasant smell, rubbing her swollen ankles. "I'm just too plain tired to eat."

Glory smiled to herself as she mixed brown beans and potatoes in a bowl. Lily might think she was too tired to eat, but once she got a taste of Poppy's recipe, she'd come alive. Poppy had fixed it twice a week—had vowed it was good for what ailed you.

Rummaging through the staples box, she located the bundle of hot peppers. There was nothing better than a dose of Poppy's Blazing Fire stew to get the blood circulating. That should get them back on their feet.

While the others dozed before the warm fire, Glory added seasoning to the skillet, humming as she worked. The mixture in the pot bubbled merrily over the red-hot coals.

Ruth finally stirred and went to the back of the wagon. Glory glanced over her shoulder to watch Ruth climb into the wagon. She wondered if Jackson would follow, but he didn't. He sat by

the fire, hat tipped over his eyes, resting from the
long day.

Wiping her hands on her apron, Glory went in
search of Ruth. She found the young woman taking
a sponge bath in the privacy of the sheltered wagon.
Ruth glanced up when Glory rounded the corner.

"Oh!" She quickly drew her bodice back into
place.

"It's me, Ruth. Sorry, didn't mean to scare you."

Ruth smiled and returned to her nightly groom-
ing. *I swear, she's going to wear a hole clean through
her skin,* Glory thought. But she envied Ruth's scru-
pulous good habits . . . and even more, she admired
the way Ruth was so happy and satisfied, so sure of
what she wanted. Glory longed for Ruth's peaceful-
ness and inner beauty, and she had a hunch it had
something to do with the Bible. Ruth understood
life and what was expected out of a person more
than most folks. Whatever it was that caused Ruth's
glow, Glory wanted it.

When Glory continued to stare, Ruth turned to
look over her shoulder. "Thought I'd freshen up a
bit while supper is cooking."

"You're not going to take a bath in the river?"

"No, it's rather shallow here. I'll just freshen up
a bit in the wagon." She flashed a wholesome smile.
"Care to join me?"

"Can't. Supper's cooking." But she would later.
It was getting to where she didn't sleep well unless
she was spanking clean. As far as she could tell, the
daily baths hadn't hurt her skin.

When Glory continued to stand there, Ruth frowned. "Did you need something from the wagon?"

"No, needed to ask you something." It was a thought that'd been going around in Glory's mind for weeks. The only way she knew to get rid of it was to come right out and ask Ruth directly so she wouldn't be thinking about it day and night.

"Ask away." Ruth's slender fingers refastened the front of her dress.

"You like Jackson, don't you?"

Ruth's brows lifted curiously. "Like him? Yes, he's very nice."

"No. I mean, you *like* him."

When the implication sank in, Ruth's smile gradually faded. "Don't you like him?"

"I like him a whole lot, but he doesn't like me."

"Nonsense." Ruth laughed. "He's been very good to you, Glory. What a thing for you to say. He's been kind and considerate and most thoughtful of all our needs."

"He doesn't like me like he likes you, Ruth."

"Nonsense." Ruth picked up the round basin and emptied her bath water in the bushes.

"But you do like him, don't you?"

"I don't think that's a proper thing for you to be asking."

"Why not?"

"Well . . . because. Whom I like and whom I don't like is a private matter. Besides, Mr. Wyatt has arranged for me to be a mail-order bride. Even if I were to find Mr. Lincoln attractive—"

"And you do?"

Ruth glanced away. "Even if I did, he isn't free to return my sentiments."

Glory couldn't let it go. It was like a worrisome hangnail that just got worse with too much handling. "But you want him to like you as much as you like him."

Ruth feigned indifference, but Glory knew better. "I can't say that I don't find Jackson a desirable man, not only in appearance but in various other ways."

Glory nodded. She knew the other ways. Confident, self-assured, powerful—he attracted Ruth all right, and Ruth's feelings amounted to more than like.

Ruth turned to face her. "Seems to me he's rather partial to you. After all, he entrusted his family Bible to your care."

That was true, he had. And it still was hard for Glory to believe.

Ruth consulted a small mirror on the back of the wagon. "Does that answer your question?"

Nodding, Glory studied the brush Ruth was pulling through her hair. The thick tresses were shiny and as black as coal. "You're in love with him."

Didn't matter, really. Glory figured most every girl on the wagon trip was in love with him, except Harper, who didn't like men, period.

"But he can't return my affection, so it doesn't matter," Ruth repeated, her tone gentler now. "Now, if I'm not mistaken, I smell supper burning."

"Yes, probably so."

When Glory returned to the fire, Harper was stirring the bubbling concoction with a large wooden spoon. Her dark eyes surveyed the pot curiously. "Girl, what in the world is this?"

Moving her out of the way, Glory replied, "Never mind. You're going to like it."

And like it they did. Jackson ate four servings, and Glory noticed with considerable satisfaction that even Ruth went back for seconds. When Lily scraped the skillet clean, Glory thought she would burst with happiness. Maybe cooking wasn't so bad after all.

The moon rose high over the campsite. After some time, however, the girls left the wagon, one by one, and ran toward the creek. Eventually Jackson staggered from his bedroll and beat a path to the bushes. By dawn, the whole party was lying on the riverbank, gripping their stomachs.

"What did you put in that devil's brew?" Harper moaned. She rolled to her side and heaved.

Lily, Patience, Ruth, and Mary wet towels and put them over their eyes.

Lying prostrate on the ground, Glory mustered enough strength to reply, "Just some beans . . . potatoes . . . chilies . . . and grease."

Grease—lots of thick, heavy lard. Guess she must have gone a lot heavier on the grease than Poppy did. She'd never paid much attention to how much of each ingredient he'd used.

Lily doubled over, holding her stomach like something was about to fall right out of the middle.

"Oh, mercy!" She moaned in agony. "In all my life I've never felt so close to death."

Patience groaned. "We may all be in heaven before too long."

"Except for those of us bound for the alternative!" Harper's glassy eyes burned feverishly in her head.

Glory felt the ground spinning beneath her as she continued to lie belly down. Oh no. They couldn't all go to Heaven tonight and leave her! She'd been sicker than this before, though it was hard to remember exactly when, but she knew she was nowhere near dyin'. And what was that alternative thing Harper was talking about? Glory didn't even know what the word meant.

She winced when she heard Jackson struggle to his feet and make another dash for the bushes.

Well, she thought, closing her eyes against a wave of nausea, if they were so fired up about teaching her to cook, they'd have to suffer the consequences.

Jackson wasn't talking. No one was, and no one wanted breakfast, even though Ruth offered to cook it. They sat around the fire, wrapped in blankets, making periodic sprints into the brush. The whole incident cost a day of travel, and Jackson wasn't too happy about it.

Glory wasn't any happier, but the way she figured it, she could have killed them all—almost did. She'd lain there on the riverbank, holding Jackson's worn black book and looking up at the sky, where she'd pleaded with someone to please not let Jackson die.

And while you're at it, I'd sure appreciate it if you'd spare the other girls' lives, too.

Someone had answered her prayer, and Glory was truly beholden to the source.

On the other hand, Jackson didn't miss the chance to tell her that it would be a cold day in August before he ate *that* stuff again.

9

In the next couple of days, the party recovered enough to eat solid food again.

But Glory was anything but a quitter. For the next few weeks, she watched Harper's cooking methods attentively, followed her directions as well as she could, and prepared a few dishes under Harper's close scrutiny.

Glory was itching to try something on her own without the teacher's continual criticism. The others were leery about what she fixed, giving her recipes a wary eye. For that reason, she'd decided not to ask Harper for help. This time she'd try a tasty treat that she *knew* was one of Jackson's favorites: apple pie. If she couldn't make a simple apple pie, then she was a plain disgrace to womanhood. During the noon break, she'd walked the horses to the stream to water them. On the way back, she'd discovered a wild apple tree. It had reminded her of the autumns she'd shared with Poppy. Early September had always brought golden days, crisp nights, and delicious apples. She'd filled her apron with ripe, tart fruit and hidden it in the wagon upon her return.

That evening as they set up camp Glory peeled, cored, and sliced the apples the way she'd seen Poppy do so many times. Now for the crust. Poppy had let her help with the apples, but he'd always fixed the shell himself. Said it was easier to do himself than to teach someone how. Claimed you had to have a feel for it, an instinct that told you when to add more water, when to add more flour, when to let it rest, how to roll it out just so.

Glory shrugged. How hard could it be? Didn't everyone say "simple as pie" when they thought something was easy? Poppy never measured ingredients, so neither would she. She began with a scoop of flour, a splash of water, a pinch of salt, and a generous handful of lard.

Everyone was busy setting up camp. Mary paused on her way to the stream, carrying dirty clothes to wash. She studied the mixture, brows arched. "What are you making?"

Glory spun around. "Nothing." She shoved a lock of hair out of her eyes with the back of her hand, and a sprinkle of flour sifted down like the first flecks of an early snow.

"Baking?" Mary smiled. "Are you making Harper's famous biscuits?"

"Hmmm," Glory smiled. "They're the best, aren't they?"

"The very best." Mary glanced around, her eyes searching for Lily.

She wants Lily to help so I won't make them all sick again. But Lily was busy gathering firewood.

"Well . . . need any help?"

"No. I can do it alone."

Shifting the basket of dirty clothes into her other arm, Mary frowned. "Best get these clothes washed—"

"Better do that." Glory spun back to her pie dough. Interruptions and distractions she didn't need. "Where was I?" she mumbled. "Oh yes." She grabbed a wooden spoon and began stirring.

The dough formed a sticky ball. She nodded, remembering seeing this step in Poppy's process. It was now that he got his hands into it. She dumped the ball onto the wooden board with a satisfying thud. Working it with her hands felt good at first, but then it got too sticky. She tossed in a few handfuls of flour and worked harder. Pretty soon, the dough got too stiff.

She rummaged around until she found the rolling pin. Now things would go better. She shoved at the dough, but it resisted her efforts. Leaning on the rolling pin, she bit her lower lip. This was harder than it had looked when she'd seen Poppy rolling it out.

Maybe some water would soften it up. She reached into the bucket and scooped out a handful and tossed it onto the mound of dough. "Oh no," she muttered when she saw specks of dough floating in the water bucket. She glanced toward the others. "I'll have to get fresh water before supper," she murmured, making a mental note for later.

Now the dough was softening up. It was also sticking to the rolling pin and her hands and her elbows. She was so exasperated she could scream. Hearing the girls' laughter alerted her that they were on their way back from the stream. She rolled faster. She had to get this done.

Grabbing the pie tin, she slapped the dough into it. Desperately, she pushed at the dough with her hands to spread it. It required so much force that the tin flipped up and down and spun like a top to the edge of the board. With a lunge, Glory caught it before it dropped to the ground.

"Enough of this," she muttered as the sound of laughter grew nearer. The dough would probably spread nicely when heated. She tossed the apples on top of the dough and then added a generous scoop of sugar, three tablespoons of flour, a gob of butter, and a dash of cinnamon. The top crust! She closed her eyes, and her head rolled back. She'd forgotten about the *top* crust. She remembered how Poppy had laid neat strips of dough across the top of his pie, weaving them, humming while he worked.

"Next time," she muttered, "next time we'll have neat strips." For now, she'd have to make do with a few stray lumps of dough that had previously escaped the pie tin. She tossed them on top of the pie and hurried to the fire.

The girls were close now. Glory spied the large cast-iron pot Patience had used to boil water. Glory had seen her pour the water into a bucket and take off with it. Obviously she was finished with it, so Glory slipped her pie into the pot and clamped on the lid. Carefully she settled the pot down into the hot coals.

Wiping her hands on her apron, she straightened. By the time supper was over, her pie would be baked to perfection. A triumphant smile spread across her face. *Won't everybody be surprised,* she thought with smug satisfaction. Poppy had been right as usual: cooking was a matter of instinct. You had it or you didn't. Tonight she'd show them all. She had it.

As the group sat around the fire finishing rabbit stew, Patience stood and reached for the pan. "Anyone care for seconds?" she asked.

Jackson extended his plate. "I would."

Glory glanced up. "Better save room for dessert."

"I didn't make dessert," Harper said. "Too much washing to do."

"What's this?" Patience asked, pointing down at the iron pot nestled in the ashes.

Glory bounded to her feet. "Allow me." She wrapped a cloth around the handle of the pot and pulled it from the coals. Carefully she removed the lid and lifted out the pie. It didn't look like the apple pies Poppy had made, but she figured in the future they would look better.

Patience approached, peering over her shoulder. "It's not how it looks that's important," Glory began defensively. "What matters is how it tastes. Jackson, if you'll pass your plate over here, I'll serve you first."

After a slight hesitation, all eyes turned to Jackson. Harper reached her hand across the circle. "Here," she said, with a beckoning wave. "No need to get up. I'll pass your plate over."

Jackson paused a beat before handing his plate to Harper. "This isn't like Poppy's Blazing Fire stew recipe, is it?"

Glory's hand shot to her hips. "I don't want to hear another word about Poppy's stew."

Harper returned his plate to him; it was laden with a huge slice of pie. "Eat up, Mr. Lincoln." She grinned.

Jackson nodded, eyeing the pie. "Looks . . . mighty good."

He cut into his pie, while Glory continued to fill one plate after another. "Oh, my," she exclaimed when the pie tin was empty. "I forgot to save a piece for myself."

"Here." All plates extended toward her.

She waved their plates away, smiling. "Oh, I couldn't."

"I wish you could," Harper murmured, staring bleakly at the wad of crust on her plate.

Glory looked at her friends, beaming now. "I have to admit I didn't want to learn to cook, but fixing this surprise for you has taught me the true meaning of . . . What's that saying? 'It's better to give than to receive.' Never made sense to me before."

She shifted, settling her hands back around her waist. "Now what else can I get for everyone?"

"Water," Jackson managed to choke out. He coughed, and Glory prayed that a chunk of dry crust wasn't wedged in his throat.

"Coming up!" She quickly filled his cup from the dipper in the bucket and handed it to Ruth to pass to him, all the while keeping her eyes on the others as they slowly ate their pie.

"What's this?" Ruth asked, staring at the white blobs floating on the surface of the water.

Glory leaned forward to look. "Oh." She'd forgotten to get a fresh bucket of water after she'd dipped her hand into it. Clumps of dough were floating in the bucket and in Jackson's cup.

"What is it?" Mary echoed, staring into the cup as she passed it to Jackson. Wide-eyed, she looked up at Glory.

Glory shrugged and snatched up the bucket. "I'll get some fresh water from the stream." She picked up the lantern and disappeared.

When she returned, she was happy to see that every plate was empty. *They must have loved my pie— not a single scrap left behind,* she mused. She would have enjoyed hearing their praise, but she guessed the moment had passed while she was at the stream.

When the last dish was cleaned and put away, Mary asked Glory to help her with the mending. Glory didn't make an excuse but willingly sat down to learn. She'd proven she could make a pie, so domestic duties weren't so bad, certainly not as exciting as hunting and fishing, but necessary just the same.

She intended to do her share of work. Truth was, she was beginning to find satisfaction in doing nice things for others. Her pie had been a hit, why not darn Jackson's socks? He'd appreciate having those unsightly holes repaired.

"Perhaps you'd want to practice mending tea towels first, dear," Mary suggested gently.

"No, I like doing things for Jackson." The words were out of her mouth before she even realized she'd thought them. Embarrassed, she bent her head to her task, drawing closer to the fire, hoping that any-one looking would believe the warmth of the flames was causing the redness in her cheeks.

● ● ●

One morning a couple of weeks later Jackson chose to walk a few miles beside the wagon, carrying his rifle and scanning the hills. For days they'd been crossing flat spaces where he could see for miles. Now they were moving along the river road that ran up to the old pueblo at the mouth of the Fontaine qui Bouille Creek.

They marched through lush, rolling hills where a man could be ambushed. Jackson doubted the law was tracking them, but he was concerned about Amos. Greed could make a man do strange things.

After noon break, he climbed onto the wagon

seat and took the reins. Amos or not, he couldn't walk another step. His feet were killing him; it felt like he'd been walking on rocks all day.

After a few miles, he handed the reins to Ruth and tugged off a boot. "No wonder," he muttered, running his hand across the bottom of his foot. "Been walking on knots the size of Texas." He glanced at Ruth. "Who did this to my socks?"

Ruth continued to stare straight ahead. "Don't ask," she murmured.

He groaned, staring at the rumps of his oxen. "Whose idea was it to have her learn all these domestic skills?"

Ruth chuckled. "Yours."

*   *   *

That evening they made camp early beside a narrow stream and a stand of trees. They needed fresh meat for their meal. While the women gathered firewood from the ample supply surrounding the campsite, Jackson set off on foot with his rifle. Glory followed not far behind, carrying his shotgun.

An hour later, they returned with six pheasants— two of them shot by Jackson, four by Glory.

"Might as well clean those while I clean mine." She reached for his two birds.

Awkwardly he handed them over, unaccustomed to having someone do his work. "You need some help with them?"

"No, sir." She headed toward the water.

Steamed, he watched her trotting off, happy as a lark.

"I'll be down after I feed the stock," he hollered. "The mare has a sore tendon that needs rubbing down."

"Already did it," she called over her shoulder.

He caught up with her in a few steps, spinning her around to face him. "You've fed the stock?"

"Of course not, Jackson. They're too hot to feed when we first break for camp." She shook her head in disbelief. "I rubbed down your mare's left foreleg with liniment on the noon break. She's still limping, so I think you're wrong about her problem being in her tendon."

He looked up and then away. "Then why don't you tell me what you think it is," he said tightly. "And don't feel like you have to break it to me gently."

She grinned. "Oh, I get it. You're kidding, right? Of course I'll tell you what I think directly, man to man, so to speak."

"Yeah, I'm kidding." He didn't like her taking over his chores, and he sure didn't like a woman telling him how to run his business.

"Good, then I can tell you straight-out I think your mare is limping because she has a stone bruise."

"A stone bruise," he repeated. His eyes met hers. "I knew that."

"I know you did. Not much we can do for that but rest her for a while."

She was right. The mare would only get worse

if they didn't rest her. Now she was sore. If he rode her, she would become lame. Just one more delay he couldn't afford.

"It's not my fault," Glory reminded him as she scanned his grim expression.

"Yeah, well, I'll feed the stock now."

"All right." She headed to the stream.

"And from now on I shoot the game," he called.

She turned to look back at him. "But I was only—"

"From now on *I* shoot the game! Understood?"

"From now on *you* shoot the game. *I'm* not deaf."

He watched her slide down the embankment, the birds bundled in her hands, his shotgun under her arm.

Women.

He was in charge, deciding what to do, when to do it. He was the wagon master, and he didn't want a woman dogging his steps, cleaning his birds, diagnosing his mare, and doing his chores.

He shook his head. It was the first time he'd thought of Glory as a woman. A girl, yes. A waif, yes. A kid, yes. A woman, no. Why, he didn't think of the other females as any more than girls, either. He trudged up the hill. He didn't need anything to upset the balance. Best to distance himself from Glory before . . . He refused to consider what he was about to think. He was feeling uncomfortable enough as it was.

●   ●   ●

Lily cooked the pheasants, and the weary travelers ate the first fresh meat of the week. Afterward, the girls started on the dishes. Glory washed slowly, knowing it would not be long before Ruth would expect her to settle down by the fire for her lessons.

She wasn't eager to begin her studies tonight. She glanced around and saw Jackson disappear around the wagon, carrying his toolbox. *Bet he's going to repair that squeaky wagon wheel,* she thought. *Bet he'd appreciate some help.* It wasn't like she was going to shoot any of his old birds.

Jackson was running a hand over the edge of a broken spoke when Glory squatted beside him. For a moment, neither of them said a word. She stared at his hands as he worked, admiring his strength. Funny, seemed to her that he was getting more handsome every day. His robin's egg blue eyes sparkled when he smiled, and the reddish gold lights in his hair when the sun shined on it nearly snatched her breath. And it was pure pleasure to talk to him about things they both understood. She enjoyed being with the girls, but she didn't have as much in common with them as she did with Jackson.

He was trying to hold both ends of the spoke while he slathered tar between them. She could see what needed to be done. Without waiting to be asked, she quickly reached out to support one end of the operation. The backs of their hands brushed and their shoulders bumped. Jackson scooted away like he'd been scalded.

"Shouldn't you be studying or something?"

Grunting, she held the spoke in place. "Not till the dishes are done."

"Wouldn't they be done sooner if you helped?"

"Might be." She let go of the spoke and straightened. "Thought you could use my help more." She stood there for an instant, expecting he'd realize how much he needed her and insist that she stay. Clearly he could use another set of hands.

He kept his eyes on the spoke. "I think you'd better join the others."

Her chin dropped. He had no cause to be so unfriendly. She'd never heard him talk to Ruth or the others like that. Sure, he gave orders, but when he talked to Ruth, it was always in gentle tones, like she was his equal. Now that she thought about it, he'd been acting strange all evening. From the time they'd gone hunting to now, he'd acted like she was bothering him, like she was stepping on his nerves.

"Go on, Glory. Those dishes won't wash themselves."

Spinning on her heel, she marched back around the wagon. She had no idea where she was headed, but she felt a powerful urge to be alone. When she strode past the campfire, she felt a tug on her elbow. She looked back to see Ruth.

"It's time you practiced your writing," she said, gesturing to the Bible, paper, pen, and ink she'd laid out by the fire.

"Don't feel like it," Glory announced, trying to hide the quaver in her voice.

Harper frowned across the fire as she looked

from Glory's face to the other side of the wagon, where Jackson could be heard working. "You're bound for a heap of trouble if you don't do your studies," Harper murmured. "A whole heap, girl."

"Oh, all right!" Glory spun around and tramped back to drop onto the blanket. It was better to cooperate than to let Harper announce to the others that she'd been annoying Jackson. "Where were we?"

Ruth took a seat beside her. "You were practicing your handwriting by writing the Ten Commandments. I believe you left off with the last one: coveting."

"Figures," Glory muttered. Ruth had briefly explained the implications. They fit Glory to a tee. Jealousy. It was a feeling she experienced all too frequently these days. It wasn't good. She thought about the other nine commandments. The one about not killing ate away at her. *"You killed Charlie! You killed Charlie Gulch! You'll hang."* She'd already broken two; how many others was she wallowing in or capable of committing? If the other sins left a body feeling as miserable as killing did, and this awful thing called envy—which she couldn't for the life of her seem to shake—she wasn't sure she could endure the pressure. More and more she was feeling like a sinner, but she didn't know the remedy or even if there was one.

Guilt assailed her. She never meant to kill Charlie Gulch, but she was a living example of someone who constantly broke the tenth commandment. Every time she saw Ruth and Jackson smiling at one another, laughing together, talking like old friends—it was as if a spike were being driven into her heart. These were two people who had been kinder to her than anyone else; she should be happy for them, want them to find happiness with each other. But she didn't, and she despised the hateful feeling inside her.

"Let me see," Ruth said, leaning over to examine Glory's efforts. "Very good, your best handwriting so far."

Glory sat back and sketched whatever came into her mind. She had no idea how to rid herself of ugly feelings like jealousy, but she knew that if she let her mind wander and let herself draw beautiful images, it would help.

"What are you drawing?" Ruth leaned over for a second look.

Glory handed her the paper reluctantly.

"Angels?" she asked. "You like to draw angels?"

"Makes me feel peaceful to draw them."

Harper glanced up. "I like pictures of things that are real, like trees and mountains. Don't see why you'd waste your time on something that isn't even real."

"Angels are real."

The young woman eyed her skeptically. "Now how do you know that? Have you seen one?"

Glory shook her head. "Poppy saw them. Saw them hovering over the bed of a dying child. Next day, the child got better. Kept getting better until she was well. Poppy gave credit to the angels."

"Do tell. And you believe in them because that old hermit believed in them?"

Glory shrugged as she reached for her drawing. "What he believed is good enough for me."

Believing in angels was a sight better than feeling envy; even Harper couldn't argue that.

"I believe in angels," Ruth said quietly. She handed Glory a clean sheet of paper. "Let's try writing the ABCs once more, beginning with the letter *A*." She smiled. "For angels, for surely they are watching over us this very night."

Ruth continued. "The Bible is full of stories of angels. The birth of Jesus had lots of angels involved: telling Mary and Joseph what was to happen, singing before the shepherds. Why, even Jesus was helped twice by angels—once after he was tempted by Satan, and also in the garden of Gethsemane."

"Jesus?" Glory asked. "Even he was tempted? You read to me about his birth and some of the stories he told. But I don't understand why, if he was God, he had to die the way he did." Ruth had read the story of Jesus' death before, and Glory had a hard time grasping the concept that if Jesus was God, he could die.

Ruth replied after a small pause, "It was because of our sins. God had to punish someone for sins. Jesus willingly took on the punishment for our sins, so we wouldn't have to face God's punishment."

Glory thought about breaking the tenth commandment and how guilty she felt. "So how does a person know if Jesus died for his sins?"

"You believe in faith that he died for you and ask him to come into your heart."

There it was again, that word: *faith*.

Glory lay in her bedroll later and stared at the stars. If angels were up there, why hadn't she seen one? She supposed it had something to do with faith. The Bible said that taking things on faith meant believing that just because a body couldn't see something didn't mean it wasn't there. She couldn't see the wind, but she felt the whisper of it on her face.

Rolling to her side, she closed her eyes, thinking about all the things she couldn't see but knew existed. Like love. She had seen the evidence of love, but she'd never touched it. Peace. That had come into her life the day she'd joined up with Jackson and the girls; but she couldn't touch it. Security. Joy. She felt those every time she looked at Jackson and his handsome features and his gentle ways, but she couldn't physically touch security or joy. Some folks might say the bag of gold she kept hidden under the floorboards of the wagon represented security and could buy a whole lot of joy. But it was only a bag of nuggets, and once they were gone, there'd be no security or joy. Look at Poppy. When he'd died, he'd taken the only thing that counted in the Lord's eyes: his soul. The gold had remained hidden beneath the floor of his cabin.

She lay there counting the things she'd have to accept on faith, until she finally drifted off. There were enough to keep her awake long after the others were sound asleep.

10

Blistering late-summer heat plagued the travelers as the prairie schooner slowly wound along the creek of Fontaine qui Bouille. The calendar that Mary kept with her personal belongings said that it was September, but the relentless sun beating down on their heads refused to give way to cooler temperatures.

They had been on the trail nearly two months, and the extra roominess in Glory's shirt and pants, and the growing holes in the soles of her boots testified to her long hours spent walking.

This morning the only conscious thought in her mind was that the walk would be shorter today. Over breakfast Jackson said that over the next ten miles the trail was rough and uneven, but that there would be an abundance of wood, water, and grass where they would make camp early tonight. The tight lines around his eyes reminded Glory that he was worried about breakdowns and additional delays.

First, crossing the river had held them up. Then, Poppy's Blazing Fire stew had kept them abed and not far from the bushes for one whole day. Last week they were detained a day and a half when an axle broke and they had to hunt up a blacksmith to fix it.

With each new setback, the lines around Jackson's eyes tightened even more. It seemed powerful important to him that they reach Denver City before late fall, so it became Glory's primary goal, too. She did everything possible to be helpful and not be underfoot.

Wildlife was sparser now. She'd seen an armadillo yesterday, a strange-looking creature with a hard shell covering its shoulders and backside. The funny-looking animal with short legs moved quickly, its strong feet and thick claws burrowing with surprising speed.

Jackrabbits were plentiful, but the meat was tough. Glory longed for the tender flesh of the small rabbits found in the woods surrounding the shanty.

At times, she even found herself missing the old cow and the mule, Molasses. Poppy had brought the little mule home before it had been weaned. Glory had had to get up twice every night to feed the animal, but because of her mothering, a strong bond had formed between the animal and herself.

She looked forward to the new life awaiting her in Colorado, but she missed her old life something fierce, with its lazy days hunting and fishing with Poppy and its cool nights lying on her small cot, the sounds of cicadas and pond frogs drifting through the open window.

If it weren't for being with Jackson, seeing his smile, listening to the stories he told around the campfire at night, she might be tempted to turn back. Because the shanty, in spite of her new friends and Jackson, was all she'd ever had to call home.

● ● ●

Shortly after noon a harness broke. Glory paused in back of the wagon, listening to Jackson mutter under his breath, wincing at his sharp expletives.

My, he surely isn't listening when Ruth reads the part about not cursing. Seemed to her there was something in those worn pages about not taking the Lord's name in vain, and the words that were coming out of Jackson's mouth this morning most assuredly weren't holy. The only time she'd heard words like that was when Molasses had stepped on Poppy's infected toe. He'd whacked the old mule upside the head and talked to him something awful.

Besides, just last night Ruth had read about being angry and not sinning. Glory would be the first to admit she didn't know much of anything about what was or wasn't a sin, aside from the Ten Commandments. But to her blistering ears, Jackson sure sounded like he was mad as a wet hen and doing some powerful sinning while he was at it.

Shoving her hat to the back of her head, she joined the other girls as they walked toward the wagon master cautiously. Glory knew full well that when Jackson's face was red and bad words were as plentiful as weeds, he wasn't in any mood for socializing.

The travelers stood in the middle of the trail, staring at the torn strip of leather as if staring would miraculously repair it. The sun seared through their bonnets as the women shifted stances, eyes switching periodically to Jackson.

Lily finally broke the strained silence. "What do we do now?"

"Fix it."

"But that will take all afternoon!" Glory exclaimed.

Jackson took off his hat and wiped a stream of sweat dripping off his forehead. "Do you have a better idea?"

"We could switch teams. Use the mule team today and repair the oxen's harness tonight."

He nodded, but his grim expression didn't soften. "We could do that, *if* the mule team's harness hadn't broken when I went to hitch them this morning." His tone was louder and harsher than usual. "All our leather has taken a beating in this heat. I wipe it down with conditioning oil at night, but the salty sweat and the wear and tear have taken their toll."

Glory didn't have another idea, good or bad. She stared at the thick leather, then at Jackson. "So we stop and fix it now?"

"I guess we don't have a choice."

Jackson disappeared into the back of the wagon for the repair kit. Glory stayed put, knowing he didn't want her help. For the next few hours, he sat under a shade tree and patched the broken harness.

Ruth offered to help, but he brushed her efforts

aside, saying he could complete the job faster by himself. However, Glory noticed he was thoughtful enough to thank Ruth for her offer.

The girls spread out, each pursuing her own activity. Ruth and Lily caught up on mending; Harper read a dime-store novel that she kept tucked out of sight in her satchel. Patience sat in the shade and fanned herself, her young face flushed with heat.

Midafternoon, Mary climbed into the back of the wagon and slept, her coughing more pronounced today.

Glory asked, "Why does Mary cough so much?"

"Dust," Ruth explained. "She has asthma."

"What's that?"

"It's a powerful affliction affecting the lungs. Doctors don't know much about it, so it's difficult to control or treat." She glanced at the wagon, shaking her head. "Poor Mary."

Glory nodded. Poor Mary. She listened to Mary's dry coughs at night, hurting for her. Mornings, Mary's ribs were sore from coughing, and she struggled to draw each breath. When the attacks refused to let up, Ruth heated water, and Mary put a towel over her head to inhale the vapors. Sometimes that was the only thing that kept Mary breathing.

Late afternoon, Glory wandered over to the tree where Jackson was repairing the harness. She studied the tool he was threading through the leather. "What's that?"

"An awl."

"What does it do?"

"Pokes through leather so you can sew it."

She stood for a moment, waiting for an invitation to join him, but it never came. So she sat down without one. Lately he didn't seem to mind her company as long as she didn't talk too much or ask too many questions. She thought maybe he was getting used to her.

Jackson glanced up from his mending. "Where are the other girls?"

"Keeping out of your way."

He flashed a tolerant grin. His temper had cooled, but Glory noticed the worry lines were still evident around his eyes. The delays were happening more often, it seemed. Guess he had a right to be concerned.

"We'll walk faster," she promised. "We'll be in Denver City before the first snow."

"I hope you're right."

They sat in companionable silence, she watching his long, capable fingers thread the rawhide strips through the harness straps. Mary's worsening coughs filled the silence.

"You shouldn't talk bad, you know," Glory said evenly.

He bent his head, pretending interest in the harness, but he didn't fool her. He was ashamed of himself for talking that way in front of the others, and he should be. He was a good man who had let his anger get the best of him.

"There's women present—Ruth says a man isn't to talk that way in front of a woman."

"Ruth's right. I'm sorry."

"It's all right." She wasn't one to hold grudges. "I'll remind you when you do it again."

He gave her a sour look. "You do that."

Settling back, she crossed her arms over her chest and stared at the faultless blue sky. "Do you believe in angels?"

Jackson glanced at her from the corner of his eye. "Never thought much about it. Why?"

"Ever met one?" Glory turned to perch on one knee, watching him work. Her discussion with Ruth still lingered in her mind.

"For certain? No, I don't think so, though I wondered a few times."

"Really? You think you might have met one?" If he'd met an honest-to-goodness angel, she wanted to hear about it. Harper didn't believe in angels, but there wasn't much she did believe in.

However, angels fascinated Glory. It was only a couple of nights ago Ruth read where God gives his angels charge over you, to protect you, to guide you. One appeared to Mary in a blaze of light to tell her she was going to have a baby. And a whole bunch of angels sang in the sky to the shepherds. Now that'd be plumb scary—get a body's attention all right. The suggestion that there was an all-powerful God and watchful angels looking after her seemed imaginary, yet when Ruth read from the black book, Glory wanted to believe it. Wanted to believe it with all her heart. The pretty words spoke to her—made her long to know this all-powerful being, made her

want him to know her. But how could he know her?
Except for Jackson and the girls, no one knew her,
and it wasn't likely God would ever find her out here
on the trail.

Jackson worked the tool through the leather, lost
in thought. "Met a man once. I'd been shot trying
to defend a friend; I was left lying beside the road. I
thought I would bleed to death, but a stranger came
along and tended my wound. He got me to a doctor, and before he left, he told me that I would live."

Jackson paused, staring at the piece of rigging in
his hand. "There was something about his eyes. . . .
At the time, the doctor shook his head, and I could
see he didn't think that I would make it through the
night. Infection set in, and I was out of my head
with a high fever for two weeks. Then one morning,
I opened my eyes. My fever was gone, and I was
hungry enough to eat a bear."

Glory sat up straighter, leaning toward him.
"Was it because of that man? You think he was an
honest-to-goodness angel?"

"I don't know who he was, but that day he was
my angel."

Glory sat back, mulling the story over in her
mind. Poppy could have been her angel—hadn't
she fallen out of the back of a wagon, and hadn't
he been there to rescue her? She knew their prairie
schooner traveled for days, sometimes weeks, before
meeting another soul. Poppy's shanty was even more
secluded, so why had Poppy been there that day, that
hour, that moment?

She glanced back at Jackson. "You never talk about your life. Why not?"

"Not much to tell."

Glory didn't believe that for a minute. He was an interesting man with an interesting life. She bet that he had all kinds of stories to tell, adventurous stories, like meeting that angel—if it had been an angel.

"Actually, I'm boring." He laid the mended harness aside and flexed his hand. "Lived a pretty normal life."

"But you take people across country every year." She'd heard Ruth and Lily talking; Jackson was one of the most experienced wagon masters around. Folks paid a bundle of money for his services.

"That doesn't make me interesting." He smiled, and her heart leapt at the familiarity in his eyes, and she wanted—oh, how she wanted—to sit here all day and talk to him. She thought about what would happen to her when they reached Colorado. He'd go one way, and she'd go another. She didn't much like the thought. The feelings that went with it grew more painful every day.

"What about your mother?" She knew she was out of line now. Ruth had already told her that he didn't get along with his mother and didn't like to talk about her.

His features tightened. "My mother lives in Illinois."

"Do you see her often?"

"Not often." He leaned back, resting his eyes from the hot sun. Grasshoppers lifted in a dark cloud; others flitted back and forth across the road, their spindly legs whirling. He was silent so long she thought he had forgotten her question. Or maybe he was sorting out his feelings.

"No more often than necessary," he finally murmured.

Glory couldn't imagine not wanting to see Poppy. She'd loved him, wanted to be near him, though he wasn't perfect. Far from it. Cantankerous as a woodpile rattler at times, but that didn't make her love him any less. She could be a mite trying herself if the situation called for it. Yet she couldn't understand why a son wouldn't want to keep in touch with his mother. Didn't seem natural.

Jackson's eyes remained closed. "Go ahead."

Glory pulled a strand of weed. "Go ahead what?"

"Ask what you're fairly bursting to ask."

"I'm not bursting—not much, anyway. I was just wondering why a son wouldn't want to be with his mother as often as possible."

"You haven't met my mother."

She knew he was right. She hadn't met his mother, didn't know a thing about her, but she'd like to see the woman who'd produced such a fine specimen of manhood. For Jackson, with all his swearing and impatient flare-ups, was a good man. Other than a few bad words in trying situations, he was a true gentleman. He also seemed to have faith like Ruth's Bible said. He often reminded the girls about their evening devotions and prayers before each meal.

She'd seen the way he dealt with others less fortunate whom they'd met along the way. He'd given a man and his wife and infant child two sacks of flour—flour that would be needed for their own journey—but Jackson had said that they were all getting fat and could eat less for the duration of the trip.

Another time he'd given a fellow traveler a pair of boots, boots Glory knew Jackson favored. But the man had no boots, and Jackson said he had two pair. Jackson seemed to go out of his way at times to prove otherwise, but he had a good heart.

He met her eyes and sighed. "My ma ran my father off when I was a little boy. I didn't think much of her from then on."

"Ran him off? Like, 'Shoo! Go on, get out of here'?"

"No, like she complained and nagged until he couldn't take it any longer. One day he up and left, and I never saw him again."

"And you're mad at *her*?" Seemed it ought to be the other way around. Glory didn't know much about mothers, but she'd heard Ruth read something about children respecting their parents.

"Doesn't that book say something about the way we're supposed to treat parents?"

"It's not 'that book'; it's the Bible, Glory. And, yes, it does say how we're supposed to treat our parents, but sometimes it's hard to live by those teachings."

Glory thought about that. She expected that he was right; no matter how hard she tried, she messed up. And those rules Ruth read were mighty lofty goals for people. She sat, twirling the weed in her fingers, thinking about all the troubles a body faced.

"I don't know much, and I don't know anything at all about your mother, but seems to me folks would be better off trying to right their own problems than stewing about the wrong in everybody else."

Reaching for the harness, he glanced at her. "How old are you? Fifty?"

She shook her head. "Don't rightly know, but I don't think I'm *that* old."

He grinned. "That was meant to be a joke."

"Oh." She grinned, relieved. She was hoping her almost nightly baths made her look right nice, even nice enough for him to notice.

His eyes softened, and he leaned over to brush a lock of sweat-soaked hair off her cheek. "How old *are* you?"

"Best I can figure—eighteen."

"You don't know?"

"Can't know. Poppy could only guess how old I was when I fell off that wagon." Her eyes fused with his, and the sun suddenly felt like a fiery furnace. "How old are you?"

"Turn twenty-eight this spring."

Twenty-eight. He was mighty old. A lot of years separated them, but the age span blurred for Glory. When he looked at her the way he was looking at her right now, those blue eyes boring into her soul, she didn't care how old he was; she could love a man like Jackson Lincoln if he were twice her age.

"I'm too old for you," he stated, and she wondered if she'd spoken her thoughts aloud.

"Ain't looking for a husband," she reminded him. The only thing she needed was a life free of Amos and to be rid of the awful burden of knowing that she had killed a man.

His smile was crooked. "You *aren't* looking for a husband."

"That's what I said."

They stared at each other, unable to break contact. Glory wondered what she saw in the depths of his eyes. Respect? Affection? Trouble? Regret that he'd even asked her to ride along that day?

Mary's cough broke their visual standoff.

Gathering the mended harness, Jackson stood up. "See if Mary needs your help. She sounds worse this afternoon."

"Yes, sir." Glory struggled to her feet, brushing dirt off the seat of her trousers.

"Jackson," he reminded. He winked at her.

Jackson. Her heart sang as she hurried to the back of the wagon to look in on Mary.

Fiddlesticks. Twenty-eight wasn't *that* old.

11

The prairie schooner swayed along the Fontaine qui Bouille Creek. The travelers walked long into the night, trying to make up for lost time.

During noon breaks, Jackson would unhitch the oxen and tie them to the back of the wagon. In their place he would hitch the mules they'd rescued from the family who died of cholera; the mules could withstand the heat of the afternoon sun better than the oxen. Switching teams made it possible for the animals to work longer than they could have otherwise.

Sunday was a day of rest, except when rains plagued them during the week and muddy conditions forced them to stop. Then they would travel even on the Lord's Day, after a short worship time. Jackson said the Lord would understand.

Glory helped with the stock as often as he would permit her, and Ruth took on as many extra duties as she could, but the weight of responsibilities fell directly on Jackson's shoulders, which were beginning to ache on a daily basis.

He silently prayed for the weather to hold as his eyes searched the clouds. It had rained every night for the past week, bad thunderstorms with wolves howling in concert. Shoving his sweat-soaked hair off his brow, he was tempted to curse the relentless heat that raged every minute the sun was up, but he knew that it was better than the blizzards that would halt them on the trail if he didn't make up time somehow. And cursing wouldn't set well with the Lord, whose favor he sorely needed.

Lord, Jackson prayed, eyeing the ominous sky, *please help the weather hold. I won't even complain about this cursed heat if you'll just help us to not lose any more time.*

The mare's stone bruise had healed, and he'd ridden her every day, ranging ahead to check the trail or falling behind to be sure they weren't being followed. Amos was never far from his thoughts.

On a few occasions he'd seen wisps of smoke from a fire not far from their camp. When he'd ridden out to check it, he'd found freshly doused ashes, but no one present. There was no doubt in his mind that someone was trailing them. It was one more worry, but there was a more immediate concern on his mind that afternoon as he tied his mare to the back of the wagon for the noon break.

No matter how far he'd ridden from the wagon that morning, he'd been unable to avoid hearing Mary's racking coughs as she'd tossed on her fever-soaked pallet inside the wagon.

The inescapable dust that billowed around the

wagon, penetrating its canvas and even the dampened cloths placed over Mary's face, made her ailment worse. There were alarming moments when Mary was wheezing so badly that everyone waited, praying that she would catch her next breath.

Ruth disappeared inside the wagon to spoon bites of milk-soaked corn bread into the girl's mouth, but she was coughing so hard that she was unable to keep the food down. As the hours passed that afternoon, Mary grew weaker.

That night when the wind finally died, Ruth successfully fed Mary thin soup that seemed to ease her raw throat and give her a small measure of strength. When she could manage a few words, Mary's concern was that her condition was slowing them down.

"Nonsense," Lily soothed. "It's the road, not you, holding us up."

Lily climbed into the wagon to stay with Mary, and Ruth joined Jackson. They spoke in quiet tones as they walked a short distance away.

"She won't last much longer at this rate." Ruth drew her shawl tighter around her shoulders. After sunset, a penetrating chill had settled over the flatland. "She needs a doctor."

Jackson nodded. "Dodge City is half a day's ride ahead." He stopped to face Ruth squarely. "We'll find someone there to look after her."

Ruth gazed up at him. "Mary's concerned that she's creating another delay. She knows it's important to make up for lost time. And now—"

"Let me worry about time," he said. "Assure Mary that we're doing fine." He turned to head back to camp, refusing to meet Ruth's inquisitive eyes.

"Would that be the truth?" Ruth probed gently.

"Get some rest, Ruth. You've been working double time."

"I'm not the only one." She glanced at the others gathered around the campfire stealing casual glances their way.

"Leave it to me, Ruth. I'll get you to Colorado safely."

The next afternoon they detoured into Dodge City and, after making inquiries, found that it had a physician, of sorts. They arrived at his office where Jackson carried in a weak and feverish Mary. The other women trooped in behind him, crowding the cramped quarters until there was scarcely a breath of air.

"If you don't mind," said the elderly, stoop-shouldered doctor, casting an encompassing glance around the room, "I would like to examine the patient privately."

"I'll stay," Ruth volunteered. "It is customary for a woman to remain present while another woman is being examined, isn't it?"

"Very well," the doctor conceded.

Jackson gave a terse nod, and the other ladies filed out, their eyes lingering on Mary as they shuffled to the door. Jackson turned to follow them, pausing to speak to the doctor quietly. "You will step out to speak with me after your examination." It was a statement, the kind the wagon master often made, that was never mistaken for a request.

"Indeed," the doctor replied as he placed his glasses on his nose and bent to his task.

Jackson closed the door behind him and took a seat on the first bench outside the doctor's office. He watched Glory lead the mules to the water tank and return them to their positions behind the wagon.

It didn't bother him anymore to see her helping out. At first, he'd been worried that she would get herself hurt, but now he realized that she was as good a hand with the stock as he, probably better. He watched her soothe his riding mare, stroking her neck, then lifting and checking each hoof for rocks or other debris. The mare was calmer around Glory than she was with him. The girl caught him watching her and flashed a friendly smile.

He felt a tug on his heart. It was easy to like her. She was natural, honest, and too open for her own good. She used none of the feminine wiles that he'd seen in others. She could be stubborn, even confrontational, but there wasn't a calculating bone in her body. Not like his mother. Now there was a woman who could use and abuse others to suit her own selfish purposes. Amelia Montgomery could manipulate practically anyone into anything until she grew tired of the game.

Glory was nothing like his mother. Still, he kept his distance. The last thing he needed was to get involved with the orphan. He might be just a wagon master, but it was the life he'd chosen. Not a job he planned to do forever, but for now it suited him. He was taking care of people who would be otherwise helpless, and he liked his job. No commitments, no woman to run his life or run him off when she tired of him.

He watched Glory rub down the mare and decided she wasn't helpless in the wilds or anywhere else for that matter, but there were people who wouldn't hesitate to take advantage of a woman alone on the frontier. Ten years stretched between this girl and him, years that represented a world of experience. And yet there was something about her that drew him out of his shell. She could make him laugh or make him want to tear out his hair—and sometimes both at the same time.

Technically she wasn't a mail-order bride, and she swore she didn't want to be. But she'd have no choice in the matter. She had youth and natural beauty. Once Wyatt saw her, Jackson had no doubt he would want to arrange a suitable marriage for her. The prospect bothered him the few times he let himself think about it. He was trying to make sure that she learned the skills she would need as a wife. Her reading and writing were coming along faster than he'd anticipated; her domestic skills needed improvement, but then she'd had no role models until she'd joined the girls on this trip. He hoped her future husband would appreciate her spirit and not try to break it. She was a special woman, and he couldn't stand the thought of her being mistreated.

Glory stepped onto the porch and dropped

down on the bench beside him. Looking up at him in that trusting way of hers, she grinned. "Heard anything about Mary?"

He shook his head. "Not yet." He was close enough to overhear the doctor's easy voice inside but unable to make out his words.

The door opened, and the doctor motioned to Jackson, who rose to join him. Glory hopped up and started to follow, but the doctor closed the door, effectively shutting her out.

•   •   •

The day dragged on. Jackson took turns with the girls sitting with Mary, holding her hand, encouraging her to take small sips of soup the woman from the café sent over. Folks here in Dodge City were a good sight friendlier than those in Squatter's Bend, Glory decided.

She sat on the doctor's porch, hands on her chin, staring at the activity going on around her. Across the street a man and a youth loaded grain into the back of a wagon. Two women standing in front of the millinery chatted between themselves, admiring the display of colorful bonnets.

Farther down the street, music drifted from an establishment with wildly swinging doors; Glory figured the business was another one of those places with painted women and boisterous men, who drank until they had to be carried out by their arms and legs.

Her eyes caught sight of a striking young couple coming out of the general store. The woman had long, dark hair that fell to her waist; the man couldn't take his eyes off her. She laughed, smiling up at him as he carried her bundles and beamed like a besotted fool.

Sighing, Glory watched as the couple crossed the street and walked down the plank sidewalk toward her. Would a man ever smile at her that way, wear his heart in his eyes for the whole world to see? She'd told the others she didn't want a man in her life, but she supposed that wasn't exactly true. She didn't want just *any* man, but if Jackson were to decide—

She caught her wayward thoughts and dismissed them immediately. Wasn't likely Jackson would ever smile at her the way the tall, dark-haired gentleman was smiling at his lady.

The couple drew closer, and Glory could hear the two sharing another laugh. Drawing her legs back so they could pass, she smiled.

The gentleman returned the greeting, tipping his hat politely. "Good afternoon."

Glory's smile widened. "Afternoon, sir." Her eyes fixed on the beautiful lady, and Glory realized that she was not much older than she. The young woman wore a gown of lavender blue and a matching hat, and her violet-colored eyes resembled pools of cool, deep water. She slowed when she saw Glory. "Hello," she said. "Isn't it a perfectly lovely day!"

Glory thought it would be lovelier if Mary were better, but she nodded. "Yesterday was cooler."

The couple exchanged a personal look, and the woman giggled, color dotting her pretty features. Glory didn't know what was so funny about her innocent observation, but the man and woman found it amusing. Squeezing the gentleman's arm, the woman extended her hand to Glory, beaming. "Please excuse us; we're newly married."

"Oh!" Glory jumped to her feet, admiring the handsome gold band on the third finger of the woman's left hand. "It's very pretty."

Still laughing, the woman held her hand in front of her, staring for what Glory suspected wasn't the first time at the symbol of her husband's love. The couple exchanged another look, and Glory realized they'd sooner be alone than chatting with a stranger.

The man recovered first, clasping the woman's hand tightly. "Forgive our giddiness. We've been married less than a month." He lifted his wife's hand and lightly kissed it. "We're Dan and Hope Sullivan."

The couple locked gazes with each other, and Glory envied the adoration she saw in their eyes.

Mrs. Sullivan turned and looked at Glory. "My husband's work has brought him to this area, but when it's finished, we'll be on our way home—well, not home, but to Michigan to visit my aunt. Hopefully, my two sisters, Faith and June, will be there with their new husbands, and we can have a family reunion before Dan and I begin our new life in Virginia."

Hope then told Glory about her sisters and Aunt

Thalia in Michigan, and how her name had been Kallahan until a few weeks ago. Before Glory knew it, she was telling the Sullivans about Mary's asthma and about Jackson Lincoln, how he was taking five women to Denver City to be mail-order brides. But not her, she insisted.

"Mail-order brides?" Hope exclaimed. Both she and the man seemed to find that quite humorous. They laughed, and Dan leaned over to steal a brief kiss from his wife.

"Not me," Glory reiterated. "I've paid my own way, so I don't have to marry. Only Patience, Ruth, Lily, Harper, and Mary." She turned to look at the doctor's closed door. *If Mary doesn't die.*

She couldn't bear the thought of losing Mary to death. It wasn't fair. Death had worn out its welcome with her. Mary was young and alive, looking forward to the day when she would have a husband. *Please, God, please spare Mary's life.* The prayer came so naturally she didn't realize she'd thought it.

Hope leaned closer to Glory, smiling conspiratorially. "My sisters and I were mail-order brides. We were all supposed to be, but Parker Sentell came along and June fell in love. Then Dan happened along for me. Only Faith married her intended, Nicholas Shepherd, and—well, it's a very long, very complicated story. But I'm happy for your friends, and I'm so sorry about Mary's illness. Is there anything Dan or I can do to help you?"

Glory shook her head, aware of how her appearance contrasted with Hope's. Glory was wearing trail-worn pants and a shirt, and her hair was stuffed under a wide-brimmed hat. The lovely Mrs. Sullivan was all sweet-smelling and looking pretty as a sunrise. The comparison only served to remind Glory why Jackson would never look at her the way Dan Sullivan looked at Hope.

"The doctor is with Mary now. We're taking turns sitting with her. Nothing much anyone can do but wait, but thank you for offering. You're very nice."

The young woman took her hand, and Glory saw so much warmth and caring in her eyes that she felt as if she'd made a new friend. "I'll ask God to watch over her," Hope volunteered.

"Thank you," Glory murmured. "I'd be much obliged. And . . . could you ask him to help Jackson, too? He's worried about reaching Denver City; he's especially concerned about getting to the Arkansas and Platte Rivers' divide before the first snow. Seems like it's one delay after the other, and now there's Mary's sickness . . ."

"Of course I'll pray for your friends. And don't worry—" the young woman squeezed her hand— "when all looks the darkest, God works his greatest miracles if you have faith."

Glory watched the young couple continue down the walk, Dan Sullivan's arm protectively shielding his wife's small frame. She watched until they disappeared into the hotel. The scent of Hope Sullivan's perfume lingered, as sweet as the words she'd spoken. No wonder Dan Sullivan had such love in his eyes. If Glory didn't know better, she'd think she'd just met an angel.

• • •

The other girls joined Glory on the bench, and they sat quietly, lost in their thoughts, waiting for the door to open again. It seemed that hours went by. Glory grew restless and left the bench to thread her way between the mules tied behind the wagon.

Her thoughts were taking her places she didn't want to go. She sat on the back of the wagon, stroking Jackson's mare between the eyes. Jealous thoughts spiraled through her. For the brief instant that she'd stood outside the doctor's office, Glory had seen the look of relief in Ruth's eyes when she'd seen Jackson entering. The bond between them was obvious. They treated each other like trusted equals. Glory couldn't help but believe there was tenderness between them; oh, Jackson didn't look at Ruth the way Dan Sullivan had looked at his ladylove, but he still looked at Ruth kindly. Glory cared for both Ruth and Jackson and hated these angry feelings that threatened to overtake her. She reached for Jackson's Bible and held it tightly between her hands, hoping that the anger and hurt would go away.

"Glory! Glory!" Glory glanced up to see Lily rounding the wagon, looking up at her curiously. "Can't you hear me? Mary is asking for us, wants you to bring Jackson's Bible with you."

Glory scrambled down and rushed toward the

doctor's office, the Bible tucked under her arm. She filed in after the others. Her eyes fell upon Mary's face as she entered. She'd never seen her friend look so pale; her face blended into the white pillowcase. Jackson and Ruth were on the other side of Mary's bed.

The doctor turned to pour water into a basin, where he began to wash his hands. The room was steamy, the air heavy with the fragrance of eucalyptus and other oils she couldn't identify.

Mary's eyelids were heavy and her face damp, but her coughing had eased. Her breathing was raspy, yet she seemed stronger. "Please," she whispered, looking directly at Glory, "the Twenty-third Psalm, my favorite."

Glory fumbled with the Bible nervously, but Harper tugged her elbow and turned the book to the correct page. Mary's gaze remained steadfastly on Glory. With a nod, she made it clear she wanted Glory to read to her.

"Uh," Glory said uncertainly. She glanced at Ruth.

Ruth nodded. "Go on. I'll help if you need me."

Nodding, Glory began haltingly. "'The Lord is my shepherd. . . .'" The words were slow and awkward as she read, glancing from time to time at Mary's face. The girl's wan smile gave Glory courage, and she continued.

The room was silent except for her tentative words and Mary's audible breathing. Surprisingly, Glory read to the end of the lyrical passage with minimal errors. "'Surely goodness and mercy shall follow me all the days of my life.'"

Glory glanced up to see Ruth and Jackson, standing side by side, watching her with pride shining in their eyes. Glory swallowed hard against the lump in her throat, and she felt her tension ease. At that moment, she felt jealousy and anger leave her heart, replaced with a sense of peace.

When she closed the Bible, Mary smiled her thanks, and Glory took her hand and squeezed it gently.

"You did a good job, Glory," Jackson said quietly. "You've studied well." He looked around the solemn group. "The doctor wants to keep Mary overnight for another vapor treatment. He says if she has a good night, she can continue with us tomorrow, provided we keep up with her daily treatments and a liquid diet for a few days. Ruth has agreed to spend the night here to look after Mary's needs. We'll make camp at the edge of town."

The girls sighed with relief and expressed hushed words of gratitude to the doctor as he brushed past them. "I'm headed upstairs for a light supper," he stated at the stairway. "I'll be back down to treat her in an hour." Looking exhausted, he turned and left them.

At Jackson's nod, the girls whispered good-bye to Mary and began filing out. Glory waited till last. "Ruth, if you want your things, I'll bring them from the wagon before we leave."

"Why, thank you, Glory. I'd appreciate that."

Glory nodded and left, glad to be able to look at her friend without the awful jealousy that she'd been feeling so much lately. She glowed in her newly found peace. She also remembered a Scripture Ruth had shared about how God sent his Word and healed them. She was so excited she could have spit. But she knew now that sort of thing was no longer an option, seein' as how it wasn't ladylike.

Glory still wasn't quite sure who God was or if he knew who she was. But she now believed he was real. She'd listened to the other girls pray, and a couple of times she'd added her own amen. But she had never asked him for anything until she'd prayed for God to heal Mary. And he'd answered! Now she wanted to pray more, but she wasn't real sure how to go about it, since it was only her second time.

With childlike faith, she looked up to the heavens. He sure must be a long ways up there, she reasoned. 'Cause for as far as she could see, she still couldn't get a glimpse of him.

As if he were hard of hearing, she leaned her head way back and yelled, "Thank you! Thank you much for what you did for my friend Mary!"

And she meant every word with all her heart.

Later, when she handed the personal items to Ruth, Glory smiled and teased, "Wouldn't want you to miss your nightly scrubbing."

Ruth chuckled. Her face was tired, but her eyes brightened with mischief. "And I trust you won't miss your nightly scrubbing just because I won't be there to remind you."

"'Course not," Glory responded playfully. It felt good to shed the tension between them. Over the past few weeks, Glory had found it difficult to talk to Ruth, to share her feelings with her like she had at the beginning of their trip together.

As Glory returned to the wagon, she hoped her jealous feelings would stay away. As the wagon rumbled down the street toward the edge of town, Glory resolved to read the Twenty-third Psalm every day if that's what it took to feel peace in her life.

• • • •

By the third day the doctor pronounced Mary well enough to travel.

Jackson watched Patience and Glory help the ailing girl into the wagon and settle her on a pallet, wrapping a soft blanket around her skeletal frame. She'd lost weight this past week, weight she couldn't afford to lose.

The prairie schooner rolled out of Dodge City at daybreak, heading west. Midmorning Jackson handed the reins to Ruth and stepped into the wagon to check on Mary. The girl's drained features were pale as death, dark circles ringing her sunken eyes.

Harper sat beside Mary, dipping a sponge into a water bucket, bathing the young woman's face with infinite tenderness.

"Are you comfortable, Mary?"

Mary's eyes fluttered open, and she smiled wanly. "I'm fine, Mr. Lincoln—don't mean to be a bother."

Jackson patted the frail, white hand lying limp on top of the blanket. "You're no trouble, Mary. Let me know if you need anything." He met Harper's eyes. "Get her to drink often and as much as she can."

Harper nodded, rewetting the sponge as Jackson stepped to the back of the wagon and parted the canvas. His eyes skimmed the thick underbrush for signs of trouble. Glory chose to walk in front of the wagon this morning, chatting with Lily and Patience. His rifle was tucked under her arm out of habit. Lately, she was careful to point out game birds and remind him a squirrel, quail, or pheasant would taste good, but she let him provide the meat for their table.

Jackson's biggest concern at the moment was that one of the girls would wander out of sight. Should he remind them that Amos might be following and they were to stay close? He weighed the possibilities. If he did, Ruth would be scared, and then Patience would sit up all night stewing if she knew Glory's uncle was close by.

Jackson could deal with Amos if he could see him. It was the long stretches of road when he couldn't that kept him awake nights. An ambush worried him; so did the possibility that Amos could kidnap a girl if she wandered out of sight. Despite his concerns, Jackson decided to keep quiet and see what the day brought.

Stepping down from the wagon, he mounted the saddled mare tied to the back. Loosening the reins, he cantered the horse alongside the wagon. "Ruth, I want you to keep the other girls close. No one walks more than a few feet from the wagon!"

Ruth nodded, urging the team along the rutted trail. "Are you going somewhere?"

"Up the road a piece. I'll be back shortly." Whirling the horse, he galloped off, tipping his hat to Glory, Patience, and Lily as he rode past.

Patience frowned. "Wonder where he's off to in such a hurry?"

Glory watched his tall form disappear down the road. "Don't know, but I wish I was going with him."

●   ●   ●

Late that afternoon, Glory ventured farther down the trail. The road was washed out, and Ruth was busy concentrating on maneuvering the wagon through the rutted channels. Jackson was out of sight and couldn't help. The oxen balked, their heavy bodies straining to pull the load. The old wagon rocked back and forth, rattling pots and pans and banging the tin washtub against its side.

When Ruth spotted Glory drifting farther away, she hollered, "Jackson said to stay close."

Glory acknowledged the shouted warning with a friendly wave over her shoulder but kept walking. Keeping pace with the wagon was tiring; it was too slow, and she felt the need to stretch her legs and walk faster.

Up ahead, a covey of quail took flight, startling her. Her hand automatically switched the rifle to her shoulder, and she took aim. But the image of Jackson's scowl brought her up short. *"I shoot the game. Understand?"* She lowered the rifle and walked on, peering over her shoulder at the quail that skittered across the road and thinking they'd look a whole lot better in a frying pan.

The wagon bogged down again; she could hear Ruth and Lily yanking the harness, trying to drag the animals now. Voices grew fainter as Glory veered off the trail and headed for a grove of saplings. The sun was blistering hot; a few minutes in the cool shade would feel good before she tackled those stubborn oxen. She was a good half mile up the road, but Ruth hadn't noticed. Glory dropped down under a tree and sat there, listening to the girls wrestling with the team, feeling a little ashamed. But the shade lessoned the guilt. She was exhausted. She just had to rest a spell.

It was cooler here, quieter. She leaned back and closed her eyes, listening to a blue jay chattering overhead and enjoying the peaceful reprieve. She could still hear the oxen snort and Ruth, Lily, and Patience talking to each other.

A twig snapped.

She opened her eyes slowly and froze. Standing not twenty yards away was a deer. A small doe, nibbling grass in a clearing. Sunlight filtered through overhead branches, putting the deer in a perfect light.

Glory lay quiet as a rock, observing the animal. A deer that size would last the party for a good two weeks. Lily could make fresh jerky; there'd be venison roasts and thick tasty steaks. . . .

The animal lifted her head, her tail fluttering up and down. The doe had caught her scent.

Glory's fingers slowly closed around the rifle butt.

The deer stamped her front foot, snorting.

Glory eased to a sitting position, settling the weapon onto her shoulder, taking careful aim.

●　　●　　●

Jackson whirled when a shot rang out. Kneeing his horse, he galloped back to the wagon.

When Ruth heard the shot, she started, almost dropping the reins. "What was *that*?"

Lily and Patience spun around, eyes seeking the source of the gunfire. "I thought it was Jackson hunting."

"It wasn't me," Jackson declared as he rode up. His eyes scanned the road ahead. Glancing over his shoulder, he searched for Glory. "Where are the others?"

Ruth followed his eyes. "Harper!"

"Back here, with Mary."

Ruth glanced at Jackson. "Glory!"

Silence.

Jackson cupped his hands to his mouth. "Glory!" He glanced at Ruth. "Where is she, Ruth?"

"The last time I saw her, she was heading up the trail. I assumed she came back, though, and was with Mary. I warned her not to go off."

Ruth looked to Patience and Lily. "Have you seen her?"

The girls shook their heads.

Patience and Lily rounded the wagon. Both girls cupped their hands to their mouths and yelled for their friend: "GLOOOOOORY!"

Wheeling the mare, Jackson took off, shouting, *"Glory!"*

• • •

Jackson rode the trail, searching side roads and overgrown paths until darkness closed in, forcing him back to the wagon. Without a lantern, he was wasting his time.

Jackson found the girls huddled around the wagon. They were hungry, scared, their eyes dark with fatigue.

Ruth anxiously stood up as he approached. "Did you find her?"

"No." He dismounted, dropping the reins so the horse could graze. The girls were silent; only Mary's occasional cough broke the stillness.

"She stayed close to the wagon most of the day," Lily ventured.

Ruth leaned forward. "We were busy with the animals. I'm sorry, Jackson. I thought she was with Mary. I never thought she'd go off on her own."

Jackson took off his hat and ran a hand through his thick hair. "Did anyone see anything? Did you see anyone following the wagon?"

One by one, the girls shook their heads. "There's

someone following us?" Harper exclaimed. "I didn't
see anyone; 'course, I was in back with Mary most
of the day."

"I didn't see anyone," Lily agreed. Her voice
caught. "Is it Amos?"

"She'd have said something if she thought Amos
was following," Patience said. She struck a match
and quickly lit the lantern. "Are you worried that
Amos might be trailing us, Jackson?"

"I don't want to worry you, but someone's been
trailing us for the last few days. Nothing I can't
handle, but you need to stay close. Ruth, I told you
that no one was to wander more than a few feet
away."

"I'm sorry, Jackson. My mind was on the animals."

Jackson released a pent-up breath. Where was
Glory? Lying somewhere wounded, unable to help
herself? Had the fool girl gotten herself shot? Had
Amos shot her?

They stood in a circle, looking at each other,
afraid to voice their growing fears. Ruth sank to the
ground, wringing her hands. "What do we do? We
can't leave her out here alone, maybe injured."

Harper bounded up onto the wagon seat, her
dark eyes wide with fright. "Maybe she wandered
off and got lost."

Jackson didn't believe that for a minute. Glory
knew her way around the woods. She had a tracker's
instinct and a familiarity with nature that he envied.
She could spot a trail quicker than he could, and

he'd pit her sense of direction against a Sioux's any day of the week. "She's not lost."

He glanced at the girls and knew they were near the breaking point. They hadn't eaten since noon, and they'd traveled over twelve hours of rough road today. They'd gone as far as they could go.

His eyes scanned the edge of the trail. They had no choice but to camp where they were. At first light, he'd search the area. If Amos was out there, he wasn't going anywhere either, hindered by the same conditions. No one was leaving until morning.

"We camp here tonight."

"Here?" Ruth stood up, her eyes skimming the area.

"There'll be no fire. Ruth, Lily, can you fix a cold meal?"

Lily nodded. "We have bread and cheese."

Jackson would give a month's pay for a cup of hot coffee, but food didn't interest him. "Fix what you can—"

"Hey, you!"

The party whirled, eyes searching the darkness for the source of the voice. A lone figure with a rifle slung over a shoulder came down the road, whistling.

Jackson took a step, reaching for his shotgun.

"Well, you going to sit here all night?" Glory walked into the ring of light. "Hi, folks." She grinned. "What's taking you so long? Had supper ready for half an hour."

The group, speechless, simply stared at her. Then confusion broke out. Ruth sprang forward and grabbed Glory around the neck and hugged her. Lily, Patience, and Harper jumped up and down, waiting a turn to express their relief.

"Is that Glory?" Mary called weakly from the wagon.

Jackson watched the exchange, his exasperation rising. Wading into the middle, he parted the women until he reached Glory.

She grinned up at him. Her shirt was splattered with blood, and her hair was loose from her cap. "Hey, how ya doing, Jackson?"

Jackson set his jaw. "*Where* have you been?"

She stepped back, her smile receding. "Waiting for you. Where have *you* been? It's dark."

"Where have *I* been? I've been scared half out of my wits, looking for you for the last hour!"

She frowned. "Scared? Why would you be scared? I wasn't but a half mile up the road." She turned to point the way. "Right up there."

All eyes pivoted up the road. Straining, they could see a faint light glowing in the far distance, a light that they hadn't been able to see in the twilight.

"Got a surprise for everyone."

She struck off, and the girls scrambled into step behind her, while Jackson got Mary and put her on his horse. Glory led them to the clearing, where a side of venison browned over a rosy fire. The smell of roasting meat flavored the air. She stood back, hands on hips, looking pleased with herself. "Shot me a deer. Thought you might enjoy something other than beans tonight."

Squealing, the girls attacked the meat, juggling the hot pieces in their hands as they tried to eat it.

In the midst of the chaos, Glory approached Jackson. Head hung low, she murmured, "Didn't mean to cause a scare. You were off somewhere, and the wagon wasn't going anywhere, so I decided to take a rest before I helped. I meant to come back . . . till I spotted the deer." She sighed. "I know I promised to let you put meat on the table, but you were busy and—but you have to admit meat will taste mighty good tonight."

Jackson wanted to wring her neck. And he wanted to draw her into his arms and hold her until the fear left him. She'd scared a year off his life, but he was so relieved that she was safe that he had a hard time staying mad.

She slowly lifted her eyes to meet his. "Don't be mad at me, Jackson. I'm only trying to help."

Removing his hat, he knocked the dust off on his wool-clad knee. "Right now, the only thing I'm mad about is the fact that you don't have hot coffee to go with that venison," he said gruffly. He didn't want her to think she could pull this a second time.

Her sunny smile resurfaced. "I can fix that. If you let me use your horse, I'll go back and get the coffeepot. I'll have a pot made by the time you bring the wagon around."

He caught her arm as she was about to skip off to jump on his horse. Meeting her gaze, he said softly, "Don't ever do that again, Glory. You scared me to death."

"Yes, sir," she replied. Then she flashed a grin. "Honest?"

"Honest what?" he snarled, looking away.

"Honest you were worried about me?"

"I was worried," he conceded shortly.

"That makes me feel real good." Riding off with the lantern, she turned to wave at him over her shoulder. "I am going to write your folks, just as soon as I learn to write better!"

Shaking his head, he reached for a piece of venison before he set off to follow her on foot. He'd been far too worried; she was becoming more important to him than he cared to admit.

12

A fearsome windstorm came up on Saturday, banging pots and pans against the side of the wagon, threatening to rip canvas and spook the animals.

The girls and Jackson battened down their belongings, shouting at each other above the gale. Lily made Mary get inside the wagon and close the flap, securing it tightly to keep the dust out. The wind blew so hard as they worked that at one point the party was forced to run for cover among some bushes. With the wind came rain. When the storm finally abated, they were all soaked to the skin, grateful for their lives. Ruth stood in the middle of the road, arms held aloft, praising God for safe delivery. Glory had climbed a small rise to watch the storm whirling off into the distance. Two small twisters rose into the clouds moving off, leaving a sky now stunningly blue.

The next morning Glory woke with a fearsome chill, her teeth chattering as she pulled on a heavy sweater Jackson had lent her. They walked eighteen miles that day. By late that night, she was huddled in a blanket in the wagon, too feverish to eat her supper. Mary shared some of her tea, but it left a bitter taste in Glory's mouth, and she pushed the cup aside.

She rode most of the next day on the back of one of the mules tied to the back of the wagon. Every time she tried to drink or eat anything, it left a brackish taste in her mouth. But she refused to slow the group down because she felt poorly.

Every day brought them closer to Denver City; yet every day the remaining distance seemed formidable. Glory's thoughts turned to the time when she would say good-bye to Jackson and the others. Sometimes she couldn't bear the idea; other times she was filled with trepidation. What would she do when she was no longer a part of the daily lives of Jackson or the girls? The girls would marry; Jackson—well, she didn't know what Jackson would do. Maybe he would marry Ruth, and they would return to Illinois and buy a small farm, start a family. She wanted that for Ruth, truly wanted it, but try as she might, she didn't want it for Jackson. In her heart she couldn't hand Jackson over to another woman, though Ruth had insisted there was nothing between her and the handsome wagon master.

Something in Glory wanted to hang on, to pretend that it was real interest that she saw in his eyes occasionally, maybe even a special look meant just for her, the kind a man gives a woman when he thinks she's not watching.

But Jackson was mad at her these days. She'd

given him a dose of his own medicine, and he hadn't liked it. It had happened two days ago, when she'd rounded a corner and found that a skunk had him cornered against a big rock. Jackson had been pinned there like a gnat; the area around the rock stank something fierce. That skunk had fired off several pernicious rounds, and Jackson looked a mite shaken though he hadn't been touched.

When she'd walked past, Jackson had waved his arms, trying to get her attention. She'd paused, sizing up the situation from a safe distance. She felt ornery that day—real ornery. The way she figured, he needed to notice her a little more and find fault a little less.

He'd mutely implored her to shoot the animal, motioning toward the rifle and pretending to pull the trigger.

She'd motioned back, shaking her head.

He'd scowled. *"Why not?"* he'd mouthed.

"Can't kill anything—you'll get upset." She grinned, hoping the Lord wasn't watching.

His scowl had darkened. *"Kill the skunk!"* he'd mouthed, jabbing the air with his finger to emphasize his demand.

She'd slowly wagged her head, pantomiming someone choking her around the neck, and her falling to the ground, dead. She'd lain there, pretending to be out cold.

A vein had pulsed in his neck. *"Stop playing around and kill the skunk!"* he'd mouthed.

Shaking her head, she'd gotten up and walked

on. She'd been in enough trouble for shooting out of turn, thank you.

Of course, that skunk would leave a powerful smell, one they'd all have to suffer with for a few days.

"Glory." The voice of conscience boomed in her head.

Heaving a sigh, she'd turned around and fired the gun in the air. The skunk bolted and ran for safety.

"I was only funnin'," Glory explained. She glanced at Jackson and grinned, noticing he wasn't laughing.

● ● ●

They passed fewer wagon trains now. When they reached the fork in the road, Jackson explained that most travelers chose the large Indian trail that crossed the main creek and took a northwest direction toward Pikes Peak. Jackson said the longer one would be safer, but he preferred the less traveled road because it had more water and better grass along it. He believed that his route would cut off some miles. Glory and the others were in favor of the shorter route.

Jackson pulled his horse to a stop and raised his hand to halt the wagon. "We've been pressing hard, following this stream for days, but I believe this route could save us a week or more. So if you'd like, we can detour a couple of miles and follow the Indian trail, where I can show you the mineral spring that gives the Fontaine qui Bouille Creek its name: The Fountain That Boils."

"Yes!" came a chorus of feminine voices. The girls were eager to take a break from the routine for a little sightseeing.

When they arrived, they hopped out of the wagon and scrambled over large ledges to see two springs bubbling up out of solid rock. Following Jackson's example, they scooped up a handful of water to drink. Though strongly infused with salts, it was fun to taste.

Glory giggled as the tiny bubbles tickled her nose as she tried to sip. She glanced up to catch Jackson watching her. The warmth in his gaze was more exhilarating than the bubbles tickling her tongue.

As they doubled back to the fork in the road, Glory watched Jackson's handsome form riding ahead of their wagon. Their little excursion to the springs was a memory she would treasure in her heart. She savored the look in Jackson's eyes, his pleasure in her delight.

The following Sunday dawned disagreeably. The October wind was blowing hard, and it was bitter cold. Large flocks of snow geese flew overhead, getting a late start for warmer climates. The women wanted to observe the Sabbath today, but the incessant rain had slowed them. They decided to walk on, only not so far today. Tonight they would have services and go to sleep early.

Jackson was keeping an eye out for signs of early

snow. The worsening weather made Glory think it couldn't be far off. *Please, God,* she prayed as she walked ahead of the wagon, winding her scarf tighter around her neck, *Jackson said we needed three more weeks, that's all. Three weeks, and we'll be in Denver City. Can you please hold back the snow until then?*

They passed herds of buffalo and antelope grazing in the fields. The wind whistled across the expansive valleys.

Late one afternoon, the wagon came upon a crossroads trading post. The adobe building crouched beneath a watery sun looked lonely to Glory. Not having seen a fellow explorer in days, the girls were eager to stop.

"All right, ladies." Jackson steadied his mare as he brought her even with the wagon. "We'll make a brief stop. The animals need water." He glanced back at the road they'd traveled. "Be careful now. Keep your eyes out for trouble."

"We will!"

"Thank you!"

The inside of the trading post was a wondrous delight. Glory's eyes roamed the crowded room, and the sights fascinated her. Eight or nine male Indians sat around a large woodstove fashioning crafts. Some wove colorful baskets, others strung jewelry using glass beads, and still others worked with a reddish metal.

"Copper," Ruth whispered over her shoulder. "Isn't it lovely?"

A beautiful young woman moved from behind a counter to wait on them. *"Je t'aide?"*

Glory and Ruth smiled, moving on down the aisle. "What did she say?" Glory whispered.

"I believe it's French for 'help.' She wants to know if we need help."

"She's so pretty."

Ruth nodded. "Like someone you'd see in a picture book."

Turning ever so slightly, Glory checked to see if Jackson was in the building. She was relieved to see that he was busy outside watering the animals. Her eyes traveled back to the beautiful girl wearing a beaded dress sewn from buckskin. That was the kind of woman Jackson deserved: large dark eyes; waist-length, raven black hair; a body slender and strong.

When Jackson came into the post, the girls had browsed through most of the merchandise. Everything was so pretty Glory couldn't decide what she liked the most. Lily and Patience made a game out it, going through the rings and bracelets like excited children. Mary chose a shiny bracelet made from red beads and an eagle feather. Lily decided on a copper bracelet that fit around her tiny wrist. Patience liked the beadwork and chose a necklace. Harper favored the woven blankets, sorting through the colorful patterns several times before deciding on a favorite. Ruth fell in love with the pottery: vases and containers painted the colors of the desert.

Glory loved everything. Beads, bracelets, pottery,

and blankets—it was impossible to choose a favorite, but she relished the game, thinking how wonderful it was to simply be in such a grand store.

"Do you like it?"

Glory jumped when she felt Jackson's warm breath on her cheek. He stood looking over her shoulder, staring at the beaded mirror she was admiring.

"It's very pretty." She'd never taken a close look at herself in a real mirror. The image had surprised her. She had freckles across her nose, and her eyes sparkled like dew on a frosty morning.

"Then it's yours."

"Oh no!" She whirled, thrusting the mirror at him. "I couldn't spend money on that."

He grinned at her, his eyes softer than she'd seen them lately. "I'm buying it for you. A pretty girl should have a mirror to look at herself." Turning to the other girls, he called, "Pick out one gift apiece, girls. My treat."

The male Indians winced as the girls' squeals of delight filled the adobe.

"Are you sure, Jackson?" Ruth asked. "This is so generous of you. . . ."

"I have nothing better to spend my money on than beautiful women. Pick anything you want— just don't break the bank." He winked at Glory. "Especially you."

Glory felt a blush color her cheeks. She didn't know how to take his teasing, but she liked it, liked it a lot. And he was doing it more often lately. The lovely clerk behind the counter smiled, coming over to help the girls make their selections.

Glory had never had a more exciting time. Why, it felt like Christmas when Poppy would put an orange and a peppermint stick in her stocking hung by the stove! The clerk wrapped the gifts in soft cloth for the girls.

When the wagon pulled away from the trading post half an hour later, Lily held her wrist aloft, admiring her new copper bracelet; Patience preened in her beaded necklace. Harper had a red-, blue-, and black-striped blanket on her lap while she ooohed over Mary's shiny beaded bracelet with the eagle feather. Ruth happily sat on the seat beside Jackson, cradling a large pottery vase painted like the desert.

Glory, too excited to sit still, walked behind the wagon, staring at herself in her new mirror.

All in all, it had been the best day of the journey, maybe the best day in her whole life. Certainly one she wouldn't soon forget.

* * *

Days later, Mary's condition took a turn for the worse; her deep, racking coughs echoed as the wagon lumbered between boulders. Her coughs were sometimes as painful to hear as they must have been to experience. Walking beside the wagon, Glory found herself wishing that she could accept Mary's affliction for a few days so the poor girl would have a chance to rest and regain her strength.

Jackson rode past Glory without looking at her as he headed to the rear of the wagon. She turned her head to watch him canter by. He'd been circling the wagon for the past few hours.

"Whew," Glory muttered, waving her hand in front of her face, "as if we don't have enough dust flying, he keeps it stirred up. Mighty antsy today." She wondered what was bothering him and then figured it must be his concern for Mary as the girl fell into another fit of shuddering coughs.

Glory decided to spell Patience, who was caring for Mary today, and turned to walk to the back of the wagon. She was ready to climb inside when she spotted three riders down the road about a quarter mile. Surprised to see anyone out in the middle of nowhere, she raised her hand to shade her eyes and squinted through the dust. Three dark silhouettes loomed on the horizon.

"Hey, no gawking," Jackson warned as he brushed by her on his mare. "You're falling behind. Get in the wagon."

"Look!" Glory pointed at the riders.

"I know," Jackson said gruffly. "Been following in plain sight for two hours. Get in that wagon. Now."

Glory reluctantly complied. Grabbing on, she swung over the tailgate. Once inside, she stared at the three figures who sat astride spotted horses. The horses walked steadily, keeping pace with the wagon.

At first she wondered if one of them might be

Amos. She dismissed that notion quickly. None of the figures was large enough to be Amos, and to her knowledge, Amos had never ridden this far in his whole life.

As the prairie schooner topped a rise, Glory could see above the dust cloud and realized the figures were actually Indian braves. At that moment, she heard Jackson call to Ruth, his signal that it was time to pull off for the noon break.

When Ruth reined the oxen team to a halt near a stand of towering pines, Jackson pulled his mare up behind the wagon. "Glory, change out the teams now. I want fresh mules harnessed and ready to go."

Usually Glory swapped the teams at the end of their break, not the beginning. Her gaze shifted to the riders, who had stopped for a moment on the rutted trail, watching them. Without his saying it, she figured Jackson wanted to be ready to make a run for it if necessary.

"Who are they?" Glory asked as she dropped the tailgate and scrambled down.

"Shh," Jackson replied, shaking his head. "Ladies, we're taking a shorter break than usual. Just get out the leftover biscuits and what's left of the water."

Ruth joined Jackson at the back of the wagon. "I see them," she said evenly, keeping her eye on the three figures on the road. "But we're going to have to get Mary out of that stuffy wagon and into the shade for some fresh air, and we have to heat some water for her tea."

"Okay," Jackson conceded, "let's make it snappy."

He dismounted, tied his mare to the wagon, and pulled his rifle out of the scabbard. Handing the Winchester to Ruth without a word, he climbed into the wagon. "Okay, ladies, time for a short break." He scooped Mary into his arms and carried her to a tall pine, where he gently settled her against the trunk.

The girls climbed out, squinting in the noonday sun, moving to their chores. Lily had gathered an armload of firewood when she glanced up to see the visitors. The sticks tumbled from her arms. "Who's that?" she cried in shocked dismay.

"Indians," Glory replied matter-of-factly, pausing with a towering red mule standing on either side of her.

"Indians!" Lily exclaimed, her jaw slack. Even Harper looked worried.

"Are they going to scalp us?" Patience whispered, her hands flying to the thick blonde bun coiled at the nape of her neck.

"Calm down, girls." Jackson took the rifle from Ruth's grasp and tucked it under his arm. "Go about your business. Don't stare. Act like they're not there."

The girls tried to comply, but their movements seemed awkward and jumpy. After hitching the team, Glory knelt in the shade beside Mary. The girl began to cough harder, her eyes wide with fright. "It's okay," Glory soothed. "Jackson won't let anyone hurt us."

Glory rose to her feet and walked to the campfire to get the mug of tea that Lily was brewing for

Mary, but Lily's hands were shaking so badly that she nearly scalded herself trying to pour the boiling water. "I'll get it," Glory volunteered, bending to steady the cast-iron pot.

When she straightened, her heart sprang to her throat. The Indians had now dismounted their horses and were walking straight toward them.

"Jackson!"

Jackson stepped into the middle of the road, lifting his right hand, palm in front of him, pushing it forward and back.

The Indians stopped abruptly. Silence settled over the area.

Jackson continued to signal with his hand. "I do not know you. Who are you?"

The lead Indian flashed a succinct signal.

Shaking his head, Jackson raised both hands and grasped them in the manner of shaking hands.

The Indian responded in kind.

Glory sidled up closer to Jackson. "Who are they?"

Placing a hand on each side of his forehead with two fingers pointing to the front, one of the Indians fashioned the narrow, sharp ears of a wolf.

"Pawnees."

"What do they want?"

"We're about to find out."

The oldest Indian, a middle-aged man, stepped away from his two younger companions and moved closer. His eyes looked past Glory at Mary, who was bent double, coughing in spasms.

Glory studied the look in his eyes. Until a few months ago, she had been unable to read or write; she had spoken with few people besides Poppy. Her communication skills had been largely nonverbal. Poppy had taught her to observe closely and trust her instincts. He'd warned her that men could twist their words to mislead, but if observed carefully, they would eventually give themselves away.

"Trust your instincts," Poppy had always said, like woodland animals that depend upon their intuition for survival. If a rabbit senses danger ahead, Poppy had said, it doesn't say to itself, *"Oh, well, it's probably nothing,"* and then proceed—not if it wants to live another day.

Glory observed the Indian—his body language, his eyes, his facial expression—for clues to his intentions. She saw no hostile pose, no aggressive move; his eyes were filled with curiosity and . . . concern. She sensed no danger.

The Indian slowly removed a leather pouch from his belt and extended it toward Glory.

"Glory," Jackson warned in a low timbre, "take the pouch."

Glory nodded, stepping closer to meet the Indian.

"Easy," Jackson said softly.

"It's okay, Jackson." Glory accepted the leather pouch in both hands. "They mean us no harm."

Glory looked straight into the Indian's eyes, and she saw wisdom and kindness there. With a roll of his hand, he gestured that the pouch was for Mary.

Glory peered inside the bag and looked at the Indian with raised brows.

In a lithe motion, the man moved to pick up an empty mug beside the fire. Gently, he took the pouch from Glory and shook out a small amount of the powder from the bag into the cup. He imitated the motion of adding water from the pot boiling over the fire. Glory carefully filled the mug from the pot as the Indian held it out to her.

They moved slowly, carefully, as in a dance, trusting each other in small increments. He handed the mug to Glory. With a swirl of his fingers in the air, he communicated that Glory should stir the brew, which she did with a spoon. With a halting gesture of his palm, the Indian signaled that she should wait. She sniffed the concoction, figuring that the wait was to let it steep, like tea.

The Indian pantomimed bringing a cup to his lips and drinking from it. Then he pointed to Mary.

"Oh," Glory said, for the first time unsure. "He wants Mary to drink this."

Jackson balked. "No one drinks anything until I know what it is."

The Indian seemed to understand the doubt apparent in their voices. He held up both hands, grasping them in a shaking manner, as Jackson had done earlier. Every eye rested on him. He pointed to Mary, then clutched his own throat and pretended to cough—harsh, racking coughs like the ones that had come from Mary all day. Then he pointed to the mug in Glory's hands and then to Mary. He pretended to drink from the mug. Then he stroked his throat in a soothing manner and inhaled long, slow, audible breaths and exhaled them with ease.

"It's for Mary," Glory announced, "to make her feel better."

"Yeah," Jackson said cautiously, "but I still don't know what's in that powder. Maybe medicine, maybe not."

Glory looked at the Indian, pointed to the leather pouch, and shrugged, lifting her palm in the air, trying to ask him what it was.

The Indian nodded and moved to one of his companion's side. He opened a bag strung over his companion's shoulder. Carefully he removed a dried flower with its root still intact. He pointed to the root, imitated a grinding motion, and then to the pouch.

"What is that flower?" Glory asked. "Looks like a daisy, only it has a bigger center."

"Coneflower," Jackson said. "The Indians grind the root and use it to ward off illness, especially breathing ailments. They've used it for years, trading it from tribe to tribe. I'd forgotten about it."

"Then I think we should give it a try," Glory said.

"Not so fast." Jackson restrained her. "Mary hasn't had solid food for days. She's weak and exhausted. What if this medicine gives her a bellyache or worse? I can't risk that."

The women nodded their agreement at the wisdom in his caution.

"We don't know these men," Ruth warned.

"How do we know they really mean to help?" Harper seconded.

Glory looked around, taking in their fixed expressions. She shrugged, figuring it was the least she could do for these folks who'd done so much for her. "You're right," she announced. "We should test it." She raised the mug to her lips and took a long swallow.

"Glory!" Jackson snapped, knocking the cup aside. "You are the most impulsive, *stubborn*—do you realize what you may have just done?"

"I helped my friend," Glory retorted defensively.

"You should have asked me. There's nothing I can do now. If something happens to you . . ."

The women looked at him, startled. Ruth looking curiously from Jackson's distraught expression to Glory and back again. "Seems if she wanted to put herself at risk, it's her choice, Jackson," Ruth whispered.

"She should have *asked* me." His gaze scanned the group. "We should have voted on it, at least. I'd be worried if *any* of you had decided to do a fool thing like that."

"Hmmm," Ruth said, lifting a brow. "Do tell."

Uncomfortable with the tension rising around them, Glory blurted out, "Well, no harm done. I'm fine, feel better than ever. Seems like a safe medicine for Mary to try."

"I don't know," Jackson said.

"I do," Mary said in a small voice, beckoning the Indian to come to her.

Glory met Jackson's scowl with lifted brows. She didn't want to lead the Indian to Mary and then to have Jackson shoot him. Jackson released his breath in a long, defeated-sounding sigh and nodded.

Glory refilled the cup with the powder and water and let it steep for a couple of minutes. Motioning for the Indian to follow her, Glory led him to Mary and handed her the cup. Mary tipped the cup to drink, looking into the Indian's eyes over the rim.

When she finished, she set the cup aside and held out her wrist. With her other hand, she untied the rawhide that held the new bracelet with red beads and an eagle feather. She gestured toward the Indian's arm in a request for him to extend it. He leaned down, bringing his arm close to her hand. With a small smile, she tied the bracelet around his wrist.

The Indian's eyes lit up. He touched the shiny beads with reverence, then nodded to her.

As the three men turned to leave, Ruth approached them, carrying a five-pound sack of sugar. She extended it to them with a murmur of appreciation. They nodded as they accepted the token from her.

The ladies broke camp quickly, and when they returned to the trail, the Indians were nowhere in sight. And though no one mentioned it, Mary's cough seemed to have subsided.

13

That evening the group camped on a small plateau. The air was windless, the sky full of stars, except for along the north, where a long bank of growing clouds glowered.

"Storm's brewing," Jackson muttered. Scanning the valley below, his gaze pinpointed a narrow wisp of smoke rising from a campfire less than a mile away, and his heartbeat accelerated. Whoever had been trailing them was closing in. Many a morning before dawn, Jackson had doubled back to corner the culprit, but instead, he'd always discovered a doused fire and an empty campsite. He needed to take care of business now, before any storm hit and they became more vulnerable.

Tonight he was going to ride under the cover of darkness and surprise the intruder. Was it Amos? He felt sure of it. He'd catch him off guard and get the drop on him. He knew he needed the advantage that darkness could provide. By day, his group was too cumbersome to flee, and there weren't too many places ahead where he could avoid an outright ambush.

The girls didn't seem to notice him saddling his mare that evening. Some were busy fixing a late supper; others were beside the campfire, reading and mending. He slipped his rifle into his scabbard, checked his Colt pistol, and strapped on his holster. He'd had a bellyful of Glory's uncle, and tonight he intended to finish this once and for all. He'd send Amos on his way and be done with it.

Glory didn't need the crazy old coot on her trail for the rest of her life. He'd leave camp and return before anyone missed him. Quietly he led his mare out of the camp, keeping to the far side of the wagon, so as not to be seen.

"Where you headed at this hour? Storm's a-brewing," Glory reminded from not three feet behind him.

Jackson jumped and spun around, his hand resting on the butt of his Colt. "Don't go sneaking up on me like that!" His heart was pounding like a blacksmith's hammer. Hearing her voice right behind him scared a year off his life. He'd better be more adept at sneaking up on Amos than he'd been at slipping away from her.

Her eyes widened. "What's going on? I've never seen you wearing a sidearm."

Jackson looked the other way. "I'm going for a little ride, Miss Nosy." He reached inside the wagon, grabbed his shotgun, and handed it to her. "Look, I didn't want to upset anybody here, so I was hoping I could come and go without an interrogation."

"What's that big word mean?"

"It means you ask too many questions."

"You don't have to get so cranky about it," she said, disappointment in her voice. "You've told us to stay alert. I was just following orders."

"Oh yes," he murmured, "you're good at following orders all right." When he saw the hurt look on her face, he softened. "Look, I need your help." He noticed that she immediately brightened. "I need to check on something. Do me a favor: Stay here and guard the camp with my shotgun. Only please don't upset the others. They'll never get to sleep if we get them stirred up, and Mary needs all the rest she can get."

"You got it," she said, her eyes bright even in the low light. "Where are you—? Oh, that's right. I'm not supposed to know where you're going."

The corner of his mouth lifted in an involuntary smile. "I shouldn't be too long," he said, turning away. Then spinning back around, he added, "But no matter how long I'm gone, you stay here. That's an order."

"Yes, sir." She gave him her best rendition of a salute.

He shook his head and swung into the saddle. One touch of his heels, and the mare took off in a soft trot.

He was careful to approach the campsite from the woods. He tied his mare to a tree and walked the last quarter mile, staying low and moving stealthily. When he neared the campfire, he stayed behind a low bush, from where he could spy one man, squatted low, pouring himself a cup of coffee. There was only one bedroll on the ground and one horse tethered nearby.

Slowly Jackson drew his Colt from his holster and waited. Ten minutes passed as he waited to make sure there was no one else around.

The man looked to be around thirty, slim and broad-shouldered. Jackson focused on his gun belt. Somehow, he didn't think this man fit Glory's description of Uncle Amos, but the girl tended to exaggerate at times, and Jackson was taking no chances. He waited till the stranger had both hands busy, his coffeepot poised in the air ready to refill his cup.

"Put your hands in the air nice and easy," Jackson called solemnly from the underbrush as he cocked his pistol. "Try something foolish, and I'll shoot."

The man set his cup on the ground and the coffeepot beside the fire. His eyes narrowed. "You might join me for a cup and a chat," he said in a measured, even tone, slowly unbuckling the belt of his holster and removing it. He tossed it aside a few feet. "Might be, we could straighten things out before somebody gets hurt."

"Could be." Jackson lifted his head and scanned the clearing. "You alone?"

"Usually am. Tonight's no exception."

Jackson paused, listening intently. Hearing no sign of anyone else nearby, he stood and slipped through the underbrush into the clearing. "We'll start with your name."

The man raised his hands and looked Jackson up and down. "Name's Dylan McCall." He paused for a beat. "U.S. marshal."

Though he tried to maintain a neutral expression, Jackson knew his eyes registered surprise. "Don't see a badge. Wouldn't have proof of that, would you?"

The corner of the man's mouth lifted a fraction. "Right here," he said, dipping his chin to his left, "in the pocket of my vest."

"One hand—slowly remove it and slide it on the ground my way."

The stranger complied, his eyes never leaving Jackson's face. He seemed to be assessing him calmly.

"Have a seat," Jackson said, preferring the man not be in a crouched position, ready to spring. "And keep those hands high."

The man sat down. "Mind if I take a sip of my coffee before it gets cold?"

"Not yet." Jackson kept his gun trained on him, while squatting to pick up the flat leather square the man had tossed on the ground. He opened it and dropped a quick glance down. The silver star flashed in the firelight. Opposite the badge was a card identifying one Dylan McCall, U.S. marshal. Jackson locked eyes with the stranger. "Looks real enough," he said, smoothing his thumb over the star. "How do I know it's yours? Could be you took it from an unfortunate Marshal McCall after you met up with him?"

"Well, take a look at my horse, bears the U.S. brand on his hip. Check out my gear, strictly government issue. And in my saddlebag here, you'll find an extradition order to fetch one nasty little gunslinger from Denver City back to Kansas City to stand trial."

Jackson promptly dragged the saddlebag to his feet, reached inside, and drew out a long envelope. His fingers lifted the flap and withdrew the paper inside. With a flip of his wrist, the paper unfurled. Quickly he scanned the contents. He looked up and assessed the man across from him. "Well, you look as official as the documents you're carrying."

The man nodded. "You're not the trusting type."

"You've been tracking us for weeks. I'd like to know why."

"I haven't been tracking you. This happens to be the only halfway reliable trail in these parts. I've been about my business, checking in with the county sheriffs as I pass through their territories, sometimes escorting some unsavory types to their new quarters in jails and penitentiaries along the way."

Jackson looked at the man for a long moment, made a decision, and uncocked his pistol. After slipping the Colt back into his holster, he motioned toward the coffeepot. "Believe I'll take you up on your offer and have a cup."

Dylan reached inside his pack, drew out another cup, and filled it. As he handed it to Jackson, their eyes met.

"I owe you an apology, Marshal. I'm not in the habit of sneaking into camps with my pistol drawn."

"Call me Dylan. And I don't get the feeling you're a dangerous felon on the loose."

"Lately," Jackson chuckled, "I'd have to believe that would be an easier life. I'm Jackson Lincoln, wagon master, escorting a group of mail-order brides to Denver City."

"Women?" Dylan exhaled. "That would tend to make a man a little jumpy."

Jackson nodded. "Especially since one of the girls has a crazy uncle who's threatened to do her harm. That reminds me, I can't leave the girls alone for long. I need to get back. I am sorry for busting in on you like this. Least I can do is offer you a meal. The ladies will have supper ready by now. I'd feel better if you'd join us. You can share our camp for the night. Storm's brewing and it feels like a bad one."

Dylan paused for a moment, then shrugged. "Thanks. I'm tired of my cooking, and I could use the company." The marshal loaded up while Jackson went for his own mare.

A short time later, the two men rode into camp. The girls beamed when they saw they had company. Male company. After introductions were made, there was a flurry of activity as everyone rushed to accommodate their handsome guest, everyone except Glory, who stood staring, eyes wide, the shotgun still tucked under her arm.

Jackson quietly moved to her side and gently confiscated the shotgun. "I think we can put this away for now."

She glanced up at him with a small furrow between her eyes. "What's a U.S. marshal doing in these parts?"

She looked so serious he succumbed to teasing her. "Here to bring back a dangerous murderer." He wondered only briefly at the frown that clouded her face as he hurried to the back of the wagon to stow his guns.

● ● ●

After supper, everyone lingered around the campfire, eager for conversation with a new face, and such a handsome one at that. "I feel safer knowing we have Marshal McCall in our camp tonight," Mary announced, and there were affirming nods all around.

"Call me Dylan," he said with an inviting smile. He pronounced the name *Dill-an*.

"Dylan," Lily purred, trying out his first name before the others, "I can't imagine what could bring you to this desolate place."

"The job, ladies. Where there's a felon to be apprehended or transported, I'm your man."

"Then you travel this trail regularly?" Ruth asked.

The handsome marshal rested his eyes on her. "As regularly as weather permits, ma'am, but you could say I know every mile and every town from Westport to San Francisco."

Glory felt her heart begin to thump wildly. If this lawman knew every town on the trail, then he'd surely been through Squatter's Bend and heard of the female murderer who was still at large. She was surely on his list of felons. She shrank back in the shadows.

Her crime was never far from her thoughts, especially during her nightmares, and more recently during her evening prayers. The more she read the Good Book, the more she realized the enormity of her sin. She had killed another human being. She had broken a commandment: "Thou shalt not kill." Those words haunted her. She'd killed Charlie Gulch. And according to his friend, she would pay.

She only halfway listened to the banter and giggles surrounding her. No one seemed to notice her, except Jackson. When she glanced up, she caught him staring at her quizzically. It was then that she made her decision. She couldn't tarnish the reputation of a good man like Jackson Lincoln by letting him continue to harbor a fugitive.

"I'm a murderer," Glory announced in a clear voice.

The chatter around her ceased. Gazes flew in her direction.

She extended her wrists, ready for the handcuffs. "Arrest me." She lifted her chin resolutely. "I just want to say that these people had nothing to do with my escape. They are totally innocent, especially the wagon master, Mr. Lincoln."

"Uh, just a minute, Dylan," Jackson began, looking intently at Glory in that way she'd come to understand meant that he wanted her to shut up. "This girl is overly tired and just a little dramatic at times. We've been pushing her to read, and I think she's gotten some crazy notion—"

"Please don't try to cover for me, Mr. Lincoln. I'm of sound mind, and I know what I've done. It's time to confess my sin. Every night I've prayed for God's forgiveness, but it's time for me to pay society for killing Charlie Gulch."

There were whispers all around, but Ruth cleared her throat to silence them. "Marshal McCall, this innocent girl was attacked by an evil man; she did . . . what she did . . . to protect her virtue and her life. It was clearly a case of self-defense."

Mary spoke, her voice thin but clear. "I don't think you should take her in, Marshal . . . uh, Dylan, that is. She's a good person who deserves another chance out West."

Dylan raised his palms in the air to stop the remarks that were beginning to pour from all sides. Even Harper was shaking her finger at him.

"Ladies, ladies," he began; then glancing at Jackson, he added, "and gentleman." His authoritative tone settled a hush over the group. "Let's clear up a few things before we jump to any more conclusions, shall we?"

There were nods all around.

"Good. Then I'll ask the questions, and Glory will answer first. Then if anyone has a comment, we'll speak one at a time. Clear?"

Glory sat up straight and tall, feeling as pale and luminous as the moon above. She nodded that she was ready.

"Glory," Dylan began, "could you be speaking of Charlie Gulch of Squatter's Bend?"

Her eyes widened in surprise and then sadness. "Did you know him well?"

Dylan nodded. "Still do, if I'm correct. He's the town drunk. Everybody knows Charlie Gulch."

"No, sir. I killed him three months ago."

Dylan shook his head. "I shared a card game with him two months ago, and he was very much alive that night, I assure you."

"But," Glory said, confused for a moment and then certain as the memory sprang to her mind, "I hit him with my rifle. His friend touched the blood that was everywhere. He said—I'll never forget his words as long as I live—he said: 'You killed Charlie. You killed Charlie Gulch. You'll hang for this. You'll hang.'"

"And that was three months ago?" Dylan asked incredulously. He shook his head. "I remember . . . around three months ago Charlie was wearing a bandage around his head. Claimed he'd been hurt when he'd apprehended a gang of thieves trying to rob the bank. But his sidekick said Charlie got frisky in a dark alley with a girl who whopped him upside the head." Dylan's features colored. "Excuse me, ladies."

"No offense taken, Marshal," Ruth assured him.

Dylan nodded, returning to his story. "Town was pretty evenly split over which version of the tale to believe. I figured there wasn't a shred of truth to either one. Most likely Charlie had fallen down drunk and banged his hard head against something harder."

There was an audible sigh of relief around the campfire, but Glory still looked confused. "You mean he isn't dead?"

"No, ma'am, not unless he's passed on in the last several weeks since I stopped in Squatter's Bend. I think your conscience can be clear, young lady." Dylan smiled at her. "The deceased is probably tipping his glass as we speak."

Glory felt an enormous relief. A terrible burden had been lifted from her heart. Then she looked at Jackson, who was smiling at her, and she felt foolish. Once again, she'd done an impulsive thing without checking with him first. She sighed and looked down as the girls around her reached to hug her.

Glory met Jackson's eyes over Ruth's shoulder as Ruth embraced her, and he was shaking his head and grinning at her.

Starting first thing tomorrow, Glory resolved, she would never do another impulsive thing. Never, ever would she give Jackson Lincoln another moment's grief.

● ● ●

Later that night, Glory dissolved into tears, crumbling into Ruth's arms. The past few hours had taken an emotional toll on Glory. To be free of the awful burden of taking another person's life left her feeling drained.

Holding her tightly, Ruth soothed her, tenderly consoling her as Glory poured out her heart.

"I've been so afraid, Ruth." Glory sobbed, hot tears washing away three months of misery and self-recriminations. She hadn't killed Charlie Gulch, and Amos wasn't following her. Could *he* be dead? No, he had been breathing when she ran off. *Thank you, Lord,* she silently cried.

"I know, dear. I know."

Patience and Lily drew near. By now, sleet pelted the sides of the wagon, but inside, the girls were warm and cozy.

Draping her new blanket over Glory's shoulder, Harper scooted closer into the friendship circle. "Now don't go crying," she sniffed. "You'll have us all bawling, and we should be celebrating. Won't have to worry about some lawman breathing down our collars when we reach Denver City. And it looks like that mean uncle of yours just plain gave up on finding you."

"I know, Harper, and I'm grateful, honest. It's just that what if I had killed a man? The Bible says, 'Thou shalt not kill.'" She'd written the Ten Commandments over and over until she knew them by heart. Killing was powerful wrong; how would she have explained to God what she'd done?

"Oh, Glory, the Lord understands if we kill in self-defense," Ruth consoled. "He wouldn't hold you accountable for defending your life."

Glory sniffed, wiping her nose on the handkerchief Mary discreetly pressed into her hand. "You're always so confident, so sure, Ruth. Why can't I be more like you?"

"You are like me." Ruth's smile was close to angelic in the dim lantern light. "We are all nothing, the lowest of sinners, without God's grace." She took Glory's hands, holding them tightly in her own. "Grace—the love and forgiveness of God—is a gift. You have everything you will ever need to claim his love."

Frowning, Glory sniffed. "I don't have *anything* except the clothes on my back, you, and Jackson's Bible." Her eyes traveled the circle of friends, meeting eyes that looked back at her with love and affection. "And you and you," she whispered, reaching out to touch the hands of each one of them.

At that moment she realized that she *did* have everything: people who loved her, the knowledge that she wasn't alone in the world. A worn Bible entrusted to her care by a man she admired more than any other.

Her eyes returned to Ruth. "But you have something more: an inner peace, a contentment, a joy. You never get upset or mad or yell or scream or cry, even when you have every right to fuss. You hardly raise your voice to the animals. How do I get to be like you, Ruth? How do I get up each morning, sure that whatever happens, I will have the peace that the Bible speaks about, the peace that passeth all understanding?"

Smiling, Ruth touched the Bible resting in Glory's lap. "The key is right here, Glory. All you have to do is read it and accept it."

Laughter mingled with tears as the girls shared a group hug. Tonight they felt their bond grow even closer. The next day they would reach the high divide between the Arkansas and Platte Rivers. Once safely through, their time together would come to an end. The thought weighed heavily upon them all.

"We'll write each other," Lily promised.

"Every month," Patience echoed. The girls held hands tightly as Patience verbalized the pact. "We promise to write each other every month, and if we should be confined or otherwise unable to correspond, we promise to have a loved one write and inform the rest about the other's welfare. We pledge to pray each day for each other, for our soon-to-be husbands, and the children we will bear." They sealed the accord with a unanimous tight hand squeeze.

When they opened their eyes, Glory gazed at them. "What about me?"

Mary smiled. "What about you?"

"I . . . won't be marrying—leastways, not anytime soon. I paid my own way, and Jackson said I'm not obligated to take a husband."

"Well," Lily said, biting her lower lip, "you will someday, perhaps." Her youthful features sobered. "What *will* you do, Glory? You can't live out here alone. Colorado is a harsh, unforgiving land. The winters are long and hard. You won't know anyone, and you have no skills."

"I do now!" She could read reasonably well, thanks to Ruth's tutoring. Harper had taught her to cook; folks didn't clamor for seconds, but she was getting better, and she hadn't made anyone sick in weeks. Thanks to Lily, she could sew a decent stitch. Mary had taught her to add and subtract. Seemed to her she was as qualified as anyone else to find work.

Harper, who'd been silent, said softly, "Maybe I could get a job, pay Mr. Wyatt back, and then you and me could stay together."

The girls turned to look at the mahogany-skinned girl. Ruth frowned. "Why, Harper, I thought you wanted to get married."

Harper's words were barely audible. "No, I never wanted to get married. The orphanage said I had to. Don't like most men," she said, her voice dropping lower. "Most men—they're mean to a body."

"Mean?" Ruth leaned over and took her hand. "Why ever would you say that?"

Shifting to her hip, Harper lifted her blouse and showed them her back, crisscrossed with deep white scars.

Patience's soft gasp covered the stunned silence.

"Dear Lord in heaven." Lily turned away.

"You never said anything," Mary whispered.

"Wouldn't have done no good. Folks at the orphanage knew about it, said they wouldn't let Ma have me if she came back. She brought men home—"

Glory's cheeks burned hot. "They had no right to do that to you. Poppy said a man who'd beat a woman was no better than a rabid animal."

"Men are mean when they're drinking," Harper whispered, tears pooling in her dark eyes as she trembled beneath the heavy blanket. "I've . . . I've been thinking that I don't want to get married to some man I've never met. I don't want no man beatin' me every night till I bleed. Glory and I can get us a place—"

"Oh, Harper." Mary hugged her, switching turns with the others as they comforted her.

"Not all men are bad," Glory argued. "Look at Jackson. He's kind and protective, and I can't imagine he'd lift his hand to a woman. We've all seen him about as mad as he could be, and he didn't treat us bad."

Dabbing her eyes with her handkerchief, Harper managed a weak grin. "Guess that's true, Glory. He'd have beat you silly weeks ago if he was turned that way."

That brought a laugh from everyone. Glory's reputation for stepping on Jackson's nerves was legendary.

"I'll bet Mr. Wyatt has a wonderful young man waiting for you," Mary said. "Handsome, strong, just itching to be a proud papa and a loving husband to you."

The girls shared a nervous laugh this time. Glory, for one, wasn't so sure about marriage. If she'd been stuck with any of those men that Poppy had tried to pawn off on her, she wouldn't be happy about it.

"Harper, you'll be just fine. We pray that Mr. Wyatt will be a kind man and that he'll find a good husband for you. It's Glory we have to worry about." Lily reached up and turned down the lantern, and the girls settled into their warm blankets. Gusts shook the wagon, and sleet peppered down on the canvas.

Closing her eyes, Glory thought about Jackson sleeping under the wagon, wondering if he was warm enough, if his pillow was soft enough, if his bedroll was sufficiently heavy to withstand the cold mountain air. She'd like to do so much for him: wash his clothes, fix his meals, and be the last one he talked to before his eyes closed in sleep.

Lily snickered.

Pretty soon Patience giggled.

Lifting the blankets over their heads, the two girls dissolved into guffaws. Before long, they were all giggling.

"What are we laughing about?" Ruth squeaked, her shoulders heaving with suppressed laughter.

"I don't know," Mary sniggered. "Shh, keep your voice down. Jackson will hear us."

The wagon rocked with the girls' ill-concealed giggles. Glory's sides hurt from trying to keep quiet. The last thing she wanted was to disturb the old bear, Jackson.

"Girls!"

Too late. Slapping her hand over her mouth, Glory shook harder, tears rolling down her cheeks now.

"Yes, sir?" Harper called, bending over double, pulling her knees to her chest.

"It's late!"

"Yes, sir!"

The six girls, tears rolling down their faces, laughing so hard their heads hurt, made every effort to sober. Each attempt failed miserably, and they burst into renewed peals of laughter. Burying their faces in their pillows, they gasped, chortled, sure they would die if they couldn't stop.

Eventually the spell passed, and none too soon. They expected to see Jackson part the back curtain and yank a knot in their tails.

Lying on their backs, they wiped tears from their eyes, hiccuping.

"What was that all about?" Ruth whispered.

No one knew, but the thought produced another brief round of snickers.

"I know," Patience whispered.

"What?" they said in a hushed chorus.

"It has to be those silly rules Lily was teaching Glory yesterday."

Glory sat up, wiping her eyes. "My lands, I'd forgotten those—" She started giggling.

"What rules?" Mary scooted closer to Glory.

"Some old rules Lily thinks I should learn so I can be a proper lady."

By now the girls were sitting up, eyes brimming with curiosity, dying to know what was so funny.

"What are these rules?" Harper asked.

Glory glanced at Lily, and they both grinned. "You tell them, Lily."

"Okay." The girls lay back down and got quiet. "Promise, no one laughs?" Lily fumbled for a match, lit the wick, and then took out her book.

They all promised to stay quiet, certain Jackson would skin them alive if they woke him a second time.

"All right. This book, I think it comes from Boston, but I'm not sure. It has rules men and women are supposed to abide by."

"And they are?" Ruth plied.

Clearing her throat, Lily began to read: "'Ladies and gentlemen, when meeting on the sidewalk, should always pass to the right. Should the walk be narrow or dangerous, gentlemen will always see that ladies are protected from injury.'"

"That doesn't sound so bad."

"It gets worse. 'Ladies should avoid walking rapidly upon the street, as it is ungraceful and unbecoming. Running across the street in front of carriages is dangerous and shows want of dignity.'"

Glory giggled. "That lets me out."

"'When walking with a lady, a gentleman should insist upon carrying any package that the lady may have. Before recognizing a lady on the street, the gentleman should be certain that his recognition would meet with favor.'"

"How would he know?" Glory asked.

"An educated guess, maybe?" Harper ventured.

"'No gentleman should stand on the street corners, hotel steps, or other public places and make remarks about ladies passing by.'"

Patience snickered. "Especially about her weight."

"Or the size of her caboose," Harper whispered.

"'Upon the narrow walk, for her protection, the

gentleman should generally give the lady the inside of the walk, passing behind her when changing corners. A gentleman walking with a lady should accommodate his step and pace to hers. For the gentleman to be some distance ahead presents a bad appearance. And last but not least, the gentleman accompanying a lady should hold the door open for the lady to enter first. Should he be near the door when a lady, unattended, is about to enter, he will do the same for her.'"

"What's wrong with that?" Glory murmured, getting sleepy from all the merriment. "I think that's nice."

"Me too," Harper said. "Better than letting the door slam in her face."

That brought on another round of giggles, but the long day finally took its toll. Soon the wagon settled down, the lantern was turned down, and the occupants rested quietly, listening to the howling wind.

Just before Glory drifted off to sleep, she thought about the rules and decided that Jackson would observe every one of them.

Because Jackson Lincoln was a gentleman.

14

Marshal McCall stayed the night, sleeping under the wagon beside Jackson.

The next morning the sleet had changed to a steady snowfall—big white flakes that Glory tried to catch on her tongue.

"Hop back in this wagon, girl," Harper warned her. It was Glory's habit to be the first one dressed and out every morning. "You can't go out there in those worn-out boots."

Glory scrambled back into the wagon. "I put on my flannels, wool dress, and jacket," she explained.

"Well," Harper said, "that's good, but you can't wear those thin boots. Time to be wearing your winter boots."

"Don't have any." For most of the trip now, Glory had been wearing whatever change of clothes another girl wasn't wearing at the time, but she had only the holey boots she'd been wearing when she'd joined them.

"Lucky thing." Harper handed her a pair of dark

leather boots. "Jackson picked up a spare pair when we stopped at that trading post some time back. Thought someone might need them, and we all wear close to the same size."

Glory's eyes widened in surprise. Jackson seemed to think of everything. Despite all the trouble she'd caused him, with all the responsibilities he had, he still kept her—well, all the girls'—needs in mind. A rush of tenderness for this man filled her heart. To think he cared enough to be sure the women had what they needed, even clothing. Even for her.

"Thanks," Glory murmured in awe, lacing the boots up to her calves. She couldn't remember ever having a good pair of boots to keep her warm and support her ankles on the rough trails.

Moments later, Glory was helping Jackson harness the oxen. When he walked around the team to join her on her side, she glanced up at him warmly. Time to show him her gratitude. She reached down and gathered her skirt with both hands and hefted it up to her knees. "Well," she said with a big smile, "what do you think?"

Drawing a thick strap over the ox's broad back, he paused to glance over. When she looked down, his eyes followed hers to the pair of shapely legs she was revealing to him. "Good grief," he muttered, glancing up to her face incredulously and back down to her legs again, seemingly before he could stop himself. "What are you doing? Drop your skirt, girl." His eyes shot left and right, looking for a safe place to look, his expression guilty. "What will people think if they see you—you can't go around hiking up your skirt and asking a man what he thinks!"

Glory's shoulders stiffened. "I'm asking *you* what you think of the new boots," she huffed. "What do you *think* I was asking about?"

"Well, I . . . uh, you kind of took me by surprise," he stammered. "I didn't rightly know what to think." His tone turned defensive. "You should be more specific when you're asking questions."

"It's a sad thing when a person can't thank another person for her new boots without him getting all cranky." She looked away, feeling stung by his reaction. If anyone else had tried to thank him, she felt sure he would have been gracious. "I declare, sometimes you are fussier than Poppy after two weeks of snowed-in cabin fever."

She turned on her new heel and marched to the back of the wagon to saddle the marshal's horse. Why was it, she thought in a fit of pure frustration, that she couldn't even try to return a kindness without Jackson taking offense?

Ruth banged two pots together to signal it was time to gather around the campfire for a hearty breakfast of biscuits and gravy. They crowded around to warm themselves and share a meal that would have to hold them through a cold morning's work. Ruth said the blessing and began serving, handing the first plate to their guest.

"Dylan," Jackson began, studying the marshal over the rim of his coffee cup, "I'd sure be appreciative if you'd accompany us for the next several days."

The girls watched the handsome lawman expectantly, their smiles inviting. Harper shoved another biscuit onto his plate before he could refuse, and then followed it with a ladle of cream gravy. Mary refilled his coffee cup before he had a chance to ask.

"Thanks," he said with an appreciative nod. "I must say, Jackson, if I hang around too long, I'll get fat and spoiled."

"I don't think that'll happen too soon. The girls and I will have all we can handle today climbing to the divide." He glanced at the threatening sky. "If possible, I'd like to be through it before nightfall. Having you with us will increase our chance of making good time."

"Seems the least I can do for the kind hospitality you've shown me."

Glory stepped up with the reins to Dylan's black gelding. "I saddled your horse, Marshal. I know we'd feel better if you rode along with us."

He smiled at her in a teasing way. "I imagine you feel better knowing you won't be wearing my handcuffs today."

"Yes, sir," she replied, blushing quickly, her gaze dropping away. Everyone chuckled and smiled at Glory sympathetically.

Dylan looked at Jackson and then glanced around to include the ladies. "I accept your invitation."

"Good." Jackson nodded, looking relieved. "Let's gather round," he began. "We've got maybe our toughest day ahead of us." A gust of wind whipped around them, sending up sparks from the campfire to swirl with the snowflakes. "The weather is going to make it slick going. Each of you will have to walk as much as you can to lighten the load. The animals will struggle just to pull the weight of the wagon." He sent a meaningful glance in Glory's direction. "And stay close. Don't wander away even for a minute. If you need a break, let Dylan or me know, so we can stop the wagon. Too easy to get lost in a snowfall, and it will get heavier the higher we go."

The girls murmured their agreement and dropped their heads as Ruth, then Jackson, led them in a brief prayer for safe passage.

Because she didn't have her stamina back, Mary was chosen to sit on the back of a mule tied behind the wagon. Glory gave her a boost, and Mary scrambled aboard, clutching the mule's heavy leather collar for support. Patience climbed aboard the other mule to keep Mary company. The girls planned to alternate throughout the day with one or another of them sitting on the back of the other mule tied next to Mary's. It gave them an occasional rest from walking, and the gentle mules accepted their slight weight without a problem.

On the trail, Jackson ranged ahead to check conditions while Dylan rode beside the wagon. Ruth was at the reins, and three girls walked beside the oxen, helping her keep them in the middle of the trail.

As the trail grew steeper and slicker, Ruth slapped the reins and called encouragement to the oxen that trudged slowly, leaning into the traces, dragging the wagon behind them. Glory and Harper smacked the oxen on their wide rumps and pulled at their harnesses when they veered off the rutted trail.

Glory kept an eye on the marshal, who was riding alongside the wagon and staying real close to Ruth. As the wagon climbed higher, the wind almost snatched their breath away. Glory moved to the back of the wagon.

"Care for a break?" Dylan asked Ruth amiably, touching the brim of his hat with his right hand. "I can climb aboard and take the reins for a while. Your arms have to be tired."

Ruth turned her head and looked into his crystal blue eyes framed by lashes dampened from the blowing snow. She stared for a long moment, then blinked suddenly and looked away. It was then that one of the oxen stepped in a hole and nearly jerked the reins out of her hands. "Ouch!" she exclaimed at the sharp tug on the leather that pulled her shoulders and lifted her off the seat for a second until she could lean back.

"Got him!" Harper shouted as she pulled up on the ox's halter until he regained his footing.

Ruth huffed a moment, catching her breath. Then she gasped in surprise as Dylan settled his weight on the seat beside her. He leaned away to secure his horse to the side of the wagon and then turned to reach across her. His gloved hands wrapped around her gloved hands on the reins.

"I-I can handle it," she stammered defensively,

stiffening her arms to lean as far away from him as she could.

"Just trying to keep the tension on," he said, his hands tightening on hers. "Just ease out from under me."

Glory punched Harper, who'd join her behind the wagon, and the girls grinned.

"Looks like the marshal's sweet on Ruth," Harper whispered.

"It surely does," Glory said. "Sweet as honey."

Ruth pulled her hands out from under his as quickly as she could, but his firm grasp slowed her. "You can loosen your grip," she said sharply.

"Let's take it slow. Wouldn't want those oxen to take a crazy notion and run off now, would we?" He chuckled. When he glanced her way, their faces were scarcely inches apart.

She cleared her throat and slid to the far edge of the wagon seat. "I hardly think the oxen could run anywhere at this point." Ruth's face flushed despite the icy snow pelting it.

"I'm kidding, Ruth," he said reassuringly. "It is Ruth, isn't it?"

"It is." She rubbed her shoulders with her hands.

"You okay?"

"Oh yes, fine," she said quickly. An awkward silence stretched between them. "Uh, I want to thank you for the way you treated Glory last night."

He nodded. "She seems like a fine girl, more sincere than most folks I meet."

Ruth's eyebrows shot up. "You mean more sincere than most criminals, don't you?"

"I generally say what I mean, ma'am," Dylan responded evenly.

"Well," Ruth said with a sigh, "it's a good thing you know this Charlie Gulch." She paused a beat before continuing, "If you hadn't, I dare say you would have arrested her, right?"

"I . . . I hope it wouldn't have come to that. I'd have had a long chat with her."

"An interrogation, I believe it's called."

His head swung around, but Ruth's gaze was fixed on the snowy trail ahead. "It would have been more of a conversation," he explained, "much like the one we had last night."

Ruth nodded. "So after you'd arrested her—"

"I don't think it would have come to that."

Ruth shrugged. "If you'd arrested her," she persisted, "you would have hauled her back to Squatter's Bend."

"Where she would have been cleared and released."

"Then she would have been separated by hundreds of miles from the only friends she has. It would have been too late to make the journey to Colorado this year. As it is, we're hitting the passes a little late."

"It's my job." He snapped the reins. "I don't always like it."

Glory punched Harper again. "That's real nice of Ruth to take up for me like that."

Harper nodded. "Push!"

Ruth ignored his remark and continued, "On

the other hand, if Charlie Gulch had died from the head wound she gave him, what would've happened to her then?"

"I think they would have weighed the circumstances."

"Of course, he's a town resident; she's a stranger."

Dylan whistled to the oxen to move them up the steep slope. "I'm not the judge and jury, ma'am."

"No," Ruth agreed, "but it's not hard to see her motivation. Glory makes no pretenses. It would be your choice to let her go."

He shook his head. "Not my call."

"And if she found herself at the end of a rope?" She looked at him directly. "And you knew in your heart that she was innocent of murder, despite what she claimed in her statement?"

He shifted his shoulders, looking somewhat uncomfortable. "If it had come to that, I would've spoken on her behalf."

"That girl is no threat to society, no matter what happens to the likes of Charlie Gulch."

"Not the way the law works, ma'am."

"Hmmm. I imagine there are a goodly number of fugitives who move out West to start a new life and do so successfully."

He nodded. "I imagine so."

"Unless, of course, they are arrested and taken ck to stand trial."

"You're a hard woman, Ruth."

On the contrary, Marshal McCall. I happen to e that vengeance belongs to the Lord."

"Well, miss, it's not within my authority to choose whom to arrest and whom to let go."

"Forgiveness is appropriate in some circumstances, don't you think?"

"I'd have to agree, but in our country that's up to a court of law." He lifted his shoulders. "Just stating a fact, miss. Don't shoot the messenger."

Suddenly the oxen hit an icy patch. As their feet began to slip, they balked. The wagon wheels locked and started sliding sideways. Dylan slapped the reins and shouted, but the oxen were paralyzed with fear. Glory and Harper jumped aside as the wagon slid another couple of feet and a back wheel dropped off the edge of the trail. The undercarriage of the wagon slammed down on the ice at a precarious angle.

Dylan grabbed Ruth to keep her from falling out as she looked down to see that the drop-off was hundreds of feet straight down the mountain. "Oh, my," she exclaimed, desperately throwing her arms around his neck.

Harper and Glory were up front now, pulling on the oxen to no avail. Jackson galloped back to the wagon. "Hang on," he shouted as he shook out his lasso, tied it securely to the back of the wagon, and looped it around his saddle horn. He backed his mare, keeping the rope taut as Glory rushed to his side. "Hold my horse steady," he told her as he slid to the ground.

Mary and Patience had slid down off the mules tied behind the wagon. "Untie the mule team, girls," Jackson ordered as he moved to the back of the wagon. "Bring them to me. Now back them up and hold them steady." Jackson secured the mules' harness to the corner of the wagon where he'd tied his rope to stop the slide. "Now, girls, lead those mules toward Glory. Steady, steady," he repeated, as the mules began to pull the wagon as far back onto the trail as the dropped wheel would allow. "Whoa," he called. "Hold them right there."

With that, he untied a long wooden pole strapped to the side of the wagon and pried it under the corner of the wagon that was resting on the edge of the precipice. Leaning hard, he applied all the pressure he could. Harper and Lily joined him. Pushing down on the end of the pole together, they got enough leverage to lift the corner of the wagon. When it was high enough, Jackson called to Glory, Mary, and Patience to lead the mules a couple of yards farther, which pulled the wagon the rest of the way onto the trail.

Everyone was exhausted from the effort. Dylan climbed down from the wagon seat and helped a shaky Ruth to the ground. Jackson and Glory switched the oxen for the mule team to pull the wagon the last hundred yards to the summit.

The snow stopped shortly after they passed the summit. They made camp that night a few miles down the trail under a clear sky. After a warm supper, an air of hope and celebration filled the air. Dylan took out his harmonica and played a square-dance tune, and Jackson took turns dancing with each girl, one at a time, saving Glory for last. As she twirled in his arms under a million stars, she felt like the happiest girl alive.

●   ●   ●

Ruth, Patience, and Glory were the last to bed that evening. The wind shifted, and clouds rolled in for a second time that day. As she changed clothes inside the wagon, Ruth had talked nonstop about Dylan. Dylan this and Dylan that. The conversation itself was unusual, especially since Glory usually had to pry a discussion out of her after a long day. Seemed she thought the handsome marshal was overly arrogant and overly confident. Seemed to Glory that Dylan was only doing his job, but she'd been too tired to argue.

"I think I'll check on Jackson—see if he's warm enough." Before anyone could object, Glory slipped out the back of the wagon and closed the canvas.

Frigid air blew up Glory's skirt as she hurried toward the front of the wagon. Sleet fell in prickly sheets, howling through the boulders. She'd never seen weather change so fast, and dresses were nothing but a nuisance! If her two pairs of trousers weren't so dirty that they could stand alone, she'd never have consented to wearing Patience's hand-me-downs. The bodice was too tight, and the dress made her look girlie—too girlie—but it was much too cold to do wash.

Rounding the schooner, she spotted a light in the distance. *Jackson must be visiting with Dylan.*

She supposed that he was enjoying time with a peer—especially since he'd been confined to female companionship for the past four months. Jealousy suddenly surged through her, but she pushed it aside. *Lord, I'm trying hard to be content with what you give me and not be envious of Jackson's time with others.*

Lately, she'd found it easier to talk to the Lord in a natural way, as if she'd known him as well as Ruth did. In many ways she was creeping closer to Ruth's certainty of belief. Sometimes Ruth spent extra time with her reading lessons; nowadays she could understand the words in almost half a Bible chapter without stumbling. Stories about the women in the Bible—Miriam, Deborah, and Esther—fascinated her; she never tired of reading about them.

Shivering, she pulled her jacket tighter, thankful that the Lord had answered her prayer and seen them safely through the high divide. With the worsening weather, even one day would have made the passage more difficult, if not impossible. Denver City was only two days away now. Two days was all the time she had left with Jackson.

She paused, wincing as icy pellets struck her, watching the light of the lantern bobbing toward her. Jackson's tall form, bent against the wind, came into view. When he spotted her, he quickened his pace, his boots crunching atop the thin icy glaze.

"You should be in the wagon," he scolded as he approached.

"I wanted to check on you—I saw your light. . . ."

Taking her forearm, he steered her beneath the

makeshift awning strung near the fire. Wood chunks blazed brightly in the midst of red-hot coals. The air was warmer here, sheltered from the blowing wind.

Retrieving the coffeepot, Jackson poured two cups, the fragrant aroma pleasantly mingling with the arctic air. Taking both her hands, he closed them around the steaming cup. "You should be in the wagon. It's not a fit night for man or beast."

She nodded, meeting the warmth of his eyes. "Is Marshal McCall comfortable?"

"Comfortable as anyone can be in this kind of weather." They edged closer to the fire, standing shoulder to shoulder. She noticed he wasn't eager to seek shelter, and she could only hope it was because of her company. They shared the silence, taking sips of coffee. After the next two days there'd be no more sharing coffee or late-night conversations. She wondered how she'd pass the hours, with no friends, no more Jackson Lincoln to argue with or hash over the day's events.

Jackson broke the stillness. "Were you frightened this afternoon?"

"No." She was never scared when he was around; only scared when he wasn't. A wagon hanging over the side of a mountain was nothing. She doubted there was anything that he couldn't fix or mend or make work, and she told him so.

He chuckled, a low male resonance that stirred the pit of her stomach. "Your trust could be misplaced. There are a lot of things I can't do or wouldn't attempt without the help of a higher source."

"You mean without the Lord?" She didn't know why folks found the source so hard to identify.

He nodded, taking another sip from his cup. "Been doing a lot of bargaining with God about that pass."

"Were you honestly worried that we wouldn't make it?" She couldn't imagine that he'd fear anything. He seemed in control of every aspect of his life.

His expression sobering, he focused on the crackling fire. "I was concerned. Even a day's delay could have meant that we wouldn't have made it through until spring. That spot is prone to sudden and severe changes in weather. One of the worst snowstorms I've heard of happened here in May of '58. We're coming through it at the end of October, but with this weather. . . ."

Glory was smart enough to know what he hadn't said, that death would have been almost certain if a blizzard had set in.

She sidled closer to him, slipping the coffee cup into one hand and her other hand into his. The act felt as natural as rain. His large hand tightened around hers protectively. They were both foolish, standing out in a cold sleeting rain, but she wasn't inclined to leave, and neither was he, she noticed.

She looked up at him. "Guess you were happy to have Marshal McCall along to help."

Jackson nodded. "Seems to be a good man." He glanced at her and smiled. "What's between Ruth and him?"

"You noticed, too?"

Their soft laughter mingled with the popping fire; they kept their voices low so they wouldn't disturb the others. Ruth wouldn't appreciate them talking about her, but it was plain to see Ruth had gotten downright flustered around the handsome marshal.

Suddenly aware of the proximity of the others, Glory gently removed her hand from his and wrapped both hands around her cup. She moved closer to the fire and sat down. Jackson came and sat next to her. They took another sip of coffee, huddling deeper into their jackets. Sleet hit the canvas, icy pellets dancing lightly in the air. Wind shrieked through the pass, howling like a banshee.

"Two more days to Denver City?" she asked wistfully.

"Two more days," he verified.

"Guess you'll be glad to be relieved of your responsibilities."

"Not necessarily."

She took a deep breath, dreading to ask the next question but knowing that she must if she were to sleep a wink tonight. "Then what?"

He glanced at her, then back to the fire. "I'll make sure you ladies are settled, and, depending on the weather, I'll either stay around for a few weeks, or I'll start back to Illinois."

"I wish you wouldn't." The admission simply slipped out. She'd meant to thank him for his care and safe passage. Instead, she'd spoken her thoughts aloud. Did he think she was being forward?

If he thought anything of it, he didn't show it. "You thought about what you'll do?"

She shrugged. "Begin my new life."

"And that will be?"

"I don't know. Guess I'll have to see if there's work available in Denver City." She found it hard to look at him now, her emotions close to the surface. "Thanks to you, I'm a sight more capable of finding employment now than I would have been earlier."

"No thanks to me," he corrected softly. "Lily taught you to sew. Harper taught you to cook. And Ruth taught you to read and write." He turned to meet her eyes. "You were a good student; you learned your lessons well." A teasing light entered his eyes. "Do you realize that I am close to eating one of your pies without choking or dipping dough out of the water bucket?"

She accepted his good-natured ribbing gracefully and tossed a measure of it back at him. "And you can shoot a squirrel at thirty feet and still have enough meat to put on the table. Aren't we amazing?"

"Thanks to you," he conceded. They shared a smile. "We make a good team," he said softly.

"We sure do." She wished it were a permanent team, like man and wife. . . . She stopped her train of thought. She didn't need a man or a husband. What was she thinking? She was sad only because she knew how little time they had left together.

He picked up a stick and stirred the fire. "Haven't changed your mind about marriage, have you?"

She shook her head, her chin firming. "Going to

make it on my own. Well, I'll need the Lord's favor, but he's the only one going to tell me what to do."

"I understand." He watched the flames. "Feel the same way about taking a wife. Don't need a woman around, making life miserable."

"Like your mother?" she supplied.

"Like my mother."

They fell into a companionable silence.

"Not all women nag and complain," she reminded him.

"How would you know?"

"Don't for certain. Just know I wouldn't be like that."

"You wouldn't?"

"No. When I marry, I'll make sure I don't nag or complain. And if I do, I'll give myself a sound talking to, like I do when I get in your way. Remind myself that I'm lucky to have a good man, and he's lucky to have a good woman, and folks are just folks. Never met a perfect person, and seems more likely every day that I won't. So when a man and a woman marry, they ought naturally to expect there'll be times when they get on each other's nerves. Considering no one's perfect, they ought to make up their minds right off to forgive and go on." She took another sip of coffee, avoiding his gaze. "Don't you think?"

He sat for a long moment, apparently considering the likelihood. "I suppose so . . . if a man and woman love each other."

"And if they don't," she said simply, "then it's not likely they'll overlook a thing. They'll always be getting in each other's hair, looking for a way out, in which case, no one can help because it's up to the person whether he chooses to overlook fault or find fault. If anyone's looking for fault, he's going to find it; and if he's looking for good, he's likely to find that, too. Poppy used to say, 'Be happy with what you got before you get a whole lot worse.'" She studied Jackson out of the corner of her eye. "Can I ask you something?"

"Is it one of those things you're bursting at the seams to ask?"

"Might be." She dropped her gaze, cradling the coffee in her hands.

"What's the question?"

"Are you sweet on Ruth—are you going to marry her?"

His jaw dropped. "What?"

"I see the way you two look at each other, all soft and caring. You never look at the other girls that way, so I think that maybe you've fallen in love with her and you're hoping to marry her once we reach Denver City."

Strained silence closed over them. A twig snapped, shooting up a shower of sparks. Glory lifted her cup for another sip. Finally she couldn't stand the awful suspense. "Well?"

"Where would you ever get the crazy idea that I'm in love with Ruth?"

"I told you . . . the way you look at her, the way you talk to her—"

"I look and talk to Patience the same way."

"No, you don't."

He took a sip of coffee. "Your imagination is working overtime, Glory."

"You don't look at Lily or Mary that way, either."

"You don't look at me like you looked at Dylan this afternoon. Does that mean you're in love with the marshal and you dislike me?"

"Of course not. I didn't look at Dylan in an unladylike way."

He turned to face her, lifting a brow. "Every single *one* of you has looked at him in an improper way. All day long."

They turned back to study the fire.

She held her ground. "You're avoiding my question."

"How can I answer when the question doesn't make sense?"

He understood the question only too well, and he didn't want to answer. His reticence confirmed her worst fear: What he felt for Ruth was personal, and he didn't care to discuss it with her.

"Okay. I don't believe you," Glory said.

"Fine," Jackson answered.

"Fine with me, too."

They sat for a few more moments.

"If I married Ruth," he said teasingly, "I'd have to borrow the money from you to pay back Wyatt."

"That's not true and you know it."

The hour grew late. Sleet pelted the overhang, and wind rattled the canvas. The coffee warmed her insides, but the long day finally claimed her.

Slumping against Jackson's broad shoulder, she realized that Ruth would say she was being too forward, but his shoulder was too tempting. Although he didn't look at her the way he looked at Ruth, tonight he had talked to her the way he talked to Ruth.

●　●　●

Jackson glanced over, smiling when he saw her nodding off. In the past few months, she'd gone from a dirty, orphaned waif to a lovely, desirable woman. She had no idea how lovely or how desirable. There were times lately he'd had to remind himself that she was his charge, not his soul mate. She matched his zest for life where no other woman had ever come close. Was he in love with Ruth? The thought amused him. Ruth, like the other girls, claimed a part of his affection, but the girl whom—he was startled by his thoughts and surprised by their intensity. What was he about to think? That walking away from Glory wasn't going to be easy? He shook the thought away. The cold was numbing his brain.

Dumping the remains of his coffee, he turned and removed the cup from her small hand. She stirred slightly, snuggling closer to the warmth of his body. He carefully eased her back into a sitting position. Then he stood up, bent down, and lifted her tiny frame into his arms.

Pausing at the back of the wagon, he tapped on the closed canvas. A moment later, Patience poked her sleepy head out. When she saw Glory in his arms, she spread the opening wider, and he laid the drowsy girl on her pallet. Settling the blanket over her sleeping form, he gently tucked her between the soft covers. What did he feel for this woman-child?

Lord, help me—what do I feel?

"Good night," he whispered.

"Good night," Patience whispered back. She quickly secured the back canvas against the whistling wind as he turned to leave.

Turning his collar up, he adjusted the brim of his hat. By morning, the ground would be a solid sheet of ice. That meant no traveling tomorrow.

It also meant one more day in the company of a woman who was about to cost him a night's sleep.

15

Storm clouds built overhead as Jackson led the prairie schooner along Cherry Creek to the main street of Denver City on the first day of November. Six expectant faces peered out of the wagon.

Marshal Dylan McCall, riding behind the wagon all day, nudged his horse into a trot to catch up with Jackson at the front of the wagon. They rode beside each other in silence until Dylan pointed toward the sheriff's office. "Here's my stop, friend. I leave you now to meet my new traveling partner, and I'm sure he won't match the pleasant company I've recently enjoyed."

The two men reined to a halt and shook hands, and the wagon stopped behind them. Jackson met the marshal's even gaze. "I appreciate your help this past week, Dylan. Don't know how we could have gotten through the high divide without you."

"Would prefer present company to my next companion, I assure you." Dylan circled his horse to face the wagon. His gaze met Ruth's as she sat straight and stiff on the wagon seat, watching him. "Farewell, ladies."

When Jackson moved on, Ruth paused a moment. "Farewell," she finally replied. She lifted her chin and shook the reins. Grinning, Dylan tipped his hat as the wagon passed him for the last time. The girls leaned out from under the canvas to wave and call good-bye, a soft sadness filling their eyes.

Excitement broke out as the party traveled the remaining distance to a house several miles outside Denver City. Chatter faded as their eyes scanned the crudely built structure.

"Is this it?" Lily asked.

"Seems rather . . . bare," Patience murmured.

Ruth smiled, and the girls reached for each other's hands. "It will be fine. Perhaps our soon-to-be husbands are already waiting for us."

"Mercy, let's hope so." Harper's eyes took in the shabby farmhouse.

Jackson dismounted, and the girls slowly climbed out of the wagon, each clutching her valise. Stepping on the porch, he rapped on the door and waited until a harsh voice responded, "Come in. It ain't locked."

The door creaked on rusty hinges as Jackson swung it open and stepped inside to hold it for the six girls who slowly filed past him. Their eyes cast about, taking in the broken chairs and filthy bed-rolls scattered on the floor. Three unkempt men sat around a table piled with poker chips.

A blond man with long, matted hair folded his handful of cards and laid them facedown on the table as he stood up. "You must be Jackson Lincoln," he rumbled.

Jackson nodded. "I am." An awkward silence followed as the wagon master waited for the man to identify himself.

"Name's Wyatt." The man's pale eyes narrowed. "Been expecting you for two weeks now."

"Had some delays on the trail, early snow in the high passes."

Wyatt grinned at his two unshaven companions. "Yeah, that's what we figured the first week, didn't we, boys? Along about the second week, we figured you'd decided to keep the girls and go into business for yourself."

The two seated companions roared at this. "Good one, Pa!"

"Excuse me," Jackson interrupted coldly, "but there are ladies present."

This prompted a few more hoots until the men took in the granite expression on Jackson's face. The laughter subsided, and Wyatt's mouth thinned. "Oh yeah, well, I'll get your money, and you can be on your way."

"I know it's getting late," Jackson began, "but I was hoping to meet a couple of the prospective husbands you've arranged for these five ladies."

Wyatt lifted his head to survey the women. "I count six." He grinned at his companions. "You throwing in a bonus?"

"Not exactly." Jackson frowned, and Glory moved up behind him to peer at the men. "I was hoping you could arrange work and proper quarters for a young lady we met along the way."

"Which one is that?"

Jackson shifted Glory around to his front, keeping a hand on her shoulder. "Her name is Glory."

Wyatt's eyes skimmed the comely girl. "Won't have no trouble finding her work; she can join the others. Got us a nice little silver mine—always need a few more to sort rocks. Can you cook, honey?"

Glory mutely wagged her head.

A slow grin spread across the man's malevolent features. "Don't matter if you can. You can load rock, can't you?"

She shook her head.

Jackson's shoulders stiffened. "A mine? These women are mail-order brides." Behind him, the girls drew together in a tight knot, their arms wrapping around each other for support.

"Really?" Wyatt's tone took on a confrontational tone. "No mention of that in your contract."

"Your letter said—"

"Things change." Wyatt shrugged as his right hand dropped to rest on the butt of the pistol strapped to his hip. "All your contract says is that you will bring me five orphans from Westport for the amount agreed upon. I'll even throw in a bonus, seeing as you've brought me one more. Whatever my letter to Potter said—" Wyatt shrugged again—"well, now, a letter ain't a binding contract, is it? Now these ladies signed a contract, and a contract is nice and legal."

"Why, you—"

"Jeb, get me the strongbox." Wyatt's eyes hardened. "Let's pay this man, so he can get back to town before dark. He looks a bit road weary. Long trips can make a fella disagreeable. Round here a man can get hisself killed if he don't take a proper tone with the locals."

Grinning, the man called Jeb slammed a heavy box down on the table. Wyatt lifted the lid, took out a large pouch, and set it on the table. Glancing at Glory, he selected a smaller pouch and placed it beside the large one. "Put the box away, Son." He turned to the other man. "Luther, make yourself useful and show the wagon master out."

Wyatt threw the money bags at Jackson with enough force that he had to catch them or be bowled over by them. When Jackson looked up, Wyatt and Luther had their pistols drawn. Jeb had joined them, carrying a sawed-off shotgun.

"Now let's not quibble over details," Wyatt said, his pale eyes icy. "Mail-order brides or mine workers, either way these unwanted, too-old-to-adopt orphans are going to have to work off their expensive passage west. When they've done that, why, you can ask my boys here, I'm a reasonable man. The girls will be free to go wherever their little hearts desire."

Jackson met the cold gaze with a clenched jaw. "You bought these women to work in your mine?"

"Well, now, that's a little harsh. As I said, once they pay off their passage, they're free to go."

"But that would be hundreds of dollars," Ruth argued.

Wyatt smiled. "Ain't it ridiculous what prices are these days?"

"It will take years for us to work off the debt," Lily exclaimed.

Wyatt chuckled, a humorless sound. He gestured toward the door with the barrel of his pistol. "Better be on your way, wagon master. After dark it's hard to see in these hills. Easy to mistake a man for a thief or an intruder. A fella could get shot." Wyatt's gaze dropped to the pouches in Jackson's hands, and his brows lifted with interest.

Jackson's eyes moved from pistol to pistol to shotgun.

Glory's gaze flew to Jackson. "Shoot him, Jackson. He's plain no good."

Shrugging, Jackson backed toward the door, holding his hands up in surrender. "Ladies, I've done my job. You'll have to talk to Mr. Wyatt if you have a complaint."

"Jackson?" Glory exclaimed in shocked disbelief, reaching for his arm as he opened the door. "Are you nuts! You can't leave us here with this—this polecat!"

"You can't," Ruth begged, as Lily and Patience clung to her sobbing.

"Please, Mr. Lincoln," Mary wheezed, despair flooding her face.

"That's it, run like a yellow-bellied coward." Harper stepped in front of Jackson and blocked his path. Her eyes locked with his. "Just like a man. All those nice things you did for us—just an act. Once you got your money, you run out on us. So high and mighty in front of us, then some flea-bitten curs point a gun at you, and you're gone."

"Hey, who you calling flea-bitten curs?" Jeb shouted.

"Well," Wyatt said coldly, "she's right about one thing. Money changes a man. Say good-bye to your knight in shining armor, ladies."

Jackson opened the door, tipped his hat to Harper, and left.

Glory listened to the jingle of harnesses. After three and a half months, she knew it was the sound of the prairie schooner pulling out. As the sound faded, cold dread filled her heart. She couldn't believe what had just happened. Jackson hadn't lifted a hand to save them. She looked at Ruth, who turned away, handkerchief pressed to her mouth.

"Hey, Daddy, you want me to show these women their new temporary quarters?" Luther asked with a salacious grin.

"Why, that's right good of you, Son, right hospitable." Tom Wyatt grinned, revealing broken, tobacco-stained teeth. "You do that, boy. And, ladies? Better get to bed right after supper. Got a lot of rocks waitin' for you in the morning—say around four thirty?"

● ●   ●

Jackson Lincoln was furious. Blood pounded in his temple, and his chest hurt with tightness. His face was dark with rage.

Halfway down the mountain, he secured the wagon and teams in a protected grove. Saddling the mare, he bounded aboard and rode into Denver City with a crisp wind at his back. Pewter-colored clouds promised a heavy snow by nightfall.

Springing out of the saddle in town, he strode to the sheriff's office and entered with the rage of the impending blizzard.

"Whoa." Dylan McCall whirled to identify the commotion behind him. "Montgomery?"

"Marshal, am I glad you're still here." Jackson grabbed hold of Dylan's arm and took a deep breath.

"Looks like I'll be around for a while. Seems my prisoner hanged himself in his cell rather than share my company on the trip back for trial. I just sent a telegram to my superiors, requesting my next assignment."

Jackson turned to the sheriff. "I need your help." He quickly told the two men about his encounter with Wyatt and his sons and what Wyatt intended to do. "We have to get back there before he puts those girls to work in the mine."

Dylan frowned. "Where's Ruth?"

"She's with the others. Wyatt won't move them until morning, not with bad weather closing in."

The whipcord-thin sheriff shook his head. "Not so fast. We know about Wyatt and his boys. Already contacted state authorities, and they're sending investigators to check Wyatt out for fraud. We've heard similar stories about other kids he's brought into town. No doubt Wyatt is a snake, but what he's doing may not be technically illegal. The experts from the state will figure that out."

"We can't wait for experts!" Jackson exploded. "Those girls are up there scared to death. They think I walked out on them."

The sheriff shrugged. "You can't interfere with a state investigation. Tell him, Marshal."

Dylan laid a hand on Jackson's arm. "Easy, friend. Let's hear him out."

The sheriff continued. "Seems we have a pattern so far. From what we've heard, Wyatt contacts a slick solicitor in a territory, who then makes the arrangements at a local orphanage, offering to take the older children off their hands while greasing a few palms. Then he tells the girls that he represents a fine man who has assembled some eligible bachelors willing to pay their passage west to meet them. He tells the young boys that he has high-paying jobs waiting for them. Then he whips out contracts so full of legal wording that the kids have no idea what they're signing. After that, he makes arrangements with a wagon master to bring them west."

Color drained from Jackson's face. "That's how I was brought in on the deal. I was doing Frank Potter a favor."

The sheriff shook his head. "I hate to add to your troubles, but you may have a more immediate problem."

Jackson frowned. "What could be worse?"

"There's a man here in town," the sheriff began, "by the name of Amos, staying at the hotel. Seems he's searching for a wagon full of mail-order brides due to arrive any day. Says he's looking for his niece, a girl named Glory. Heard she was traveling with a small group of women when he stopped at a trading post. Folks there remembered a pretty girl by that name, who bought a mirror, it seems. He's convinced she's the niece who knocked him cold and stole his gold. A mean fella, if you ask me. Little gal is in a heap of trouble if he catches up with her."

Jackson took off his hat and ran an agitated hand through his hair. "That's all we need."

The sheriff moved to the stove to pour himself a cup of coffee. "I insisted he let the law handle it, but he only wanted to know her whereabouts. No law against that."

"Does he know about Wyatt's little scheme?" Dylan asked.

"I didn't mention it." The sheriff tasted his coffee and grimaced. "That doesn't mean he won't get wind of it."

Jackson met Dylan's eyes. "All the more reason we need to ride out to Wyatt's right now."

"There's nothing we can do about it tonight," the sheriff announced with a tired sigh. "I trust everything will be straightened out in a few short weeks."

"We haven't got weeks!" Jackson snapped.

Dylan turned him around and pushed him back through the door. "I'll have a chat with him, Sheriff."

Outside, Jackson shook off Dylan's restraining hold.

"Look, McCall, if you're going to tell me to wait

for the state boys to mosey down here, save your breath! Glory's in trouble, and I'm going after her. If I hadn't been outnumbered earlier, she'd be with me now."

"Glory? Ruth's up there too."

The two men faced off. Jackson's eyes steeled. "Look. There are six women up there who need our help. I don't intend to stand here and split hairs."

Shoving past the marshal, Jackson strode toward his horse.

"Wait a minute, hothead. You did the right thing—it would have been nuts to take on Wyatt and his two boys alone." Dylan blocked Jackson's path, motioning with a sideways nod to start walking. When they stepped into a deserted alley, he turned to face Jackson. "What you have here is a lawman willing to help you take those ladies into protective custody until the state investigators have this thing sorted out."

Jackson released the breath that he'd been holding. "I'd be much obliged."

Dylan clapped him on the shoulder. "Well, if Wyatt and his boys are as nasty as you say and Amos is on the prowl, we have a little short-range planning to do."

• • •

"Didn't I tell you so?" Harper sat down on the hard bunk and crossed her arms, her dark eyes openly accusing. "Men are worthless, lying, sneaking . . . no-good . . . stinking, useless, vile—"

"Men," Lily finished.

Harper nodded succinctly.

The old bunkhouse was drafty, wind whistling through the cracks. A woodstove in the middle of the room gave off little heat in the icy mountain air. Wyatt didn't have to lock the door; the mountains and impending storm held the women prisoners.

Glory sighed. "Jackson isn't like that."

Harper snorted. "He's a man, ain't he?"

"He's not *that* kind of a man."

Harper sprang to her feet. "How can you defend him? Look what he's done to us." She snapped her finger. "Poof. He sold us out, Glory. Took the money and walked out the door. You saw him, same as us."

"I know it looks that way." Glory felt awful. It *did* look as if Jackson didn't care a whit about them, so he'd left her no choice but to suspect the worst. She turned her eyes on Ruth. "Do you think Jackson could really betray us?"

Ruth shook her head. "I would have never thought he would, but you saw what he did."

"I won't believe it," Mary whispered. The young woman lay on her cot, dark circles under her eyes, the high altitude making her breathing even more difficult. "I saw what he did, but I refuse to believe Jackson would desert us."

"Any man worth his salt wouldn't walk off and leave a woman in our position." Harper jerked her blanket over her shoulders. "We've been bought for hard labor, ladies. And I fell for Jackson's act—pretending to be oh-so-nice, pretending that he cared about us and that he'd protect us no matter what." She yanked the blanket closer to her neck. "He's just like any other man. Thinks of himself and doesn't give a hoot about others."

"Not all men are traitors," Lily contended. "I've met some very nice men who were thoughtful and considerate. Jackson was wonderful . . . until tonight."

Patience sneezed. Rummaging in her valise for a handkerchief, she said softly, "Rats. I'm coming down with the sniffles."

Harper eyed her imperiously. "Well, honey, if you do, don't expect Wyatt and his gentlemanly sons to bring you hot soup."

The girls shivered at the thought of Wyatt's repulsive sons, Luther and Jeb.

Patience had been unusually quiet, sitting through a supper of cold corn bread and water and looking miserable. Glory glanced at the shivering girl. "What about you, Patience? Do you think Jackson will turn us over to Tom Wyatt without a fight?"

"Looks to me like he already has. I'm sorry, Glory. I know you believed in him; we all did. But maybe your trust, and ours, has been misplaced."

Mary started to cry, tears wetting her thin pillow. "If I can't work and pay back Mr. Wyatt for my journey, what will he do with me? I'm useless."

Glory crossed the short distance to her bunk and took the sobbing girl in her arms.

"Don't worry," Harper said gruffly. "I'll do your share of the work, and if Wyatt complains, I'll show him what for."

"I'll help too," Lily offered.

Patience sneezed again. "Me too."

"We'll all help, Mary." Glory held the girl tightly. "Dry your tears. Jackson won't let this happen to us."

Glory didn't feel nearly as confident as she sounded. She didn't know about Jackson. What *would* Wyatt do with a sickly girl? Would he sell her to some uncaring, thoughtless animal every bit as vile as he? Mary wouldn't last a week. . . .

Straightening, Glory lifted her chin. "I don't care what you say, Jackson won't do this to us. He . . . he has a plan. He's only pretending to go along with Wyatt because he was outnumbered. It would have been foolish for him to try to take on all three of them. Why, I bet this very minute he's arranging a rescue."

"Right." Harper rolled her eyes. "And I'm the Queen Mother."

Wind battered the bunkhouse; Glory huddled on Mary's cot, more scared than she'd been in her whole life. *Please, Jackson, don't do this to us. I love you.*

"We'll run away. We can do it," Lily whispered. "The door isn't locked; we can slip out when the others are asleep and—"

"We'd die, Lily!" Glory exclaimed. "We haven't any food or water. It looks like it's going to snow any minute. It's miles and miles back to Denver City." Glory glanced at Mary. "We can't leave shelter; the mountain roads are narrow and dangerous. It's pitch-black out there, and we have no lantern, barely adequate clothing—"

Lily leaned closer. "But you're used to the out-doors. You could lead us, Glory."

"I'm not that good, not nearly as good as Jackson."

The girls groaned.

"We can't count on him," Ruth said.

"When the storm's over," Harper began, "we sneak up on Wyatt and his no-good sons, and we knock them senseless—"

"We can't do that either, Harper," Glory moaned. She would like nothing better than to knock Wyatt and his boys senseless, but if that mission failed, then no telling what Wyatt would do. He might decide they were more trouble than they were worth and do away with the lot of them. Short of killing the three men, the plan was too risky, and she didn't want any part of killing.

"We should pray about this," Ruth murmured.

"We will, Ruth, but in case the Lord is tending other business right now, we'd be smart to help him out." Glory slipped off the cot and started to pace. "I know Jackson is bluffing. He's thinking of a plan to help us this minute."

No use mentioning that she didn't believe a word she was saying, but she had to be strong for the others.

Rolling her eyes, Harper pulled the blanket over her head.

Hope lit Ruth's eyes. "Do you think so, Glory? Do you really think so?"

Glory reached for Ruth's hand and squeezed it. She could believe what she was saying—she must. "I know so, Ruth. Now everyone listen to me. Sleep lightly, and keep a close ear out for any sound that might mean Jackson is trying to help us."

Lily lifted a brow. "Like what?"

"Like a peck on the window or the door opening softly."

"What if it's Wyatt and those awful sons of his?" Ruth shivered.

"If it's Wyatt and he tries anything funny, we'll fight him with anything we can get our hands on." Her eyes fixed on the iron poker lying next to the stove. "I'll use the poker. Lily, you hit him with your pillow. Ruth, take off your boots and knock the wadding out of him."

"I'll empty my valise," Patience offered. "It will make a weapon."

"Good."

"What about me?" Mary wheezed.

Glory's eyes swept the room.

"I know," Mary enthused. "I'll charge him from the back. I'm little and wiry, and I'll use my fingers as weapons to gouge his eyes out, if I must," she whispered.

"Perfect," Glory agreed, and the others murmured their support. Eyes pivoted to Harper.

Yanking the blanket off her face, she heaved a resigned sigh. "I'll take him from the front." Springing to her feet, she doubled both fists. "I'll make him wish he'd thought twice about lying to us."

"Okay, we have a plan. Now, everyone buck up and have a little faith. Jackson won't let us down."

"And neither will the Lord," Ruth promised. "He

might be off tending other business, but he still has an eye on all his children."

The girls knelt in prayer and joined hands. "Father," Lily whispered, "we need you to be looking right now. You are our hiding place; you will protect us from harm."

"Yes, Lord," Harper whispered. "You tell us not to worry about anything, but to pray about everything. You tell us to tell you what we need, and what we need right now, God, is for you to look after us."

Patience added softly, "You tell us not to be afraid, for you are with us. You are our God, and you will strengthen us. You will uphold us with your victorious right hand."

"You will keep in perfect peace all who trust you, whose thoughts are fixed on you, Father," Ruth reminded.

"You have loved us, even as your Father loved you," Glory said softly. "And God has given us his Spirit as proof that we live in him and he in us." Her heart overflowed with the joy of remembering the Scriptures.

"We feel your Spirit this hour. Protect us this night, our Father. For you are the only one who can," Mary prayed.

Squeezing hands, the girls extinguished the candle and climbed onto their hard cots, ready for battle.

Glory lay beside Ruth, listening to the first drops of cold rain hit the dirty windowpanes, rain that was destined to turn to heavy snow before morning.

Glory tried to imagine how dark and cold a mine would be and finally gave up. Likely she'd find out soon enough.

"Glory?" Ruth whispered.

"Yes?"

"Do you really believe Jackson will come, or were you only trying to console the others?"

"I believe he will come, Ruth. Believe it with all my heart."

Ruth lay quietly for a moment. "Then I'll believe it too."

Stillness settled over the drafty bunkhouse. Only Mary's rattling cough broke the silence.

"Ruth?"

"Yes, Glory?"

"Do you really believe there is a God, and that he loves us and cares about us, died on the cross to save us and give us eternal life?"

"I believe there is, Glory. With all my heart, I believe there is."

Silence stretched between them. Rain pelted the windows, and the wind whistled through the cracks between the logs. The uncertainty of life never felt more certain.

"Ruth?"

"Yes?"

"I believe it too. With all my heart, I believe it."

Reaching across the small space, the two girls held hands in the darkness and waited.

16

In the middle of the night, the girls still lay wide-awake in the Wyatt bunkhouse, their ears straining to hear every sound, listening to every gust of wind and their own rapid heartbeats. With every facet of her being, Glory willed Jackson to return before dawn to rescue them. She reviewed every memory, everything she'd heard him say, every expression on his face, every action he'd taken. In none of those things could she see a man who would abandon them to a fate like this. Jackson Lincoln wouldn't—no, he couldn't—leave them behind, never to return.

Glory rose to toss another chunk of wood into the stove. There were precious few sticks remaining to last the night. She shivered inside her jacket and tightened her wool scarf around her neck. They had all agreed that Mary should have the only blanket. The poor girl's breathing was raspy, the cold night and unsettling hours taking their toll. Harper had handed it over willingly.

"Where do you suppose the others are?"

Glory turned to look at Lily. "Others?"

"The other kids who work the mine."

"Hidden away, probably. Wyatt wouldn't want—"

She stiffened, suddenly aware of a noise outside the single window of the bunkhouse. Her first thought was that Wyatt or his sons were returning to torment them. But that didn't make sense when they could simply open the door and walk in. Her heart leapt to her throat. To her, only one person could be outside that window.

"Did you hear something?" Ruth asked in a hoarse whisper.

"It's them," Harper said. "Get to your battle stations."

"Hold on." Glory eased away from the stove, careful not to make a sound. "It's Jackson. I told you he'd come back for us!"

"Not so fast, girl." Harper crouched beside her cot, whispering. "We don't know it's Jackson. Better get ready for a fight."

The girls scrambled out of their beds, but Glory rushed past on her way to the window. "No, no," she whispered, "stay quiet. We've got to help him."

She shoved back the rotting curtains and peered out, but the glass was so filthy and the night so dark she couldn't see anything. But her heart knew who was mere feet away. She could hear him grunting as he strained to lift the cumbersome window.

"It's okay, Jackson," she said in a low voice as she shoved at the window, trying to raise it. "I'll help you from inside."

She pushed up with all her might while he pushed from the outside. Suddenly she heard a creaking and then a popping sound as the rusty nails gave way. The window slowly lifted from the sill, then suddenly slammed upward.

Glory sighed with relief, then gathered the shredded curtains and sprang aside to allow Jackson access. She could point him to the front door, but Wyatt and his sons might see him. The window was hidden from the back part of the house where Wyatt and his sons slept.

He landed inside with a thud, his heavy boots hitting the rotten floor planks in the thick darkness. Glory lunged forward to throw her arms around his neck. "You're here," she whispered. "I knew you'd come for me."

A man's harsh chuckle sent goose bumps down her spine. "Told you I'd find you."

"Jackson?" Glory whispered, praying that the darkness was playing tricks on her.

"Now don't tell me you don't recognize your favorite uncle Amos."

Glory sprang back and would have fallen to the floor had Ruth not caught her. "Oh no," Glory moaned.

"If I recollect, it was a dark night when you clobbered me and ran off with my gold." Amos's voice rumbled with rage. "Left me for dead, you did!"

Mary screamed.

"Making a habit of it, are ya?" Amos latched on to Glory's arm and jerked her upright. "Don't surprise me. Time you paid the piper, girlie. I want my gold. Now!"

Glory quaked with fear. There was nothing Amos wouldn't do to get Poppy's gold. "I'd give you the gold if I had it, Amos. You've got to believe me."

"I don't got to do nothing of the kind." He gave Glory a shove. "You give me that gold or I'll tear you apart."

Mary gasped, and then her wheezing intensified. She struggled for every breath now.

Amos stopped and turned in the darkness, homing in on the sound of Mary's raspy breathing. "Or I might grab me one of your friends. Is that what you want, Glory?" He had no trouble finding Mary. He fumbled in the dark until he reached her. With a jerk, he pulled the sickly girl from Harper's arms. Mary began to choke—wrenching sounds—as her fright shut off her air supply.

"No!" Glory fought her way through the inky blackness to Mary and tried to twist her free of his grip. "Let her go, Amos. You're hurting her!"

"I'll hurt her worse," he snarled. "Where's that gold, Glory?"

Patience and Lily started to sob; Ruth begged him to be merciful.

"Let her go, Amos," Glory pleaded. "She's sick. I'll take you to Poppy's gold. I have it hidden. We can make good time, just the two of us. We have to go now, before Wyatt and his sons hear the racket and come to investigate."

"No, Glory!" Ruth pleaded. "You can't go with him—"

"I'll take you, Amos," Glory repeated. "Now! But you have to let Mary stay here."

"If you're lying to me, I'll do away with the lot of 'em." He thrust Mary backward onto the cot, his left hand closing around Glory's arm, pinching her tender flesh so hard it brought tears to her eyes.

Whirling, he dragged her to the window and hoisted her to the sill. With a wicked shove he sent her flying through the opening. She landed on the ground with a hard thump, and he chuckled with glee. "If you make a run for it, Miss Glory," he sang out on a high note, "I'll bring Miss Mary with me!"

"I'm not going anywhere, Amos," Glory returned.

He grunted with rage as he climbed through the window and landed on the ground in a heap. Struggling to his feet, he gave Glory a sound slap across her face. "That's a taste of what you'll get if you try anything. I mean it. You try to run out on me again, and I'll come back here and take care of your little friends."

"I'll do whatever you say." Teeth chattering, Glory huddled against the icy wind. Snow had already begun to fall.

Snatching her arm, he ushered her to a stand of aspens, where a horse waited. He grabbed a fistful of her hair and then climbed into the saddle.

"Ow," she cried as he dragged her up behind him. She struck out at him. "That hurts!"

"Don't try anything funny, Glory. I mean it. Where did you put that gold?"

"In Denver City. I hid it before we came out here to Wyatt's."

"You better not be lying to me," he snarled as they set off at a trot.

•   •   •

Investigating the ruckus, Wyatt opened the door to the bunkhouse and held his lantern aloft. His night-shirt flapped in the howling wind. "What's going on out here?"

The women huddled close, sobbing and pray-ing in the center of the room. They shrank back as his spindly frame filled the open doorway. The only sounds were Mary's wheezing and the gusts of wind banging the door against the side of the building.

"I'm not a patient man!"

Ruth spoke up. "A man came in."

"What?" Wyatt roared, lifting the lantern higher. His long hair whipped in the wind.

"Through the window there. He took Glory, his niece. He's a horrible man. I think he means her harm. You could catch them if you leave now. They have about a quarter of an hour's start. I saw them heading into the woods—you could follow their tracks."

The other girls gasped.

"No," Lily exclaimed, "you can't send him after them."

Ruth turned to look at her. "It's the only way we can save Glory. This man is less of a danger to her than Amos. Remember, we're only worth something to Wyatt if we're alive. Glory's uncle will surely do away with her once he gets what he's after."

"Oh," Lily choked, burying her face in her hands to sob.

Wyatt strode to the open window and slammed it shut. "The next one who tries to escape will be shot, you hear me?"

"The dead could hear you," Jackson said, appearing in the open doorway with Dylan right behind him. Both men had pistols trained on Wyatt.

"Jackson!" Ruth sprang up to meet him. "Glory knew you would come. She lied to Amos, told him she'd hidden the money in Denver City. She sacrificed herself for Mary and us."

He strode into the room as Wyatt turned and extended his lantern to get a look at him.

"Are you hurt?" Jackson asked the girls as he moved toward them.

"No," Ruth said, "only scared."

"Get your things," Jackson said evenly. "You're coming with us."

"See here—" Wyatt stopped short when Jackson turned to face him.

"I don't want any trouble, Wyatt."

Dylan was standing watch at the door. "We've got company."

Outside, a man's voice filtered above the howling wind. "Daddy? It's Jeb. You want us to shoot 'em?"

"If these men step outside with the women, shoot 'em all," Wyatt yelled. He glanced at Jackson and grinned. "No trouble, wagon master. You're not going anywhere with anybody."

"Okay, Pa," came the reply from the darkness outside.

Dylan, standing behind the door with his pistol aimed in the direction of the voices outside, spoke up, "Wyatt, shine your lantern this way. I have something you should see."

When Wyatt hesitantly complied, Dylan flashed the badge pinned to his jacket. "See this?"

"You the law?" Wyatt took a step back.

"Dylan McCall, U.S. marshal. I'm here to take these women into protective custody until investigators can check the legitimacy of your claim to them."

"Now hold on," Wyatt said, backing away now. "Why didn't you say so? You don't need to go stirring up a hornet's nest. We can work something out."

"Thought you might see it that way. Here's the deal. You call off your boys, and we leave peaceably. Nobody gets hurt. I can tell investigators how cooperative you were."

Wyatt grunted, then sighed heavily, took a deep breath, and raised his voice to shout, "Boys, change of plans! Put down your weapons, and let these two men and the women leave."

"Huh? You sure, Pa?"

"Do as I say," Wyatt roared.

Dylan motioned to Ruth. "Ladies, line up behind me and stay close. Jackson will follow behind."

Spreading her arms, Ruth quickly assembled the girls behind her. She stepped behind Dylan and took hold of his shirt. "We're with you," she murmured.

"Let's go." He stepped through the doorway, pistol held aloft. Quietly the group filed out with Dylan in the lead and Jackson protecting their flank. He grabbed Wyatt's lantern just before he slammed the door shut.

"What the—?" Wyatt roared.

The group made a break for the nearest trees before Wyatt and his boys had a chance to change their minds.

Hurrying deeper into the woods, they could hear the shrill voices of Wyatt's boys. "Why you lettin' them take the women, Pa?"

"Because, you *fools*, there's more where they came from. Besides, more lawmen are on their way. Time we took to higher ground."

"We coulda shot those men, Pa!"

"If you lazy bums had rolled out of bed and come out here when I first called you," Wyatt bellowed, "we'd all been inside the bunkhouse, and those boys wouldn't have gotten the drop on me. But no, you don't listen to your pa!"

The ruckus faded as the small group scurried through the woods. They paused in an aspen grove, where Jackson bent to check two sets of footprints, one set large and one set small. He glanced up at Dylan. "Looks like this is where Amos left his horse."

Dylan nodded. "They can't be far. I'll go after them."

"You take the others and get them back to Denver

City," Jackson said. "The wagon and teams are waiting about a mile down the road. I'll go after Glory, and we'll meet up by morning."

"Be careful," Dylan warned.

"I will. See to the girls' safety. The storm is about to break, and it's going to be a bad one." The two men shook hands and set off in different directions.

Within minutes, Jackson located a set of prints in the snow. Fresh, not over an hour old. As the sprinkle of falling snow grew heavier, Jackson urged his mare into a gallop. It looked like Amos was angling back toward the road. He had to catch him before the snow covered his tracks. Kicking his horse, he rode faster.

Rounding a bend half an hour later, Jackson spotted a light in the distance. He quickly dimmed his own lantern. Amos's horse was lunging up a hillside, while Amos awkwardly held his lantern aloft. The snow, combined with the awkward weight of Amos and his passenger, made it hard for the animal to keep his balance.

Jackson reined his mare to circle around, hoping to catch Amos by surprise.

When Amos's horse topped the next rise, Jackson put his heels to his mare, and she shot out of the trees in a blur of snow and wind. The wagon master turned his mare so she'd bump Amos's horse, and then he reached out and grabbed its bridle. Amos's lantern flew to the ground and smashed.

"Jump, Glory!" Jackson shouted, but she was already sliding off the animal's back.

Jackson glanced over his shoulder to be sure she was clear. Amos struck out, hitting him in the jaw. Jackson reeled and dropped his lantern but managed to keep his hold on the bridle. The two horses leapt side by side, brushing between the nearby aspen trees.

The trail narrowed; there was hardly enough room for one animal. Amos's knee collided with a tree trunk, and he pitched backward, losing his balance and falling heavily to the ground.

Jackson wheeled his horse around and galloped back. Dismounting, he kept an eye on Amos, who by now was raising one hand in the air. "Don't shoot," he hollered, bending forward to clutch his knee.

"Look out, Jackson!" Glory cried. "He's got a knife in his boot!"

Amos sprang, slashing wildly. Jackson instinctively raised his right hand to protect himself. Amos ripped his palm and wrist, tearing open glove and flesh.

Jackson swung his left fist and connected with Amos's jaw and sent him sprawling. Awkwardly, he drew his pistol out of his holster with his left hand. Amos rolled to his knees and crawled a few feet.

"Stop right there," Jackson warned, leveling the Colt.

"You won't get away with this," Amos snarled. He kept his eyes on the pistol in Jackson's hand. After a pause, he backed up a few feet and slid down a tree trunk and sat there, glaring.

Glory rushed to Jackson. He awkwardly put his

left arm around her, pulling her close to his side. "Are you all right?"

"I'm fine. I knew you would come." She paused. "What about the girls?"

"Dylan has them. They're on their way to Denver City. We'll meet them by morning." He glanced up at the swirling snow. "Round up the horses. The storm is getting worse."

"You got it."

The two men stared at each other for a long moment in the silence of the falling snow.

"What are you going to do with me?" Amos snarled.

"Well, it comes down to this, Amos." Jackson leaned over to pick up the knife. His blood stained the mounting snow. "When we leave, we're taking your horse. I'll leave him tied about a mile down the road. Then you have a choice to make. You can give up the notion of taking the gold away from Glory, or you can continue to hunt her down and deal with me. In which case, you won't have a second chance. So you come after Glory again, and there'll be no mercy. Or you can walk to your horse, mount up, and ride on. You make the choice."

Amos glared up at him.

Jackson mounted his mare and pulled Glory up behind him. He fixed Amos with a solid stare. "May God have mercy on your soul." Looping the reins of Amos's horse around his saddle horn, Jackson set the horses into motion.

• • •

Snow pelted their faces as Jackson galloped the horse back down the trail. Glory knew if the storm kept up, he wouldn't be able to see the road in another fifteen minutes.

"Will Amos come after us?" she shouted above the whistling wind.

"That's up to him!"

She knew Jackson had been fair enough to give him a choice; other men likely wouldn't have.

The wind shifted, and snow flecks turned to cotton-ball-size flakes. They approached an over-hanging rock, and Jackson veered off to the side of the trail. Slipping out of the saddle, he tied Amos's horse to a low bush. He quickly remounted the mare, and they rode on.

"What about your hand?" she called in a worried voice a short time later. "It's bleeding!" It was a nasty wound. He was losing blood fast, and unless the gash was properly dressed, he could bleed to death. Jackson stopped the horse long enough for Glory to get down and scoop up a handful of snow and press it to his wound.

Blinding snow swirled as the horse and its riders pushed on through the mounting drifts. Conversation was impossible now. Glory clung to Jackson's waist, trying to summon faith like Ruth's.

God has his eyes on his children. Glory knew that accepting God's Word meant she had to believe that, no matter what, but she wondered if even Ruth could hold on to her faith tonight.

Clamping her eyes shut, she whispered between chattering teeth, *I believe, Lord. I just hope you're not off tending business elsewhere.*

Gradually she felt changes taking place in Jackson's body. At first, they were small, barely perceptible: a relaxing of his muscles, an inability to answer her shouted questions. Then the changes became more pronounced. He slumped, weakened from the loss of blood. Her fingers rested in warm blood pooling on the saddle. Through the faint light reflected off the snow-covered ground, she detected the gaping wrist wound, and it looked bad.

"Jackson!" Fear choked her. If he lost consciousness, he would be too heavy for her to lift. "Jackson! Answer me!"

Stirring, he tightened his grip on the reins. "I'm all right."

But he wasn't all right; he was still bleeding. Worsening weather rapidly deteriorated into blizzard conditions. Wind shrieked through the boulders, and snow piled up on pine branches.

Reaching around his waist, she took the reins and pulled the horse to a stop.

"I'm all right," he protested. "Just got to find shelter before the storm gets any worse."

"You're in no shape to do anything." All the times she used to climb all over her mule, Molasses, gave her the courage to try a desperate move. She shifted her weight to one side, stood up in the stirrup, and swung out, easing her slight weight around his frame. Grunting, she climbed in front of him and landed just behind the saddle horn. She wrapped his arms around her waist and called over her shoulder, "Hang on."

Fumbling in her pocket, she pulled out a handkerchief. She twisted it into a rope and tied it around Jackson's hand. Gathering the reins, she tapped the mare with her heels and set off again.

Snow came down in heavy, wet sheets. Inching forward in the saddle, Glory strained to make out the road. She kept the mare to the far left and slowed her to a walk when they entered a narrow ledge. *Don't look down,* she chanted under her breath as the mare picked her footing through the narrow, rutted trail. *For heaven's sake, don't look down.* She didn't need a full moon to warn her of the two-hundred-foot drop-off on the right.

Reaching back, she grasped hold of Jackson, who was slumped over her shoulder now. "Hold on. I'll get us there." Wherever that might be. She had no idea where she was going or how to get there.

She couldn't feel her face. Frigid wind whipped around her head, and her lips were numb. She had to find shelter—but where? This mountainous terrain was so different from Missouri's gently rolling hills.

The mare cleared the narrow pass and plodded into a valley. Here, the snow whirled across the exposed land, piling to frightening depths.

Glory shook her head, trying to clear her vision.

Jackson leaned on her shoulder, unconscious now. She could hear her own heartbeat in her ear. Everything began to blur; she was becoming disoriented.

Dear God, help me.

Reining the mare through another snowbank, she tried to think, but her mind was slow and unresponsive. Wind tore at her coat and seeped though her wool dress and leggings.

The horse stumbled and nearly went down. Flanking it hard and lifting the reins, she sent it surging back to its feet. At the same time, she fought to keep hold of Jackson.

We're going to die.

No! She wouldn't let Jackson die. She had to keep moving.

Ahead would be shelter somewhere: in a grove of aspens, or in a cave, maybe in an abandoned mine.

She couldn't see three feet in front of her. The mare thrashed about, trying to wade through the drifts, snorting with fear.

Suddenly, out of nowhere, a faint light appeared in the distance.

Bolting upright, Glory whispered to Jackson, "It's all right. Somebody's coming." Relief flooded her as the light bobbed closer.

Oh, thank you, God. Thank you for hearing my cries.

The light stopped in front of her. The stranger lifted the lantern to reveal his face. It looked like Poppy standing before her, moving the lantern slowly back and forth.

"Poppy?" she whispered. Grabbing hold of

Jackson's hand, she tried to squeeze it, but her hand wouldn't close. "It's Poppy," she cried.

"Go back!" The figure waved the lantern in warning. "Go back, Glory. You're going to die if you don't."

"Go back where?" She twisted to look back over her shoulder at the swirling void. "Poppy, I can't go back!" Tears slipped from her eyes and rolled down her cheeks. The wetness froze in seconds. This couldn't be Poppy; Poppy was dead. Her mind was playing tricks on her. She turned to look again.

"Go back! Turn around!"

She obeyed. She turned the mare around, and when she looked back at the figure, he and the light had disappeared.

Leaning in the stirrups, she strained to locate him. "Poppy? Poppy!"

A howling wind caught in her throat and choked off her pleas.

Guiding the mare, she waded the animal back through the fresh tracks. She was losing her mind. Poppy was dead; Poppy wasn't here in Colorado in a blinding blizzard, holding a lantern and warning her to turn back.

The horse could barely clear the drifts. Snow swelled to the mare's belly and dragged against the stirrups.

The narrow ledge. She couldn't make it back over the tight pass. The snow was getting too deep. She wouldn't be able to keep far enough over, and they'd drop over the side.

She suddenly turned the mare, veering to a sharp left. The path tapered, then widened to a small pine grove. Slowing, Glory listened to the wind shrieking through the boughs. The pungent scent of pine mingled with the awful cold. She was so frozen the scene felt surreal, and she wondered if she was imagining it like she'd imagined Poppy and the light.

Holding tight to Jackson's gloved hand, she closed her eyes, barely able to think. *Are you going to let us die, Lord? I sure would appreciate it if you didn't.*

"Jackson," she whispered, tired now, so very tired. "This might not be a good time to tell you this, and I know you can't hear me anyway, but it's one of those things I'm fairly bursting to say. If I don't say it right now, I might never have the chance again."

Swallowing, she gathered her strength and her nerve. It was possible that they wouldn't make it through the night; that's why she had to tell him now.

"I love you," she whispered. "I know you don't want me to love you, but I love you anyway. I've loved you from the moment you found me sitting on the trail and offered me a ride. I loved you when you shouted and blustered at me; I loved you when you were kind, and I loved you when I couldn't get a bad word out of you."

His heartbeat was faint against her back.

"If I were as pretty as Lily or as smart as Ruth, I know that you would love me back. But I'm not. Don't suppose my looks would scare a man, but I don't have Patience's grace and beauty. You don't like my boyish ways, but Poppy raised me to take care of myself, and that's what I have to do. There's nothing wrong with a woman being able to take care of herself—you might even be grateful to me for saving our lives—if it turns out that I have."

Right now the prospect didn't look so good.

"What I'm trying to say is that someday, if we make it out of this, you will meet a woman you love as much as I love you right this moment, and I will envy her with all my heart. Hard as I've prayed about it, I'm still jealous when you pay attention to other women, not that you do that often, but sometimes you do. I'm sorry. I suspect we'd have to always deal with that . . . if you were to ever love me back."

A noise caught her attention. A soft, mewling sound. Opening her eyes, she looked around, trying to identify the source. Bear? Her heart accelerated, and her hand slowly searched for the rifle. What should she do? If she left the saddle, Jackson would slide off, and she wouldn't be able to lift him again. That would mean death for both of them.

Clucking softly, she eased the mare a step forward. If it was a bear, he had the advantage, but it couldn't be a bear. Bears were in their dens this time of year. Her hand closed tighter around the rifle, shifting it to the saddle horn. If she had disturbed a bear's winter sleep and he charged, she would shoot by sound and pray the bullet found its mark. She'd shot a black bear once, but it had been in broad daylight, and she'd had her wits about her. Unable to feel her fingers in her gloves, she wondered if she could squeeze the trigger.

Kneeing the mare another step, she waited, ear cocked to the wind. There it was again, louder. A snort. Heavy breathing.

Bring the rifle to your shoulder, Glory.

In slow motion she brought the Winchester into position. It was there—not twenty feet away on the right, in the bushes.

Why didn't it charge?

If it wasn't a bear, what was it?

The mare took another step.

Bushes rustled.

You can do this, Glory. It's either whatever is out there or us. Jackson can't help. You have to get Jackson's wound dressed . . . Maybe he's already dead.

No! He's not dead; you can feel his breathing. He's weak, awful weak, but he's alive.

Fresh blood—the bear—the animal, it smells fresh blood.

Her heart thumped against her rib cage.

It was so close now; she could feel its presence, hear its ragged breathing.

The mare took yet another step.

A thrashing in the bushes. There it was. Dead right.

Straining to spot the enemy, Glory kneed the mare closer, positioning the rifle against her right shoulder. Jackson's weight mashed her against the saddle horn. Her shoulders shook from the weight of the gun, and she strained to hold the barrel level.

The bushes moved and against the ground's pristine backdrop, she finally saw it. An elk, with a four-by-four rack, wounded and hurting, lying on its side in the snow. Pain-glazed eyes stared up at her.

"Sorry, ole fella," Glory whispered. The animal had probably tangled with a mountain cat and lost. "I gotta do us both a favor." Taking careful aim, she willed a steady hand and slowly squeezed the trigger.

The explosion startled the horse. Rearing, it catapulted Glory, the rifle, and Jackson onto the ground. She landed with a thud in the softly packed snow. The Winchester went one way, and Jackson flew the other.

Glory lay for a moment, too tired and too cold to care anymore. "Jackson," she finally murmured after long moments, "I think the Lord is busy elsewhere." She paused, biting her bottom lip. "I'm real sorry, but I think we're going to die."

Searching the ground beside her with her right hand, she felt for him. "Jackson?"

Instead of Jackson's powerful build, she encountered something furry. Startled, she drew back. The elk. Struggling to her knees, she crawled to the dead animal. Breaking into sobs, she laid her head against the carcass and bawled with relief. *Thank you, God, thank you!*

Crawling back to the mare, she grabbed a stirrup, pulled her stiff body upright, and fumbled in the saddlebags for Jackson's skinning knife. *Jackson. Where was Jackson?*

She jerked the knife free, then dropped back to her knees and inched back to the elk. Within minutes, she'd cut through sternum, muscle, cartilage, and entered the stomach cavity. She worked methodically, scooping armfuls of entrails onto the ground. The knife sliced cleanly through hide, blessed substance that could save their lives.

"It's all right, Jackson. The Lord has sent us help," she called over her shoulder as she gutted the animal. "We're not going to die."

When the elk was field dressed, she crawled back to the mare, her hands blindly searching for Jackson. She found his unconscious form lying near the animal's hooves.

Struggling to her feet, she grasped him under his arms and pulled.

Pulled.

Pulled.

Straining and pulling, she edged him only inches with each step. His weight resisted her slim frame and threatened to undo her.

Pausing.

Pulling.

Finally she had him beside the carcass. Digging into the snow, she scraped a round ball into her hand, then pressed it against his wrist wound, praying that the cold would stop the bleeding until morning light. Summoning her last shred of strength, she rolled his still form inside the elk and crawled in beside him.

Lying spoonlike in the warm hollow space, Glory wrapped his arms around her waist and shoved, inching them farther back into the life-saving warmth before she, too, lost consciousness.

17

Ruth paced the mercantile porch, keeping an eye peeled on the edge of town. The soles of her boots scraped the planked floor as she strode back and forth, wringing her hands.

The mercantile door opened, and Dylan McCall came out. He paused when he saw her state, a slow grin spreading across his rugged features. Ruth saw him and turned to stare in the opposite direction.

Pulling the door closed behind him, Dylan joined her. "You still fretting? Jackson knows how to survive in the wilds."

She spared him the briefest of glances, then returned to her vigil. She'd been edgy and cranky all day, worrying herself to death about Glory and Jackson. *Lord, I trust you've held them in your care, but why don't they come?* "It's been a week. They should have been here by now."

The marshal calmly adjusted the brim of his hat. "Not necessarily. Snow could have held them up. We just got to Denver City a couple of days ago ourselves."

She paused to face him. Hands on hips, looking

vexed, she spouted, "We started from the same place at the same time. Snow delayed our arrival a few days, but not a week. We're here; Jackson and Glory aren't. They could be lying out there dead, for all we know."

"Not exactly at the same time. Jackson took off in the opposite direction. No telling how far he rode before he caught up with Glory and Amos."

"If, *if* he caught up!" Dropping her hands, she resumed pacing.

Dylan pulled up a chair and sat down. He removed his hat and carefully settled it on his knee. His relaxed position clearly didn't set well with the serious brunette. Ruth shot him an annoyed look.

He lifted his palms defensively. "What? I'm just trying to stay calm."

"If you were any *calmer*, they'd be shoveling dirt in your face, Dylan McCall." She craned to see around the porch post. Where were they? *Lord, I can't stand the suspense a moment longer!*

"All right. I surrender. Stew till you lose your mind. I won't say another word." Dylan crossed one leg over the other, folded his arms, and stared at Ruth. The arrogant posture only angered her more, and she stared back. He lifted a brow. "Now I suppose you're going to tell me there's a law against a man sitting on a porch?"

"Can't you find someone else to annoy?"

He appeared to consider it and then shook his head. "No, I get my enjoyment stepping on *your* nerves."

"Oooph!" Ruth gathered up her skirt and moved to the far corner of the porch.

Grinning, Dylan took out a toothpick and stuck it between his lips, rolling it to the corner of his mouth. "Yes, sir, Ruth. I'm as calm as pudding."

Across the street, Lily, Patience, and Mary came out of the café. Harper lagged behind, talking to the owner, a small, frail lady who was raising a nine-year-old granddaughter.

"Did you hear the questions Harper was asking Mrs. Katsky?" Lily asked. "You'd almost think she was interested in buying the café."

"It would be a perfect job for her," Patience admitted. The three girls agreed there wasn't another woman on earth who could make a better apple pie.

"Her pot roasts cannot be beat," Mary confessed. "Only Harper can't buy a café. She doesn't have any money."

The girls smiled when they saw the pastor coming across the street. Smiling in turn, Arthur Siddons hurried to greet them.

"Hello, Pastor Siddons," Lily called.

"Hello, girls! Been searching all over for you!" The balding, plumpish sixty-year-old paused before them, his round face beaming.

Patience waited for him to catch his breath. "Was there something special you wanted, Pastor?"

"Yes, yes!" He took her hand, squeezing it firmly. "I've just come from a meeting. The church board wants me to extend an invitation to you ladies to remain here in Denver City for the winter."

Delighted smiles lit the women's faces. "That's wonderful, Pastor Siddons!" Patience sobered. "But how? We have no means of support—"

"We discussed that," Pastor conceded. "Tom Wyatt is a heinous man, and unfortunately we have no control over what he and his no-account boys do, but the folks of Denver City are good people. We want to extend our hospitality until spring. By then you ladies will have decided what you'll need to do, and the weather will be more cooperative." He pulled his collar up closer against the bitter wind. "Harry Rexell says he can use a hand at the mercantile, and Rosalee Edwards said she's going to need extra help at the millinery over the holidays. Imagine we can find enough work to keep you all busy until spring!"

"Oh, thank you!" Patience threw her arms around the older man's neck and hugged him.

Red-faced, the pastor stepped back, grinning lamely. "Oh, my, it's our pleasure, miss. Having five pretty new faces in town won't hurt the feelings of our single men one bit. Five *eligible* ladies, I might add."

"Six," Mary reminded softly.

The girls looked at each other, sobering.

"Six, when Glory gets here."

Pastor Siddons nodded. "Your friends still haven't arrived?" He shook his head, making a clucking noise. "We can send a search party now that the weather's broken—"

"Thank you, Pastor. Marshal McCall insists that

they're all right and will ride in any time. I'll talk to the marshal again, and we'll let you know what we decide."

"Good, good." Pastor Siddons rubbed his gloved hands together. "May I tell the church that you will stay? They can't wait to lend a Christian hand. Why, old Mrs. Guffey already has all of you down for Christmas dinner at her house. She cooks a mighty fine turkey."

Patience glanced at Lily and Mary. The girls nodded happily. "And I'm sure Harper will be happy to stay. She might even find work at the café."

Pastor Siddons clamped a hand over his heart and nearly swooned. "Etta Katsky would be plumb tickled pink to find good help. She's trying to get by with her nine-year-old granddaughter waiting tables, but she's getting worn to a nubbin with all the extra work."

Mary stepped closer, extending her hand. "Thank you for all your kindness, Pastor Siddons. I don't know what we would have done without your help."

"You're welcome, Mary. And Doc says he wants to see you at his office this morning. Thinks he might have something for that cough."

Siddons walked on, calling a friendly greeting to a young couple coming across the street.

Patience, Lily, and Mary walked on, casting curious looks toward the mercantile.

"Poor Ruth. She hasn't slept a wink for the last week."

"She's terribly worried."

"We all are."

Patience frowned. "Don't know who she's more worried about, Jackson or Glory."

"Everyone's worried sick about both," Lily said. "What can be keeping them?" Silence overtook them since no one dared to speak of the dire possibilities.

Lily finally whispered under her breath. "Does it seem to you that Dylan is awfully interested in Ruth? They argue constantly, but I think they really like each other."

Mary and Patience spared a brief glance in the direction of the mercantile porch, and then looked straight ahead. A giggle escaped Mary.

"What's so funny?" Lily asked.

"Ruth and Dylan. She's so serious and he's so . . . not serious, unless he's doing his job. They would make a fine pair."

The thought of their contrasting natures resulted in a round of giggles.

Lily jabbed Patience's ribs. "Shhh, they'll hear us!"

"Can't help it," Patience gasped. "Wouldn't that be something? Ruth and Dylan married?"

● ● ●

Dylan shifted the toothpick to the other corner of his mouth. Leaning back in the chair, he watched Lily, Patience, and Mary walking on the opposite side of the street. Fine girls. They'd make some lucky men good wives one of these days.

"So, Ruth. What do you think about the price of corn?"

Ruth slowly turned around to look at him. "What?"

He lifted his brows. "What do you think about the price of corn?"

"I haven't an earthly idea what corn sells for these days."

"What about an unearthly one?"

She gave him a dirty look.

"None, huh." He removed the toothpick and stared at it.

"Why?"

"Why what?"

"Why do you want to know the price of *corn*?"

"I don't. Just trying to find a subject we can discuss without ruffling your feathers."

"Don't even try." Ruth turned back to watching the road. "And corn certainly won't do it."

"There's got to be something I can say that won't get your dander up—"

"Try 'I'll be leaving now, Ruth.'" She brushed past him, nearly toppling his chair, and he had to grab for the railing.

Springing to his feet, he spit the toothpick on the floor and yelled at her disappearing skirts. "Come on, Ruth! Hey, you want to get married? We get along so well; we would make a fine—where's your faith, woman?"

He ducked, grinning as an apple sailed over his head and hit the front window of the mercantile.

Scowling, Harry Rexell burst out a second later, broom in hand.

Dylan turned and innocently pointed at Ruth.

Snatching her skirt in her hand, she stalked off to the other end of the wraparound porch.

Grinning, Dylan flipped Harry a coin. "For the lady's apple."

Pocketing the coin, Harry stared after Ruth sourly. "Well, tell her that around here, we prefer to eat 'em, not throw 'em at folks' windows."

The men turned at the sound of a horse galloping into town. Shouts went up as Patience, Lily, and Mary ran to meet the new arrivals.

Grinning from ear to ear, Glory slowed and walked the mare through the center of town with Jackson, bandaged hand and all, riding behind her.

"Where have you been?" Patience shouted, running beside the horse. Lily and Mary raced to keep up.

"Had a little trouble, but we're here now," Glory called back. Her eyes darted to Mary. "Don't run, Mary! You'll start coughing!"

Ruth raced around the corner, holding her skirts. Her eyes lit when she recognized the riders. "Glory! Jackson! Praise God you're all right!"

"Saw me an angel, Ruth!"

Ruth frowned. "You what?"

Glory beamed. "Saw me an angel! Looked a little like Poppy!"

A curious crowd started to gather. Patience, Lily,

Mary, and Ruth pressed close as Glory dismounted and helped Jackson from the saddle.

"What's wrong? We were about to send a search party after you," Patience exclaimed.

Ruth enfolded Glory, and the two women hugged. "I was so scared something had happened," Ruth whispered.

"We got caught in the blizzard. Jackson was wounded and lost a lot of blood. We couldn't travel for a few days. I'm sorry if we worried you."

"What's this about an angel?"

Glory pressed her ear close to Ruth's. "Tell you all about it later on. Right now, Jackson needs attention."

They shared another brief embrace, and Ruth said softly, "Just so you're safe; that's all that matters."

Ruth turned her eyes on Jackson. "Are you all right?"

"Fine, Ruth." He glanced at Glory and smiled. "She took good care of me."

Glory flushed at the praise. "Shucks, anyone could do what I did. Used the snow and my hankie to stop the bleeding. The good Lord provided us an elk to keep us from freezing. When the storm passed, we set out and came to a cabin, where an old hermit who knew about herbs and such helped us."

Dylan joined the noisy reunion. He clapped Jackson on the back, relief evident in his eyes. "About to send the dogs out," he said.

Jackson smiled. "I was about to hope you would." The men exchanged a few brief words in private.

"Better have that hand looked at," someone in the crowd suggested.

"Doc's in his office now."

The crowd cheered as Glory put her arm around Jackson to help support his weight and led him across the street.

"I can walk," he protested under his breath. "Stop mothering me."

"Plan to—just as soon as I know you're going to live," she whispered back. Leaning closer, she added, "Put too much effort in you to lose you now."

Grinning, he met her eyes and said quietly, "Lady, you couldn't lose me if you tried."

●   ●   ●

Dylan caught up with Ruth as she walked toward the café. "I'm waiting."

"For what? The price of corn? I told you, I don't know anything about corn."

"For an apology. I told you Jackson and Glory were all right."

Color dotted her cheeks. "Don't start with me, Dylan. For all you knew, they could have both been dead."

"But they weren't."

"They could have been!"

Grinning, he looked hurt. "Are we going to fight, or are you going to kiss me good-bye?"

Her footsteps faltered. Slowing, she turned to face him. Her features softened. "Are you leaving?"

Their eyes met and held. The teasing light was gone from his. "A wire came through about half an hour ago. I'm due in San Francisco in a few weeks. Now that Jackson and Glory are back safe, I have to move on."

Color drained from her face. "But the weather. It's so bad—"

Laying a finger across her lips, he said quietly, "Take care of yourself, Ruth."

Nodding, she caught his hand and held it for a moment, her eyes closed. "Be careful, Dylan McCall."

"You know me, Ruthie. I'm always careful."

She looked up, tears moistening her eyes. "No one calls me Ruthie unless they're given permission."

Leaning closer, he whispered against her ear, "That's my next project."

She swallowed back tears. "Will I ever see you again?"

Smiling, he took her hand, and they walked to his saddled horse standing in front of the livery. After swinging into the saddle, he finally released her hand. A cocky grin surfaced. "Why, Ruth, I could swear that's an invitation. Am I hearing things?"

Meeting his eyes, Ruth glowered. "Of course you are. Why would I ever want to see the likes of your no-good hide ever again?"

His features gradually turned serious. "I'll be back come spring. Will you be here?"

She lifted her chin saucily. "Guess you'll just have to come back and find out."

Throwing back his head, he laughed, his breath

a frosty vapor in the cold mountain air. Turning his horse, he looked back over his shoulder and winked. "Did I mention I have two single brothers looking for wives?"

Her hands came to her hips. "And why should that matter to me?"

"Thought Patience and Lily might like to know. Chances are they'll be riding with me next spring. They're both even ornerier than me!" Nudging his horse, he rode out of town, his laughter still ringing.

Ruth turned and went into the mercantile, glancing over her shoulder.

But only once.

●　●　●

Two days later Glory and Jackson rode his horse up a narrow trail to the foothills. They tied the animal to a pine and swept the snow off a large flat rock to settle down and enjoy the view. The sun sparkled on the clear, wide stream and the mounds of white banks below. Pines hung heavy with new-fallen snow.

"Do you want to stay here with the other girls?" Jackson asked.

Glory sighed and shrugged. She'd been giving it a lot of thought. Patience and Mary had begged her to stay; Ruth had said she could make a new life in Denver City as well as anywhere else. Trouble was, there was only one thing she really wanted to do, and that wasn't possible.

"I do and I don't. I'll miss the girls something

awful when I go, but I feel restless, like I haven't reached my destination. Does that make sense to you?"

He nodded. "To a man who's traveled most of his life, that makes sense."

"I suppose you'll go back to Missouri to lead another wagon train," she said wistfully.

"No, been thinking about giving that up." He grinned at her playfully. "I'm tired of cross-country travel. This last trip about did me in."

"You mean us women."

He frowned. "It's been real trying."

She could see he was teasing her, but there was some truth there, too. "I know I was a terrible burden to you."

"You exasperated me at times." His expression sobered. "But in all fairness, I learned a lot from you."

"From me?" she asked, amazed.

He nodded. "I watched you learn and grow, always with an open heart. It made me realize how little I had grown in the same amount of time."

"Not you. You know everything."

"I hardened my heart a long time ago. When a man does that, part of him stops growing."

"You mean . . . about your mother."

He nodded. "Being around women for all these months, seeing each of you dealing with your lives . . . I got to thinking that my mother couldn't have been much older than you girls when my father left. I could imagine her as she must have been then. She used to say I reminded her of my pa. No wonder she was cross with me. No surprise that raising a child without help made her bitter." He released his breath slowly. "Because of my time with you and the other women, I started to see my mother through the eyes of a grown man instead of those of a child."

Glory laid her hand on his arm. "You're not so bad, Jackson. We all get out of shape once in a while. The trouble starts when we refuse to do anything about it."

He smiled, dimples flashing. "About time I make peace with the past, learn to forgive, and move on. For too many years, I let it eat at me, almost destroy me. Figure one of the first things I'll do is visit Ma in Illinois, try to heal some old wounds."

She looked up at him in wonder, so proud she thought she might burst.

"Used to think all women were heartless, and then the Lord sent six young women into my life who taught me what it means to care about someone. Patience, Lily, Ruth, Mary, Harper, you—you had it tough, growing up. I'm ashamed to think of how good I had it."

She nodded. "Least you had a ma."

He nodded. "What happened to you didn't make you bitter. You, especially you—" his eyes softened—"faced everything with an open, willing heart."

She sat back, thinking. He was telling her his secrets. She had a few secrets of her own. "I have my faults. For months, I was torn watching you and Ruth together, wanting the respect that you gave her, wishing I could be as wise and confident as she is, knowing in my heart that she was the perfect woman for you—"

"Ruth? You still think—" He shook his head.

"You talked to her like she is your equal . . . you depended on her . . . anyone can see why you two would be good for each other."

He leaned over and tweaked her nose. "The reason I could share responsibilities with Ruth, the reason I could talk easily with her was because I had no romantic feelings for her. She was and is a trusted friend." He paused to smile. "And if I don't miss my guess, she's a little sweet on Dylan." He lifted his brows.

Glory shrugged. "Could be, but he sure makes her mad."

"Love's that way sometimes. The one who attracts you the most is the one who can get under your skin the worst."

Glory shook her head. "I wanted so much to be like Ruth. She was everything I wasn't—wise, serene, trusting in her belief in the Lord."

"Seems to me you're the spitting image of her right now."

She thought for a moment before answering. A light came into her eyes, and she nodded. "Yes, I suppose I am . . . more than I thought possible anyway. Guess all along I felt I wasn't good enough, been trying to earn God's love on my own. Then I decided I couldn't earn it at all; it's a gift. All I had to do was reach out and take it."

"Now you know what I mean about how you've grown."

She thought about that too, realizing that so many of her prayers had been answered, gradually, without her even noticing. She turned to look at him. "Well, if you aren't going to be a wagon master, what will you do?"

"I've been giving that some serious thought. After I go see my ma, I think I'll chase my dreams, do some things I've always thought I would do some day. I love the ocean, and there's a place in California I'd like to settle down, not far from Monterey Bay. I'd like to have a little farm there. You can ride on sandy beaches . . . watch the seagulls." He reached out to brush a lock of hair off her cheek. "The sea is a sight you'd like."

She gazed back at him with wide, trusting eyes. "I've never seen the ocean."

"You could go with me." He met her gaze evenly. "We could be partners."

Her heart leapt at the thought. Partners? With him. "I have the money to buy a little spread. Poppy would approve of me using the gold for that. I could buy land . . . near you."

He shook his head. "I buy the land. You keep Poppy's gold. I was thinking more along the lines of you joining me, working the farm together."

"Oh—" she paused to absorb that—"like partners."

"Partners."

Glory thought of what she'd read in the Bible,

and she shook her head slowly. "I don't rightly think we could live on the same farm. It wouldn't be proper if . . . I mean . . ."

She was struggling, wanting to go anywhere with him, wanting to be with him, but needing it to be right. She wanted to be with Jackson more than with anyone else she'd ever known, but she'd tried to live with guilt before, and she didn't like it.

She knew herself better now, and she didn't want to start a new life with him that was wrong in the eyes of the Lord. That reminded her of the Bible that he had entrusted to her for the trip. It had served her well, and now he would be needing it back, since it appeared that they would be parting ways. "You'll be wanting your Bible back."

"I was getting around to that—"

"I haven't written your ma yet. Ruth says she'll help me, real soon—"

His fingers against her lips stopped her. "Pipe down. There's a few things about me that you should know."

She met his eyes, curious now. "Like what?"

"Well, for starters." Leaning closer, he kissed her softly on the mouth. He tasted of cold air and sunshine. "I think you're every bit as smart as Ruth, and in my opinion you're prettier than Patience, and I hope by now you know I am in love with you."

"Honest?" Her eyes searched his to be sure he wasn't teasing, and what she saw was the warmth of love.

"I'm not prone to lying about a thing like that."
He gathered her in his arms.

She closed her eyes, absorbing his words. He
loved her, but did he love her the way she loved
him? Did he feel sorry for her because she had no
prospects? Was he wanting her to tag along . . . as a
partner . . . the way they'd been on the long journey?
Traveling partners? That wouldn't be enough, not
anymore. She drew back in his arms. "Jackson, I
don't want you to feel obligated to look after me. I
can go on, make a life for myself."

"Is that what you want?" His eyes looked accepting, but she saw hurt there as well.

"Don't take me wrong. Anyone would want
to be partners with you. It's just that all my life
I've lived on the kindness of others." She looked
away at the distant mountain range. "Poppy found
me and took me in. You and the girls found me
and took me in. You see, I've always been a stray,
found and later accepted, but never chosen. My
continued existence has depended on the kindness
of strangers. I don't mean to sound ungrateful." She
studied his expression, looking for understanding,
as her words began to falter. "It's . . . just that . . .
I need to be chosen."

The tenderness in his eyes deepened. "What I'm
hoping . . . what I'm asking is that you be my partner
for life. Glory?"

"Yes?"

"I'm asking you to be my wife. If you want, I'll

get down on my knees and beg, because my life wouldn't be the same without you."

"Marry you?" Her heart leapt with joy at the miracle of it. She thought Jackson would never marry, that he was dead set against it, and here he was, telling her that he loved her, asking her to marry him! Could it be that her silent prayer, her most cherished wish, was being answered? Her heart overflowed with joy. "Yes," she said in a rush, "oh yes, Jackson—" She frowned. "Wait a minute. Honest-to-goodness marry you? Are you sure?"

He nodded. "Never more sure of anything in my life."

"Then, yes, Jackson Lincoln. I would be *proud* to marry you."

His mouth lowered to take hers, and she succumbed to the bliss of his kiss. Moments later, she gazed up at him, seeing all the love there she'd dreamed of seeing but feared she'd never have. It occurred to her that in all fairness there were things she should remind him of. She'd hate for him to later regret having chosen her.

"Don't forget that I'm not the best cook . . . and my sewing could be better, too." They exchanged a long, slow kiss.

"You're improving."

"I'm still impulsive, even when I try not to be."

"Oh, really," he chuckled, "like I hadn't noticed."

"Patience, Mary, Harper, Lily, and Ruth are staying here until spring—"

"Smart women, the weather being what it is." They exchanged another gratifying kiss. "I figure Dylan will be back for Ruth next spring," he whispered against her mouth.

"That's nice. Hopefully the others will meet someone they will fall in love with."

"They're all lovely girls. God has someone for each one of them."

She drew back momentarily. "Even Harper?"

He chuckled. "Most assuredly Harper. And I can't wait to meet that man."

"You know what you're getting then," she said, snuggling back into his arms. It was more of a statement than a question.

He winked. "No, but since it's you, I'm willing to chance it."

She sighed, wrapping her arms around his waist, reminding herself that he'd had four months of daily contact with her, six hundred and eighty-five miles to observe her, plenty of time to get to know her faults, and still he'd *chosen* her for his wife.

"Thank you, dear, sweet, heavenly Father," she murmured, "for loving me so much."

If you look for me in earnest, you will find me when you seek me.

TURN THE PAGE
FOR A PREVIEW OF

And keep an eye out for the
rest of the books in the series,
Faith, June, Hope, and *Patience*

Available soon with a new look
online and in stores

CP1614

1

On November 7, 1873, Denver City sat under a crystal blue dome. Ruth took a deep breath of crisp mountain air and fixed her gaze on the faultless sky. It was a truly remarkable day—beautiful in every way.

Sunshine warmed her shoulders as she listened to Glory and Jackson Montgomery repeat their marriage vows. Marrying outdoors was Jackson's idea. He was an outdoorsman; he wanted to be as close to God as he and Glory could get when they became man and wife. The audible tremor this afternoon in the wagon master's otherwise strong voice amused Ruth, but she supposed the quiver was natural for a man accustomed to being on his own and about to commit the rest of his life to one woman.

Ruth cast a sideways glance at the man standing next to her. Marshal Dylan McCall stood stiff as a poker, his face expressionless as he witnessed the ceremony. What could he be thinking? The egotistical man was surely commiserating with Jackson, thinking that he was glad it was the wagon master and not he about to be saddled for life.

Well, no matter. She was not like some women she'd noticed, inexplicably drawn to the marshal. Besides, it must be God's will that she never marry. True, her head still reeled and her heart ached from the unexpected news she received from the doctor yesterday—news that she would never be able to bear children. Perhaps it was just as well that the mail-order bride thing hadn't worked out for her. Wouldn't her new husband have been dismayed to learn that Ruth had no uterus. "A rare defect," the doctor had said, "but it does happen sometimes."

Ruth lifted her chin and glanced again at the handsome marshal with eyes as blue as the color of today's sky. If it was God's will that she never marry, then she would accept it as another one of life's injustices that God allowed for his own purposes. Getting married and having children wasn't the have-all-or-end-all of life. At least not for her. She'd make a good life for herself, especially now that Tom Wyatt's spiteful trick had been discovered.

Ruth understood why a man needed a wife who could give birth to children, someone to give him strapping heirs to help with the work. Knowing this didn't lessen her desire to be loved. But then most men were like Glory's uncle Amos. They made promises they never intended to keep and blamed other folks for their own shortcomings. The chances of her finding a man who would love her regardless of her barrenness were about as remote as her hitting the mother lode the local prospectors fantasized about. She had no such fantasies. Life was real, and sometimes hard, but it was the living of it in God's will that was important to Ruth, certainly not the finding of a husband.

With a mental sigh, Ruth shifted her gaze back to the happy couple. Glory was different. She loved Jackson and would give him a whole passel of kids. Ruth tried to imagine the feisty Glory as a mother. When the wagon train had first come across the homeless waif, they'd thought she was a boy—a young man *very* much in need of a good bath. It had taken several days for Glory to convince Lily, Patience, Harper, and Mary that Glory wasn't going to oblige. She was oblivious to her malodorous state, though how she missed them holding their noses Ruth would never know. The happy-go-lucky, will-o'-the-wisp Glory had no idea she wasn't socially fit. Finally the women took it upon themselves to throw her into the river, then determinedly waded in after her, wielding a bar of soap. Glory's squeals of outrage had not deterred them. When the boy-like child had been scrubbed from head to toe, the transformation was amazing.

A smile hovered at the corners of Ruth's mouth. During those days on the trail, Glory had become like a sister, and Ruth wished her nothing but happiness. Still, it was hard to imagine Glory married, nursing a child—Ruth's thoughts cut off and she forced down a tinge of remorse. She could accept God's will for her life; she really could.

The preacher concluded the ceremony. As Jackson swept his bride into his arms and kissed her breathless, the small crowd clapped and whistled. There wasn't a doubt in Ruth's mind that the two were made for each other, although for a brief and unreasonable time Ruth herself had suffered her own attraction to the handsome wagon master. She enjoyed Jackson's friendship, but Glory truly had his love and that was only right. Ruth felt not a twinge of regret about the match.

Everyone had helped to prepare the after-wedding festivities. Tables covered in lace tablecloths and adorned with bouquets of dried fall flowers had been set up in front of the church. A large wedding cake festooned with a tiny bride and groom stood amidst the decorations. An air of festivity blanketed Denver City as fiddlers tuned up.

Well-wishers descended on the happy couple as Ruth drifted away from the confusion. She'd be back to extend her best to the new Mr. and Mrs. Montgomery when things settled down a bit.

Oscar Fleming caught her eye, and she smiled back distantly. For the last few days the crusty widower had been on her trail. There had to be fifty years' difference in their ages if there was a day, but that hadn't stopped Oscar. He smiled, winked, and showed a set of brown teeth worn to the gum every time he could catch her attention.

Ruth stiffened as the old codger sprinted in her direction.

"Afternoon, Ruthie!" he called.

Ruth mustered a polite smile, her eyes darting to the marshal, who was watching the exchange with a self-satisfied grin. "Good afternoon, Oscar. Lovely ceremony." She tried to sidestep the old coot.

"Hit was, hit was." Grinning, he blocked her path. "Thought maybe I'd have me th' first dance."

"Oh," she said, her gaze swinging toward Patience and Mary, but they were both helping a group of women set food on the tables. They were too busy to pay heed to her silent plea for help.

Oscar held out his scrawny arms. "How 'bout it, Ruthie? You and me cut a jig?"

Jig, indeed. Ruth swallowed, drawing her wrap tighter as she tried to manufacture a plausible excuse. She glanced up when a hand wrapped around her left arm and Dylan McCall politely interrupted. "Now, Ruthie, I believe you promised *me* the first dance."

Though weak with relief, Ruth seethed. *Ruthie.* How dare he call her that! Still, it was a chance to escape. She stiffly accepted his proffered arm and mustered a friendly smile. Anything was better than dancing with the old miner. "Why, I believe I did, Marshal." She smiled her regrets to Oscar. "Will you excuse us?"

Oscar's grin deflated, his chin sinking down to his chest. "Maybe later?"

"Of course," she conceded. *Much, much later.*

As the couple strolled off, Ruth pinched Dylan. Hard.

Though he winced, the marshal kept a pleasant smile on his lips . . . and pinched her back.

"Ouch!" She jerked free of his grasp and flounced

ahead, pretending to ignore him. The very *nerve* of
Dylan McCall acting as her rescuer!

His masculine laugh only irritated her more.
"Admit it, Ruthie," he called. "You welcomed the
interruption!"

Ruth's face burned. "Not by the likes of you!"

He paused, chuckling as she marched to the
punch bowl. She swooped up a cup, dunked it into
the bowl, then quickly drank, dribbling red liquid
down the front of her best dress in the process. She
dropped the cup and swiped at her bodice, then felt
punch oozing through her right slipper.

Her temper soared. It was Dylan's fault. He made
her so mad she couldn't think straight. From the
corner of her eye, she saw Dylan politely tip his hat
and ease into the crowd.

"Oooooph!" Ruth sank into a nearby chair, steam
virtually rolling from the top of her head. How that
man infuriated her. If only he weren't so handsome
and charming at times as well. . . .

* * *

Forever. Whew. The vows the newlyweds had
exchanged lingered in Dylan's mind as he threaded
his way through the guests. He paused to speak to
the ladies. Lily and Harper bloomed under his attention, but his mind was on the ceremony.

Forever. The word made a man break out in a
cold sweat—at least a man who liked women but
didn't care to tie himself down to any particular one,

only one, for the rest of his life. Not unless he was planning to die tomorrow.

He'd been accused of breaking women's hearts, and he supposed he had broken his fair share. They could be as pretty as ice on a winter pond or ugly as a mud wasp, and he'd allow them a second glance. Dylan didn't judge a woman by the way she looked on the outside. He'd learned long ago that the outside didn't mean much. He'd told someone once that when he met the right woman he'd marry her, but deep down he knew he'd never see the day. There wasn't a *right* woman. Not for him. There were just . . . women. All softness and pretty curves, but inside they weren't worth a plug nickel. Sara Dunnigan had taught him that. Women were out to use men, use them up for their own purposes. Well, he had *his* own purposes, and they weren't to share with any woman.

The married women turned to watch him walk away; Lily and Harper tittered. Dylan neither welcomed nor resented the attention. A woman's naive notice made him feel in control. He could always walk away, and he intended to always be able to do just that.

The receiving line had begun to thin as he approached the newlyweds. He shook hands with Jackson. "You're a lucky man."

The sincerity in his tone wasn't entirely contrived. Jackson *was* lucky. Glory was the one woman who could tame the wagon master, and Dylan wished them well. Jackson grinned down at his bride. If

ever there was a happy man, Montgomery fit the
bill today.

"It's your turn next, McCall!"

"Don't hold your breath, Montgomery."

Dylan leaned in and kissed the bride lightly on
the cheek. Glory blushed, edging closer to Jackson.
Beaming, Jackson drew her close.

"That's my girl. Beware of wolves in sheep's
clothing."

Dylan lifted an eyebrow. "Me? A wolf?"

"The worst," Jackson confirmed with a sly wink.
"Knew that about you right off."

The two men laughed.

The new Mrs. Montgomery frowned. "Jackson—"

Throwing the marshal a knowing wink, Jackson
took his wife's arm and steered her toward another
cluster of well-wishers.

Dylan milled about for a while, exchanging
expected pleasantries and hoping he could leave
soon. Events like this weren't his cup of tea. He spent
the majority of his time alone, which he preferred.
He was eager to get going to Utah. He would have
left last week, but Jackson and Glory had talked him
into attending the wedding. Jackson needed a best
man, he said, and Dylan had reluctantly agreed, feeling torn between friendship and duty to his job.

Dylan spotted Ruth with Mayor Hopkins, her
cheeks flushed, blue eyes aglow, thick, shiny, coal
black hair hanging to her waist, laughing up at him.
She'd never looked at Dylan that way . . . but then
he supposed a woman like Ruth wouldn't. Men like

him were loners. They had to be. Keeping the law was a dangerous business. Ruth, even with her independent streak a mile wide, would avoid a man like him, as well she should.

Dylan had stepped onto the sidewalk when Pastor Siddons threaded his way through the crowd toward him. "Marshal McCall! They'll be cutting the wedding cake soon. You won't want to miss that." The pastor beamed. "Etta Katsky makes the best pastries this side of paradise."

Smiling, the marshal acknowledged the invitation. The whole town was friendlier than a six-week-old pup. It was a good place for Ruth and the other girls to settle.

The two men stood side by side, watching the festivities. Arthur Siddons's pleasant face beamed. "Nothing like a wedding to make you feel like a young man again."

Dylan refused to comment. His gaze followed Ruth as she moved through the crowd. He'd never seen her smile like that, laugh like that, so happy and carefree.

Arthur looked up at him, a sly grin hovering at the corner of his mouth. "Right pretty sight, wouldn't you say?"

Dylan had to agree. "Ruth's a fine-looking woman. All the girls are."

The pastor nodded. "Mother was just saying how nice it is to have young blood in the town. Tom Wyatt and his boys are low-down polecats. The whole town's known that for years, but I have to say the devil was taken by surprise this time. Had it not been for you and Jackson, those six young women would be working the mines right now, without a hope for the future."

Dylan bristled at the thought. "The Wyatts ought to be strung up by their heels."

"Yes, many agree, but Wyatt's not done anything he can be legally prosecuted for. We know he promised the women husbands, but in a court of law he'd say the women, the orphanage, and Montgomery misunderstood. He would eventually set them free, once they worked off their debt to him. But considering the wages he'd pay, that would take a mighty long time. It isn't the first time he's used deceit to gain mine workers. Brought eight women out last year, and one by one they escaped. Found one this spring." The reverend shook his head. "Poor woman didn't make it."

A shadow crossed the marshal's features. "I thought once that Jackson and Glory had met the same fate."

"Yes, Jackson and Glory were fortunate to survive that blizzard." The pastor beamed. "Wouldn't have, without Glory's common sense."

"No." Dylan watched the laughing bride and groom. "She's quite a woman."

Arthur nodded. "Colorado's rough territory. A man can freeze to death in no time."

Sobering, the minister rested his gaze on Mary, who was smiling up at Mayor Hopkins. The couple seemed to be enjoying each other's company.

"Now, there's the one I worry about. The poor thing coughs until she chokes. Won't be many men who'd want to take on such a responsibility."

Dylan agreed. Mary's asthma would make it difficult for her to find a husband. He looked at Harper and Lily, who were busy setting out platters of golden brown fried chicken. Harper was so independent and quick-tongued it would take a strong man to handle her. Lily would do okay for herself, and Patience wouldn't have any trouble finding a husband. She was the looker of the bunch.

His gaze moved back to Ruth. She was now conversing with a tall, lanky man who looked to be somewhere in his late twenties. The couple made a striking pair. The young man's carrot-colored hair and mahogany eyes complemented Ruth's black tresses and wide blue eyes. But Ruth was going to be trouble for any man who took her on. She was as prickly as a porcupine—and as quick to raise her defenses. Made a man wonder what was inside her.

Not him, of course, but some man—some good man looking to settle down.

Patting his round belly, the pastor chuckled softly as he followed Dylan's gaze to the couple. "They make a fine-looking pair, don't they? Conner lost his wife a couple years back. Fine man, Conner Justice, so young to lose a mate. Lost Jenny in childbirth . . . baby was stillborn. His wife's death was mighty hard on him. Conner is only now coming back to community socials."

Dylan's gaze narrowed. It appeared to him that

Conner Justice was recovering quite nicely. He was standing a bit too close to Ruth for manners. The sound of Ruth's lilting laughter floated to him, a sound he hadn't heard often. She was enjoying herself for the first time since he'd met her.

Well, good for Ruthie. Maybe Conner Justice needed a new challenge, and the saucy brunette would certainly provide him one.

The pastor patted his belly again. "Well, the bride and groom will be cutting the cake soon." He stuck his hand out to Dylan. "Guess you'll be moving on?"

"I have to be in Utah by the end of the month."

"Worst time of the year to travel."

"I'm used to it."

Dylan preferred to travel in better weather. But when he'd decided to help Jackson deliver the brides to Denver City, he knew he'd be delaying his trip to Utah and would probably face bad weather. It wouldn't be the first time he'd been inconvenienced, nor would it be the last.

"Take care of yourself," Pastor Siddons said.

Dylan smiled. His eyes involuntarily returned to Ruth and Conner, while the pastor wandered toward the cake table. Ruth looked like she was having a fine time.

"Well, I am, too," he told himself, but right now he couldn't have proved it.

A Note from the Author

Dear Reader,

When I first began the Brides of the West series, I thought I would tell only the Kallahan sisters' stories: Faith, June, and Hope. Then Glory came along, and she opened a whole new realm of possibilities. Ruth, Patience, Harper, Lily, and Mary were created—and as you see, the Brides of the West just keep involving themselves in the most unlikely knee-slapping escapades. As the Brides of the West continue, I hope you will see something of yourself and your own life in the stories of Ruth or Patience or any of the other courageous young women. My prayer is that this fun-loving fiction containing simple truths will minister to you, my reader, and put a song in your heart and a smile on your face.

In his name,

Lori Copeland

About the Author

Lori Copeland is known for her fast-paced historical and contemporary romantic comedies. She is a two-time *Romantic Times* Lifetime Achievement recipient, a RITA and Christy Award nominee, and an inductee of the Missouri Writers Hall of Fame. In 2014, Hallmark Movies produced her contemporary title *Stranded in Paradise*.

Lori has published a combined total of 120 books in both the general and Christian market.

She makes her home near Branson, Missouri, with her husband. They have three grown sons and an ever-growing family.

TYNDALE HOUSE PUBLISHERS IS CRAZY4FICTION!

Fiction that entertains and inspires

Get to know us! Become a member of the Crazy4Fiction community. Whether you read our blog, like us on Facebook, follow us on Twitter, or receive our e-newsletter, you're sure to get the latest news on the best in Christian fiction. You might even win something along the way!

JOIN IN THE FUN TODAY.

 crazy4fiction.com

 Crazy4Fiction

 @Crazy4Fiction